REMEMBER

I0837200

ISBN: 978-1-0693186-2-6

This book is written in U.K. English.

Acknowledgements

Once again, a huge thank you to my wife, who deals endlessly with my nonsense with far more patience than I deserve. To my beta readers, whose suggestions helped keep this story from getting too dark. To the sapphic writers' communities whose advice and support continue to warm my heart. To all of the queer people who came before, who faced much worse odds, who were unable to tell their stories and who continue to serve as inspiration to those of us who rail against oppression today and every other day. To the young queers who carve their identities out of spaces we didn't know existed. To my editor, Janice Crowe, who catches the mistakes that fall through the cracks and lets me know that my weird corner of the world uses words other people don't know. Thank you all, endlessly from the bottom of my heart.

Author's Note

This book takes place in Alberta, Canada and features international characters. As a result, spellings and expressions will be inconsistent between speakers

A glossary and playlist can be found at
marinestjean.ca

Content Warning

As some people feel that content warnings are spoilers, the actual content warning will be on the next page.

Actual Content Warning

This book contains depictions of graphic sex, violence, consensual violence during sex, death, reference to suicide, homophobia and adult language.

It is intended for mature audiences.

one

Regina, Saskatchewan

Lisa burst into the kitchen. Her lipstick had disappeared and glitter clung to her skin. "How close are strap-ons to the real thing?"

Her roommate took an audibly annoyed sip of her coffee. "Normally," Pat set the mug down gently. "We start conversations at this hour with *good morning.*"

Lisa huffed and tried to run her fingers through her tangled mass of auburn hair. It stuck. "Okay, fine. *Good morning*. How close?"

Pat sighed and drained her mug. "I'm going to need more coffee before I ask why." She shuffled over to the carafe, still in her black boxer shorts and the over-washed blue RCMP t-shirt Lisa had given her for her birthday.

"How can you drink that?" Lisa wrinkled her nose. A flake of glitter caught the light as it fell.

"What? Coffee? You drink coffee all the time."

"No, *black* coffee. Besides, aren't you supposed to be into tea or whatever?"

Pat rolled her eyes. She had tried hard to suppress her accent, but it was still present. She returned and set her coffee on the chipped 60's Formica table with three straight stainless-steel legs and one decidedly less so. "I like it," she shrugged.

Lisa slipped into the bockety folding chair across from her, leaning on her elbows. The table rocked and splashed Pat's coffee. She closed her eyes and took a breath, but didn't say anything.

"Am I the sunshine to your grumpy?" Lisa stared apologetically. She really *was* sorry about annoying her, but not sorry enough to stop.

Pat managed to keep herself from wincing. "We're not dating. And you read too many romance novels." Pat lifted the mug from the table before Lisa could do any further damage.

"Okay, so back to my question."

"You haven't answered mine either. Why?"

"I met someone."

"And you're planning on strapping right away?" Pat took a sip. "Bloody heteros. No concept of foreplay," she muttered.

"Hey!" Lisa said a little louder than she had intended. "I'm not straight."

"I'm sorry. I didn't mean it like that." Pat pinched the bridge of her nose to hide her grimace. "All I meant was that dating men does close to nowt in preparing you to date women."

Pat hoped that would be sufficient. She wasn't *trying* to be biphobic, she was simply trying to navigate Lisa's newfound attraction to women without doing something stupid - such as giving her the wrong idea. Lisa had given her a few opportunities to make a move. And Pat had wanted to. *Really* wanted to.

But there were complications. They were roommates, for one. A *fling* would be one thing, but if something ended badly, they'd be looking for other arrangements until they finished school. The other complication was trickier.

At least, that's what Pat told herself. And now, because of a variety of factors, here she was, sitting across the table from her absurdly beautiful roommate who had found someone else. She didn't like to admit it, but it stung. Pat flexed her jaw to hide the jealousy on her face and settled for *grumpy*. Pat did *grumpy* well.

"Anyway."

"Anyway." Pat put her coffee back down on the table now that it was a little less full. "I have no idea."

Lisa tilted her head. "You've never used a strap-on? I thought that's what lesbians did."

"No, I've never used a dick. I have nothing to compare it to." Pat took a sip of her coffee. "And not all lesbians *use* strap-ons." She cradled the warm mug. "Or other sapphics," she added.

"Do you?"

Pat stared at her pointedly.

"Fine." Lisa grinned. "I guess that makes sense."

"I get it. Most lesbians have been with a man at some point. Just not me." Pat sipped her coffee.

"Were you ever curious?"

"Nope." Pat popped the *p*.

"Why not?"

Pat's eyebrows hit her hairline. "You want me to go into detail about why I find men unappealing?"

"I mean, yeah, there are ugly ones, but look." Lisa ran over to the sofa to grab the romance paperback splayed open on the armrest. She shoved the cover in Pat's face.

Pat curled her lip. "No, thank you."

Lisa turned the cover around to look at it. "Really?"

Pat shook her head.

"He kinda looks like you though. I mean, if you take away the ripped abs."

Pat pulled her head back and frowned.

"Wait, are you hiding abs under there?" Lisa tried to lift Pat's shirt, but she ended up sloshing her coffee on herself.

"Sorry!" Lisa raised her hands apologetically. Her laugh said that she was not sorry. "What about Hugh Jackman?"

Pat grabbed a paper towel and dabbed at her shirt. "Not even a little bit."

Lisa frowned. "What about…"

Pat interrupted her before she could finish. "This sounds a lot like *Green Eggs and Ham*."

"And Sam-I-Am eventually convinced him to eat them." Lisa pointed a finger. "And he *liked* them."

"He liked them because he was delirious. The eggs were *green,* Lisa." Pat stared, unimpressed. "Why are you so intent on getting me to like men?"

"I don't know?" Lisa screwed up her face. More glitter fell on the table. "I came out to you. I guess, I just felt…" she shrugged.

Pat rolled her eyes. "That's not how coming out works. Just because you discovered something about yourself and shared it with me doesn't mean that I have anything to share with you. I've known I was a lesbian since I was ten."

"How did you find out?" Lisa leaned an elbow on the table. Pat rescued her coffee before it could spill.

"I was obsessed with Pamela Johnson in year five. She was a year older than me and a good thirty centimetres taller." Pat did not feel like sharing more than that, but she recalled the butterflies and confusion clearly. She had been old enough to know it was wrong, but young enough that she hadn't understood the consequences.

"Into older women, huh?" Lisa bit her lip, smiling. "I'll bet you were adorable as a kid."

"I was not. I was messy and had tangled hair and got in trouble for punching boys when they would annoy me. Then the teachers would tell me that that's how you knew a boy liked you and I would get sick and sit in the nurse's office with a stomach ache."

Lisa could tell she hadn't gotten over it from the vitriol in her voice. She must have made a face because Pat added, "I don't hate men. I hate the idea that I *have* to like them because everyone else thinks they're so great. And just because some people have a problem with me fucking women doesn't mean *I* care if you fuck men. Or women. Or both."

"Well, I haven't technically…"

"You're asking about strap-ons."

"True."

"Tell me about this girl." Pat needed to deflect the conversation away from herself.

Lisa practically danced over to the carafe and poured herself some coffee. She added several spoonsful of sugar. "Her name is Phaedra."

"Pretentious."

"She's a piercer."

Pat squinted. "I don't see any piercings, which means…"

"I didn't get any piercings!" Lisa crossed her arms.

Pat cracked her neck. "No need to get so defensive. I would have thought a new piercing would be kind of stupid as a cadet anyway."

"Training's almost done."

"Does that mean…?" Pat raised an eyebrow.

"No, I'm not getting anything pierced," Lisa huffed, crossing her arms tighter. "I went to get a tattoo."

"Of what?"

Lisa shrugged. "Nothing, apparently. I chickened out last minute."

"And how does your piercer fit into this?"

"She helped me calm down after I had a panic attack." Lisa's eyes lit up. "She was so sweet."

Pat couldn't help but smile. "And?"

"And we sat in the studio for three hours talking while she waited for walk-ins." Lisa beamed.

"And now you're trying to figure out how to get pregnant with silicone?"

"God, wouldn't that be amazing?" Lisa propped her head up against the table. Pat eyed her coffee nervously.

"No, that would be terrible." Pat said. "When you're dating women, you throw rational thought out the window for at least six months."

Lisa stared quizzically.

"You've never heard a U-Haul joke?"

"What?"

Pat shook her head, disappointed. "You clearly need more queer people in your life." Pat finished her second coffee. "Because I like you though, I'm going to give you a warning. Not that you'll listen."

"I always listen."

"Right. Anyway. You're going to fall hard and fast. And in two months, when you get sent to your detachment, you'll have the worst heartbreak of your life."

"What if I get posted here?"

Pat shook her head. "They'll send you to bumfuck nowhere."

"Here's bumfuck nowhere." Lisa still looked hopeful.

Pat couldn't bear to crush her. "I hope you're right."

Lisa put her coffee mug in the dishwasher.

"Where's Northton?" Lisa waved a piece of paper, still wearing her cadet uniform.

"Oh, fucksticks, I'm sorry." Pat had already changed into her pyjamas.

Lisa removed her boots. "Why?"

"I went to high school there." Pat considered how much to say. "Maybe it's changed."

"Oh no, now you have to tell me everything." Lisa ran into her room, unbuttoning her blouse along the way. Pat averted her eyes.

"How are you going to tell Phaedra?"

"Maybe she can come with me?" Lisa yelled, shuffling clothes around.

Pat didn't comment, but she doubted it. She'd met Phaedra a couple of times. Sweet, a little spicy, but definitely a city girl. Pat didn't think she would trade her wolf shag cut, tight tank and loose-fitting designer jeans for gingham and overalls three years out of style anytime soon. She had that soft-masc look that all the sapphics were after lately. Lisa didn't know it, but Phaedra would move on in a heartbeat when she left.

Or maybe that was her jealousy talking.

Lisa emerged wearing her bathrobe. Pat turned back to her carpentry textbook. "You're seeing her tonight?" She hoped she could avoid talking about Northton.

Lisa nodded, but she wasn't going to let Pat get away with it. "Now spill."

"Fuck." Pat swore under her breath. "How much do you want to know?"

"All of it." Lisa lifted her hands and let them flop back down to her sides.

"You're going to regret that," Pat warned.

"I've got my big girl panties on," Lisa insisted.

Pat eyed her sceptically. "You're wearing pants under that bathrobe?"

"Wouldn't you like to know?" Lisa smirked.

Pat inhaled, trying her best to ignore the comment. "When I arrived, I was the only openly queer kid in town. I was still the only one the day I left. Because they killed the other one."

Lisa clapped a hand over her mouth.

"You sure you want me to continue?" Pat raised an eyebrow.

Lisa nodded.

"Her name was Willow." Pat flicked her eyes up to meet Lisa and lowered her gaze. "Willow was dating some douche."

"As we all do in high school," Lisa said. Pat raised an eyebrow. "As some of us do," she corrected.

"He proposed. Willow said *yes,* but then dumped him later. Caused a stir in town." Pat flicked her fingers, like she was trying to brush the memory away. "He called her a dyke and word got back to her parents."

"Was she?"

Pat shrugged. "Bi, maybe. I don't know. It's not like she gave herself a label. She kissed me once." She sighed and slouched in her chair. "Apparently that's too queer for Northton."

Lisa winced. "That's a hard way to find out your daughter's gay."

"Yeah, except that we all thought they'd be cool about it." Pat's voice was laced with a seething Lisa had never heard before. "Willow's parents were old hippies. They owned a shop with incense and crystals and cack. When they found out, they were going to send her to a conversion therapy camp."

"What?" Lisa grimaced.

"Turns out their *divine feminine* bullshit meant *women in the kitchen and pumping out babies is a sacred calling and has nothing to do with patriarchy*. But in a self-righteous *we use organic deodorant, so it's okay to be misogynistic* kind of way."

"So, she ran away?" Lisa asked.

Pat stared into her empty coffee mug before shaking her head. "She O.D.ed on her parent's meds."

"Jesus." Lisa rushed to wrap her arms around Pat. She hadn't done that since Pat had made it clear she wasn't interested in Lisa. After she'd embarrassed herself like a preteen at a Kpop concert.

That had been a bizarre experience for her. Guys had *always* chased Lisa. Flirt a little and they'd flirt back without fail, even if it didn't go anywhere. But flirting with girls was like trying to get a cat to pay attention to you. It might turn to look in your direction, but then it would saunter off like you hadn't just humiliated yourself.

She hadn't anticipated how foreign it would be to date women. It felt rude to ask. Predatory, even. And then Lisa had stumbled into Phaedra's arms. Things felt so much more *right* than they ever had before, but she had no idea what she'd done to get there. Or how to repeat it.

Pat didn't flinch or move away. Instead, she placed her hand on Lisa's arm and held her there. Lisa let it linger a little too long. She pulled away before she did something stupid like kiss her.

"Let's talk about something else."

Lisa nodded and let go. "Is there anything good about Northton?"

Pat thought for a moment. "I still own a place outside of town, but I haven't visited since I left. It needs work, or I'd offer to put you up."

"You own land in a place you hate?"

"My parents left for B.C. No-one wanted to buy it at the time, so they transferred it to me." Pat bobbed her head back and forth. "And I don't *hate* the place, but the people? They all talk about small town values and raising kids and no crime - if you fit in. I didn't, so I left."

"They bullied you too, huh?"

Pat curled her lip in pride. "They tried."

"You're just full of tantalising information today, aren't you?" Lisa leaned on the kitchen counter. Her bathrobe fell open a bit too much for Pat's comfort level. "Keep going."

Pat blinked, as if doing so would make Lisa's cleavage disappear. It didn't. She stared at her textbook instead. "It was your standard high school bullying. One of them took it too far. Tyler. He thought he'd impress Caleb – the douche Willow dumped, if he started a fire in my locker."

Lisa made a face.

"I don't know either. Teenage boys, I guess. You know men better than I do." Pat raised her hands defensively. "Anyway, I hit him with the Bronco."

"You what?" Lisa clapped her hand over her mouth for the second time today.

"Not *hit* hit. Just a gentle nudge. His dad was right cheesed, but I was a minor and didn't have a license, so I got off with some community service." Pat shrugged.

"I don't even know what to say about that." Lisa blinked. "You're insane. You know that, right?"

Pat raised her hands as if she were weighing the consequences. "Rules are a little different in small towns. He did RCMP training right out of high school. You'll probably get to work with him, if he's still there."

"Okay, I'm going to have to ask him for his side of the story." Lisa kept shaking her head in disbelief.

"Whatever. Don't you have a date with *Phaedra* to get ready for?" Pat mocked.

"Why? Living vicariously through me?"

Pat frowned. "I get plenty."

"What? When? I never see you go out."

"That's because I'm discreet."

Lisa smiled, mouth agape. "You've been holding out on me? And here I've been sharing every detail about my love life."

"None of which I've asked for." Pat shooed her away. "Go. Enjoy your time with women before it becomes too scandalous."

"Damn, Pat. Now you're just making me depressed," Lisa groaned.

"It'll be okay. Phone me when the heartbreak gets too bad." Pat was not at all sure how good of an idea that would be, but it sounded like something she should say.

"You're not helping," Lisa whinged.

"You've known each other two months. If it was some man, you'd have some mediocre goodbye sex and then ride off into the sunset, grateful never to have to pick up his Y-fronts again." Pat turned the page, trying to avoid thinking of Lisa having sex.

"Why didn't you warn me I'd feel like this?" Lisa slumped back into the cabinets.

"I distinctly remember warning you," Pat stood and took Lisa's hands. "Fine then. Go and have some unforgettable goodbye sex. Then you'll have something to dream about when you're with some boring cis white boy you found in Northton."

"Okay, that's not fair." Lisa allowed herself to be dragged off the counter.

"Then call me in a year to tell me all about the mind-blowing sex you're having with the Hugh Jackman look-alike who, for some reason no-one can fathom, lives in Northton, even though I'm fairly certain they're all related." Pat pushed Lisa into the bathroom.

"You're still not helping," Lisa protested.

"You're right. I really don't want to hear about any of that. Spend less time here with me and more time out with Phaedra." Pat shut the door. "And call me. I'm serious."

two

Northton, Alberta. Sixteen years later

License and registration, please."

"You know who I am, Lisa." Caleb flashed a smile. His new red Chevy Silverado 3500HD looked ridiculous in the paved parking lot with only patches of melting snow on the ground.

"We're gonna pretend I don't. Just like we're gonna pretend I don't know what you're doing here."

"C'mon Lisa," he whinged. "It's not like I haven't been with everyone else in this dump." Caleb held his vape pen with three fingers and blew a cloud of mango peach vapour out the window.

Lisa cocked her eyebrow.

"Only because of Josh. But if you ever change your mind…"

Lisa curled her lip and pulled out her citation pad.

"Oh, come on!" Caleb threw his hands in the air. He might have gotten away with it when he was younger, but Caleb was finding out quickly that his greying temples, receding hairline and the fine, but deep wrinkles carved into his face pushed him further into *creepy* rather than *charming* every year."

"Look, Caleb. I don't care who you pick up – if they're legal. But it's Walter's property and he doesn't want you here. Move along or I write the ticket. We've been over this."

Caleb muttered a string of curses and rolled up the window. He sped off, leaving Lisa in a cloud of diesel exhaust.

Lisa coughed and checked her watch. If she headed back to the detachment now, she could finish up her paperwork and be home by a reasonable hour.

"Fucking hell." Tyler brushed the snow off his muskrat fur hat.

Lisa swivelled in her chair. "It's not that cold out."

Tyler grunted and narrowed his eyes. "Not that. Bill was right. Fuckin' goth kids."

Sherri rounded the corner with a fresh pot of coffee. "Bill was right? Who was it?"

"Willow."

Lisa blanched. Pat's Willow? She hadn't thought about Pat in years. A decade? Maybe more?

"Should we phone her parents, or is that Bill's job?"

Tyler took his hat off and shook his head. The fluorescent lights highlighted his bald spot making him look a lot older than he was. "They died last year in Arizona. Some sort of contaminated organic nonsense on a hippie commune."

Lisa's stomach lurched at the callousness, but she had come to expect that from Tyler.

"So, who owns the plot?" Sherri poured the coffee down the drain.

"The commune did, but they didn't renew the lease, so now it's back to the town." Tyler hung up his jacket.

"I can call them, but it would be a waste of time. Bill sent out the legal notice last year."

"Didn't she have friends? Won't they want to know?" By the glare she received from Tyler, Lisa was guessing *no*.

"Willow died decades ago. She had a falling out with everyone and then killed herself," Tyler spat as if he was still angry about it.

"Eighteen years ago." Jacob corrected.

Tyler shot him a look. Jacob slumped his shoulders and went back to his paperwork.

Lisa had heard the rest from Pat, but she wasn't about to tell Tyler that. "Nobody felt bad about that?"

Tyler shrugged a little too intensely. "Everyone feels bad when it happens. They forget. They move on. Especially after what she did."

"What did she do?" Now was Lisa's chance to hear the whole story.

"She was gonna marry Caleb. They had a whole wedding planned. His parents spent a fortune. Then he caught her with some dyke."

Lisa made a face at the thought of anyone marrying Caleb. "Okay, then." She turned to look away, but Tyler continued.

"Her parents left, which was just fine with us because they were fuckin' weird. No-one's thought about her or them in years." Tyler turned to Jacob. "Eighteen years, you smartass shit." Jacob buried his face in his computer. Tyler pulled up a chair and sat. "It's best to let sleeping dogs lie."

Lisa wasn't going to protest. She may have lived here since leaving cadet training, but she still felt like an outsider. It was hard not to when daily life still revolved around who's dad owned what and grudges you'd held since high-school.

In the beginning, she'd held a faint hope that moving here would be like a Hallmark movie. She'd find a ruggedly handsome man that needed help saving a Christmas tree farm. Instead, she found Josh, the skinny tow-truck driver. Sweet, kind, caring. Perfect for *someone*. It satisfied an itch. Kind of. It also kept people from talking.

She'd thought about letting him go multiple times, but go *where?* On the one hand, she felt guilty about using him as a placeholder. On the other, why break the poor man's heart for no reason? He certainly wasn't going anywhere. And then she'd have to see him around town. People would pester her and pressure them to get back together. *A love story written in the stars.*

She hated to admit it, but Pat had been more-or-less right about this town. If her transfer requests ever got approved, she would happily leave rural life behind. She sighed and turned around. A bit more paperwork and then she would go home.

She found Josh's tow-truck parked in her driveway, Lucifer, his black lab stuck his head out the window. His tongue lolled ridiculously. Lisa swore under her breath. *That's not how you should feel about a boyfriend.* Thinking about Pat after all these years had put her voice in her head. Her straight friends would have told her that this feeling was normal. Everyone hated it when their boyfriends interrupted their peace.

Josh was everything a girl could want, she tried to argue with the Pat in her head. He listened when she spoke. Bought flowers. Seemed really enthusiastic about community. He fit in here. He tried to make everyone see the good in this town. Lisa felt angry at herself that she didn't buy into it as much as he did.

Josh stepped out of the truck. "Hey!" He waved with a ridiculous grin. She could find a boyish charm in it if she made an effort. But right now, she could only compare it to Pat's subdued smirk. *Stop thinking about Pat!*

"Hey Josh. What are you doing here?" Lisa pitched her voice higher to try and sound bubbly. The effect felt more like she was cringing. Josh didn't seem to notice.

"Just bringing you these." He held out some flowers. "Can I come in for a bit?"

"Thanks." Lisa accepted the flowers. *Be grateful,* she scolded herself. *Most women would kill to have their man bring them corner store carnations.* "You know I have to work tomorrow, right?" She scratched Lucifier's ears as she walked past. "Hey Lucy," she cooed.

"I know." Josh swayed nervously. "I just wanted to talk."

"Okay, I guess. Come on in."

Josh followed Lisa into the house and found a place on the sofa next to a cream-coloured Scottish Fold. Oatcake hopped down, indignant at being disturbed. She licked herself twice and then sauntered off to another room.

"What did you want to talk about?" Lisa took off her jacket. *Straight to business. Very romantic. The problem is definitely you.*

"So," Josh lifted the brim of his snapback. "we've been dating for a while."

Lisa's stomach tightened, but she tried not to let it show.

"And you said you never wanted to get married," he continued. Lisa's stomach relaxed just a hint.

"But I thought, it would make more sense if we moved in together." Josh pawed at the back of his neck. "Your place, my place, it doesn't really matter," he added.

Lisa had only ever had one roommate – Pat. And she didn't have a lot, but what she did have felt comforting – like it belonged there. Her blender. Her coffee pot. Warm flannel left draped over the back of the bockety kitchen chair.

The thought of Josh's stuff littering her house felt like a violation. It made her queasy. Lines formed on Lisa's forehead. A lot of lines. Enough lines that Josh mumbled "okay, I guess not."

Lisa hadn't been aware that she was frowning, but she always did have trouble keeping her face from giving her away. She tried to force an expression of sympathy, but all she could feel was annoyed at him for dropping this on her. Now she'd have to think about *this* all night.

"I just... I like my space, Josh. I might get transferred, or... I don't know."

Josh raised his eyebrows for a moment. "Wow." He turned to stare at an invisible fly. "I guess I thought this was more serious. I didn't think you wanted to leave."

Lisa was bad at this part. She didn't want to hurt him. She also didn't want him around all the time. Or even most of the time.

Lisa had given almost no thought to this part of her future. Unlike some of her friends, her dreams of cohabitation were hypothetical at best. But as her forties approached, those friends and now even strangers openly wondered when the appeal of a white picket fence and kids would set in.

But she simply couldn't picture it. And moving in together should be something you *wanted*, shouldn't it? But she didn't, and now, she had hurt a great guy. A great guy who should probably find someone else who *did* dream about that sort of thing.

The fact that you're not upset about him finding someone else should tell you something. Pat had told her that about an entirely different boyfriend once. Clearly Lisa had learned nothing since then.

On the other hand. The amount of new people who had moved here since she had arrived was closer to zero than twenty. Who would Josh even date? Marissa? Lisa sighed.

"It's not that, I just... I'm not that type of girl. You know I never wanted to get married. Or move in with anyone." *There,* she thought. That shouldn't cause a breakup, but it will at least plant the seed needed to make *him* think about breaking up with *her*. That would avoid uncomfortable questions later.

Josh slumped a little, dejectedly.

Pity is a terrible reason to stay with someone. Another bit of sage advice from Pat, also about a different boyfriend.

"What do you know about Willow?" Lisa hoped changing the subject would break the tension.

"Who?"

"Bill phoned in a vandalism incident in the graveyard. Her grave."

"Oh, *that* Willow." Josh perked up. He liked feeling useful. "She O.D.ed in grade twelve. I was in grade ten at the time, so, there were a bunch of counsellors that showed up. Kyle knew her better."

"Huh." Lisa unlaced her boots. "Tyler said something about a wedding."

"Yeah, she was engaged to Caleb. She called it off and he got angry. A lot happened, but, well," Josh clapped his hands against his knees. "I'm sure you know all about that."

"A lot happened?" Lisa wasn't sure how much she should prod, but it might give her a clue as to who vandalised the grave.

Josh tilted his head back and forth. "Caleb's parents had a lot of money. At least, a lot for here. They own the car dealership the next town over and a couple commercial properties here. I don't know everything, just that the rumour was they'd spent a lot on the wedding." Josh inhaled deeply. "They refused to renew her parents' lease on their business."

Lisa's eyebrows shot up. "Is that rumour too?"

Josh shrugged. Everything in Northton is a rumour.

"What about the rumour that she was found with another woman?"

"Pat? Yeah," Josh laughed. "She was something." "The town lesbian, I guess, though people said a lot worse things than that."

Lisa turned so Josh couldn't see her wince. He didn't know she knew Pat. Or that Pat had been her roommate. Or that she had dated Phaedra.

"Pat caught a lot of heat for that," he continued. "She left around the same time as Willow's parents."

"So, it's true?" Lisa said.

"Pat was the one who told me what happened. Kyle used to hang out with her. He was about the only one who did, until Willow started hanging out with them, too."

"And your parents were okay with Kyle hanging out with the *town lesbian*?" Lisa felt dirty when the words left her mouth.

Josh rubbed his hands against his knees. "They were just happy Kyle had a friend."

Lisa nodded slowly, attempting to put everything together. Josh's cellphone went off. "I gotta go. Another rollover." He stood and moved in for a hug.

"Sorry about...bringing up moving in together."

"It's okay. I'm just sorry that I'm not..." Lisa shrugged, "you know. That type."

Josh closed the door quietly. She released the breath she'd been holding and then chastised herself for the spark of relief she felt when he left.

Why had she stayed here so long? Inertia, maybe. It was too easy to remain. Boredom is a poor motivator for change. It's not like this place threatened her. Not like it threatened Pat.

Pat.

That was what she had been planning to do once she got home, except that Josh had interrupted her. Find Pat's number.

Lisa pulled an old and yellowed Xerox box out from the bottom of her closet. She tipped it over. Old shirts. Her Cadet Commendation Pin and a bunch of journals fell out. Lisa smiled at the photos pasted to the pages - back from when you'd still print them out.

There was Pat, wearing her flannel and Carhartt's. She always did look more threatening wearing that than Lisa in her RCMP uniform. It fit her broader shoulders and slimmer hips. If it weren't for her round face, it would be easy to mistake her for a man - something Pat played to her advantage when rescuing Lisa from unwanted advances. Pat had always been the best wing-woman a girl could ask for.

Lisa had been startled when she had first met her. The poster in the student hall had said *female roommate only*. Then she saw a man answer the door and thought it was a creep. Until Pat opened her mouth. God, she had embarrassed herself. So many things she thought she'd known for certain had crumbled into dust in that year she'd spent with Pat.

Back then, Lisa had been so sure she'd had no interest in women. And when an ex-boyfriend had suggested a threesome, she'd declined immediately. She could probably kiss one. But more than that? Girl parts were gross and dirty, weren't they?

And then they'd had *that* conversation. She remembered every detail about it, down to the sagging cream and rust patterned sofa. She'd been drinking Moroccan mint tea out of her blue and white RCMP coffee mug, complaining about a hook up.

"And then after all that, he wouldn't even reciprocate." Lisa leaned back, her mug cradled warmly between her crossed legs. "But that's normal, I guess."

Pat looked up from her textbook. "What's normal?"

"Guys not going down on you. It's like, gross or whatever, so they don't do it."

Pat squinted. "Gross?"

"Yeah, you know? All the blood and hair and... smells." Pat's lack of reaction made Lisa feel a lot less sure about what she thought she knew for a fact.

Pat nodded slowly. "I see. Are you sure he likes women?"

Lisa pulled her head back. "You think he's gay?"

"You don't have to be gay to not like women." Pat laughed. "But why would you think your body is less appealing than a bloke's pasty skin tube that he's had crammed into his sweaty pants all day? At least your parts are self-cleaning. Better hope he took a shower that day."

Lisa felt her forehead tighten. She *had* heard that last part in health class at one point.

"Personally," Pat placed a hand on her chest, "I love women." Her hazel eyes met Lisa's. Something stirred that she hadn't felt before.

"I would go down on a woman all day." She bit her lip, eyes closed. The way Pat had said it, like she was giving testimony in a church. Hallelujah, Praise Jesus.

Lisa sipped her mug of tea.

After that, she kept catching herself staring. At first, she'd dismissed it as curiosity. Pat looked *different* is all. Of course she'd stare. Then the daydreams started. What would it feel like to press her lips against Pat's? How would her tongue feel against hers? Was it the same as a man's? Would she taste different? *Idle thoughts,* she told herself. *They didn't mean anything.* That was a lie.

Night after night of trying and failing to get herself off to the hot corporal, her ex-boyfriend, and even Hugh Jackman, she kept waking up soaking with Pat on her mind. The way she had looked when she locked eyes with her. The way she described loving women. The way she had said it with such reverence. What would it feel like to be worshipped by her?

"I think I'm bi," she had blurted out the next morning before she lost her nerve.

Pat sipped her coffee and set it back down on the table. She looked up at her. "Do you want to tell me about it?"

Lisa realised that she did *not* want to tell Pat about it. How could she tell her about what she wanted Pat to do to her? About what she wanted to do to Pat? "No. I just thought you should know." That was safe enough, wasn't it? It opened the door for Pat to make a move.

Instead, nothing changed. Pat drank her coffee black in the mornings and went to bed at a reasonable hour. She did take her to a gay club once, but Lisa didn't catch her looking at anyone. Which was just as well, she supposed. If she had, Lisa would have tried to cut her hair and style her clothes after whatever girl had caught Pat's eye. She really did read too many romance novels.

And then she'd found Phaedra. Lisa had never given up on Pat, but Phaedra had *really* scratched that itch. A little too well, maybe. After the intensity of those feelings, Lisa wondered if it had destroyed any chance at finding love again. Pat was frustratingly right again.

She flipped through the pages, looking for Pat's number. All she found was page after page of pictures and journal entries gushing about Pat and then Phaedra. A surge of regret washed over her. That had been the last relationship where she had been truly happy. Why had she let that slip through her fingers? For what? A mediocre job? Pulling over drunks and rerouting traffic during the town's annual parade?

And then she saw it. A number on a yellow sticky note. It looked familiar, but she hadn't written a name.

Lisa dialled the number and hoped it was Pat.

"Hello?" It wasn't Pat's voice, but it brought a smile to her face nonetheless.

"Phaedra?"

"Oh my God, Lisa! How have you been? Are you in town? Is that why you're calling?"

"Oh no, I'm so sorry." Lisa stumbled over her words. How could someone's voice cause such a flood of emotion after this long? "I thought I was calling Pat."

"You don't have her number? I thought you two were besties."

Lisa imagined Phaedra's lips forming the words. She salivated. *Stop it,* she chastised. "Yeah, it's been a while and I was trying to reconnect. You don't have her number, do you?"

"Yeah, I've seen her a few times. Are you far away?"

"Kinda. It's a long story. We didn't have a falling out or anything, just life, you know?"

"Yeah, life does that to you." Phaedra paused. "Anyway, I gotta go. My wife is calling me. I'll text you her number. Call me when you're in town, we'll hook up."

Wife? The thought made her unreasonably jealous. Lisa was the one who broke it off. It would never have worked. But she still couldn't help feeling like *she* should be a woman's wife. *What is wrong with you?* She scolded herself. *Didn't you just tell Josh you weren't marriage material?*

A ray of hope invaded her overactive imagination. *Maybe Pat is still single?* Lisa shook the thought from her head. She didn't need to start daydreaming about *that* only to be crushed again. Pat had made her feelings clear, hadn't she?

What even was this? Only ten minutes ago she was hoping to push Josh to break up with her. Josh. A perfectly good man. An attractive one. *Not one that makes you wet from a wrong number after more than a decade, though,* she thought.

Lisa fell backward and sprawled against the floor. Why was she like this?

Minutes later her phone pinged. Phaedra had texted her Pat's number, along with a winky face emoji. *Why are you doing this to me Phae?*

And then the moment of dread. Would her body do this to her when she phoned Pat? No. It had been too long. They had never dated. She'd never had a chance with Pat. Pat was a friend. A friend who probably already had someone.

Lisa ignored the way that thought made her wince and dialled the number.

three

Hey, it's Pat."

"Pat?" The smell of the apartment they'd shared came rushing back. Fresh paint and old books. Like a school library. And Pat herself smelled like Neapolitan ice cream. How, she didn't know. She'd once used her body wash and shampoo and it didn't at all make *her* smell like that.

"That's what I just said." There was a hint of annoyance in her voice.

"It's Lisa."

"Holy shit, Lisa? Where are you?"

"I'm in Northton."

"Still? I thought you would have bailed on that shithole as soon as you could."

Lisa smiled stupidly. She had forgotten how much Pat swore. Lisa was about to speak, but Pat interrupted. "Ah fuck, I'm sorry, I shouldn't have called it a *shithole*. You've probably got a guy you're too good for and you're president of the PTA. You love it there, don't you? And I just called it a shithole. I mean, it *is* a shithole, but it's *your* shithole."

"Uh, not exactly. Where are you?"

There was a pause. Lisa heard a fan turn off. "I'm at my place. Near the shithole. Sorry, Northton."

"What? For how long?" Lisa felt her pulse rise. Why had she never seen her?

"Er..." Pat sighed. "I did my apprenticeship and then set up shop here. Industrial rent is bollocks, and I already own this place, so I might as well set up shop here."

"A shop? Doing what?"

"Cabinetry. Furniture. Pays a lot better than framing and everyone is always renovating."

"How come I've never seen you in town?"

"Because I never *go* into town." Lisa heard her scuffle against something. "I *hated* Northton, Lisa."

"But *I'm* here."

She heard Pat exhale. "I know that *now*. I thought you'd transfer out as soon as you could. Especially after how much of a mess you were after Phaedra."

Lisa flushed at the mention of her name. *This is not normal. Normal people don't do this. Normal people don't pine for their ex and their roommate when they have perfectly good men.* "She said you'd seen her."

"Yeah, I made a couple pieces for her and her wife, Andi. You knew about Andi, right?" Lisa heard a bit of trepidation.

"I found out a few minutes ago." It came out colder than she had intended.

"Anyway, I assume you're still with the force then? Or did you actually marry some country boy and pump out a bunch of babies? Are you making tradwife videos now?"

There was the Pat she remembered. It caused a bloom of warmth in her chest. "How do you know I didn't marry a woman?"

"Because it's Northton."

"Fine. No marriage or babies. I'm with a guy. Josh. He's sweet," she said flatly.

"Oh God, Lisa."

"What?"

"Don't *what* me. You're miserable." Pat delivered her verdict with the confidence of a therapist who'd seen a thousand clients with the exact same issue.

"What? No! I'm not miserable!"

"I can hear your disappointment over the phone. Break up with him and go marry Phaedra."

"Phaedra has a wife, remember?"

Before she could blink them away, fat tears gathered and streamed down her face. Why was she so emotional all of a sudden? Her period wasn't for another two weeks. She had literally everything any woman could want. Her own job, her own house, stability. Oatcake currently wrapping herself around her leg. *You forgot Josh.*

Pat interrupted her thoughts. "Are you...are you crying?"

Dammit Pat, how do you know this? Lisa wiped at her face. Her fingers came away wet.

"Text me your address. I'm coming over. I'm on RR9, so it'll take me an hour to tidy up and get over there. And then we'll go to Boots. Boots still exists, right?"

"Okay." Lisa's voice broke. "Thanks, Pat."

Lisa hung up and knelt down to clean up the mess she'd made. Oatcake made a nuisance of herself until Lisa spent ten minutes petting her. She got bored and wandered off, leaving Lisa to finish putting her mementos away.

Lisa sighed. Why was she acting this way? She wasn't *gay* gay, was she? She couldn't be. *You find men attractive, right*? But she'd never felt this intensely about men before. Did she just not know what love felt like? Was she really that stupid?

Oatcake meowed in the kitchen. Lisa fed her dinner and took a shower. She could be mature and put her attraction aside. She was just confused, is all. She would ask Pat about it later. Once she'd calmed down. Pat knew everything. Just like old times.

The doorbell rang. Lisa answered in a towel. Pat stood, hip cocked slightly to the right, hands in her loose-fitting trousers. She looked like she'd stepped directly out of one of her photos.

"Oh my God, Pat!" Lisa squealed and threw her arms around her. She still smelled like Neapolitan ice cream.

Pat laughed softly and hugged her back. "I'm so sorry. If I'd known you were here, I would have visited ages ago. Even if it meant coming back to this shithole."

Lisa let go and took a step back. "How the hell do you look exactly like I remember you? What have you been eating? Spill your secrets!"

"Black coffee." Pat turned away, bashful. "You know I'm domestically challenged."

"Do I ever!" Lisa laughed again. "Remember that time you tried to make risotto, and the house smelled like burned rice for a week?"

"Yeah..." Pat bit her lips. "That'll teach me to make something just because a pretty girl says she likes it."

Lisa's stomach twisted. She had been the one who said she liked risotto. Pat wasn't flirting, was she? *Jesus, Lisa, get yourself under control. Pat's just giving you a compliment.*

Oatcake strode confidently up to Pat and brushed against her leg. "Ooh, who's this?"

"I wouldn't..." Lisa cautioned, but Pat had already picked her up. "Oh."

Pat cradled Oatcake like a baby. Lisa had never heard her purr so loudly.

"She, uh." Lisa stammered. "She doesn't like people. She usually bites them."

Pat rocked Oatcake in her arms. "Cats seem to like me." She grinned.

"I guess they do." Lisa stared for a few more moments. "I'm going to go finish getting ready."

Lisa threw off her towel and rummaged around for something appropriate to wear. Boots may be a shitty bar with VLTs and a warped pool table, but it stayed in business because it was the only one in town. So, why did she feel like she needed to dress up? It couldn't be for Pat. Pat was wearing buffalo plaid and tan doek trousers with too many pockets. Lisa suppressed the urge to put on a dress and settled for skinny jeans and a crisp cream-coloured button up that complimented her hair.

Pat lowered Oatcake gently to the ground. She required a bit of coaxing to leave her arms, but she eventually crawled out with only a quiet mewl of protest.

"I have no idea how you did that."

"Well, I kind of moved my arms a bit so she got annoyed and let me go." Pat shrugged.

Lisa eyed her from the side. "I meant…never mind." She knew Pat loved to wind people up by misrepresenting what they said. "Your truck or mine?"

"We'll take yours. You never did trust my driving." Pat hung her head. "And, I've only got the lorry right now. My Bronco is in pieces."

Lisa raised her eyebrows. "That's true. I'm still amazed you never got a ticket the entire time we lived together."

"See," Pat pointed her fingers, "that's why it helps to have friends who are cops."

Lisa shook her head.

"The beauty of a small town," Lisa pulled up next to Boots, "is that you don't have to park five blocks away or stand in line forever to get in."

"Because the only people that show up are the same six drunks," Pat muttered.

Lisa shot her a look.

"I'm serious!" Pat flailed her arms. "That plant pot has the same dead grass in it as the day I left."

"How can you tell? It's half-buried in snow."

Pat grumbled, but didn't say anything.

The corner of Lisa's lip curled upward. "C'mon. You can play grumpy to my sunshine, just like old times." She stepped out of the truck feeling a lot more sunshiny than she had in months.

Boots smelled about the same as Pat remembered. Stale beer, staler sweat, and cheap cologne. The country music had changed with the times - gotten louder and somehow, more misogynistic. The pool table leaned a bit more, though the VLT's were newer. She didn't recognise any of the patrons, but there were only three of them.

"Go find a spot, I'll order us a pitcher." Lisa walked away. Pat caught herself staring a little too long at her hips in those jeans. Thankfully all three of the patrons were focused on their VLTs.

Pat reprimanded herself. She knew it could never work, for the same reasons it couldn't work before. Even if she didn't have a boyfriend. *God, she was stupid.* Either that or whoever had cursed her life found it endlessly amusing to drop Lisa back into her lap after all this time, just waiting for her to fuck up. Pat took a deep breath and found a table in the corner. The last thing she wanted was to be recognised.

Lisa arrived with the pitcher, sloshing only a little. Pat poured herself a beer. "So, tell me about your man troubles."

"Definitely like old times then, huh?" Lisa sighed. Pat filled her glass.

"If you really want it to be like old times, I can just tell you to toss him and we can be done with it." Pat raised her glass. Lisa clinked it, and took a gulp of beer quickly so she wouldn't have to respond. Pat saw through it.

"Oh balls, that's *exactly* what you want me to do, isn't it?" Pat set her glass down without taking a sip. "What the fuck happened? He didn't hit you, did he?" Pat's eyes turned a murderous shade Lisa hadn't seen before. Her heart fluttered in a way it really shouldn't have.

"Jesus, Pat, no. No-one hit me." Lisa took a drink. "I don't know how to explain it."

Pat sat back in her chair, but her muscles remained tensed. She watched Lisa intently, waiting to spring into action.

"I know that look, Pat. It's the one you used when you were about to threaten a guy who wouldn't leave me alone at a club."

"Yeah?" Pat picked up her beer. "Well, we're in a pub, that's close enough. And there's a guy who won't leave you alone."

Lisa groaned. "Not like that. I just…" She lolled her head about, moving her hands absently as though they could conjure the words she couldn't say.

Pat put her glass down hard enough that it made noise. It caused Lisa to startle and look up at her. "Look. I know Josh a smidge. I used to hang out with his brother, Kyle. He's a good one, but you're not into him. Simple as that."

Lisa exhaled and stared at the wall. "How do you always know?"

Pat snorted. "You'd be shocked at how common that is."

"I think," Lisa looked around the room to see if anyone was listening. "I think I'm still in love with Phaedra." Lisa was grateful she hadn't accidentally said *you.* "How is that even possible?"

"Okay?" Pat took a sip of her beer. "Tell me more."

Lisa sighed. "It's like, I've *never* felt about anyone the way I felt about her." *That's a lie and you know it,* Lisa thought, but she wasn't about to make a fool of herself in front of Pat again.

Pat stared at her half-full beer glass. Her eyes followed the thin lace of foam slowly dropping into the straw-coloured liquid below. "No-one?"

Lisa looked up at her. She was certain Pat could hear her heart slamming against her ribs. She shook her head.

Pat could hope. Even if Lisa decided to direct her affection on her, it would still be stupid. She still couldn't. She had already wasted her one chance. And monsters don't get what they want in the end. Those are the rules. Best to tell her what she needed and hope she made the right decision.

She finished her beer. "You already know what I'm going to say."

"I still need you to say it." Lisa grabbed the pitcher and refilled Pat's glass.

"The only people you've ever felt this way about are women? This place isn't for you."

Women, not *woman.* Pat had seen through her omission. Lisa scoffed. "It's not for you, either." She drained her own glass and refilled it.

"You're learning."

"I wish learning felt good."

Pat looked around the bar. No-one new had entered in the half-hour they'd been there. "Let's play some pool for a bit. Don't want the town's finest being caught drink driving."

Lisa shook her head. "Tyler drinks and drives all the time."

Pat shook her head. "Of course he does. Just like every other yokel here. Keeps Fred in business."

"You knew Fred?"

Pat nodded. "Fred and his wife were about the only people in this town that weren't utter shite."

"What about Josh's brother, Kyle?"

"Kyle left as soon as he could. Came out about a year later, only visits at Christmas. He's never brought a boyfriend home."

"His parents object?" Lisa gathered the balls from the pockets.

Pat finished her second beer. "His parents don't know. The only person he's ever told has been your boyfriend."

Lisa winced. "Please don't call him that."

Pat raised her shoulders. "You know what you have to do to get me to stop."

"You're the worst."

Pat grinned and organised the balls in the triangle. "Hurry up and take the shot before they roll away. This table hasn't gotten any less rickety in the last twenty years."

Lisa leaned over the scuffed maple rail. Pat averted her eyes, or rather, tried to. While modest standing up, Lisa's blouse was anything but in this position. Pat pinched the bridge of her nose to block out the way her breasts strained against the poplin. It didn't help.

"Don't look at me like that." Lisa stared, indignant.

Pat had a momentary panic attack.

"I know I'm a terrible shot. It's not like I play pool that often."

A wave of relief washed over her. She pulled her eyes from Lisa and saw that the triangle remained intact, save number eleven, which had drifted a bit on its own. The white ball had only made it a third of the way across the table. Pat flashed a smile. "I thought you'd be better at this after living so long in Northton. What else is there to do here?"

Lisa pursed her lips. "Solving the mystery of who stole Wilma's keys at least three times a month." She leaned on her pool cue. "Also trying to find excuses to avoid going fishing."

"Very important, that last one." Pat set her cue back on the rack. "Practically a full-time job around here."

Lisa laughed. Pat looked at the floor before she fell in love. She hadn't realised how much she'd missed that sound.

"Here," Pat reached for Lisa's pool cue. "Let me show you how to line up a shot."

Lisa stared up at her sceptically. "You're aware that several men around here have tried to teach me."

Of course they had, Pat thought. *Who didn't love a little male validation. And men love feeling useful around women.*

"And it didn't work?" Pat put a hand in her pocket. "I'm shocked."

"Your tone says otherwise." Lisa knocked her with her hip.

"If I say any more, you'll accuse me of male-bashing."

Lisa laughed again. Pat didn't look away this time. Her hazel eyes lingered on Lisa's for a few moments longer than they should have. "That's never stopped you before."

"Alright then," Pat shrugged. "Take the cue and put it in your fingers like this." Pat took Lisa's hand and placed it correctly on the table. She leaned over her, sliding the cue steadily across her knuckles.

Lisa nearly fainted in her scent. How the hell was a pool cue sliding between her knuckles making her think about sex? Was she fourteen? Maybe it was the alcohol. Maybe it was because her jeans felt like too much material between her and Pat's thighs. Was there something else there? Was Pat packing?

Which was when Josh walked in.

four

Josh who had just bought her red grocery store carnations. Josh who had left disappointed because she didn't want to move in with him. Josh who was the sweetest, nicest guy in town, which was a low bar, but still, he rose to meet it.

Lisa's brain reeled making eye contact with him. How did she look bent over the pool table under Pat, practically taking her from behind and making suggestive motions with a pool cue. Wondering if she was packing. Wondering if Pat could feel her pulse racing. Wondering if Pat knew she'd already ruined her underwear.

"Pat?"

Pat stood up and stuffed a hand in her pocket. "Hey Josh."

Josh looked from Pat to Lisa. Lisa stood up and straightened her blouse.

"You know Lisa?"

"We were roommates when I was doing cadet training." Lisa walked over to Josh and put an arm around his waist. Josh kissed the top of her head. Pat felt the absence, but knew better than to let it show.

Because that's what women did, wasn't it? They always chose their men. Make fun of them, complain about them, warn others about them, but at the end of the day, you spare men's feelings at all costs. Especially when that cost was other women.

Pat knew she had no right to feel this way. It was just her bitterness talking. She couldn't pursue whatever Lisa might be playing at. But she also couldn't help gripping the pool cue a little harder than necessary.

"When did you get into town?"

Pat frowned. "I live here."

"What?"

Pat laid the pool cue on the table. "I'm a ways out of town. Remember? Kyle used to hang out there all the time."

"I thought you'd left after..."

Pat shrugged. "Nope."

Josh looked at Lisa as though she might have the answer. Lisa looked straight at Pat, hoping to communicate telepathically that she should keep her mouth shut. *About what though? Nothing happened. Pat doesn't even like you in that way.*

Josh spun his keys around his finger. "How come we haven't seen you around?"

Pat jerked her head back in disbelief at the question. "Because you're fucking rubbish."

Josh's keys stopped spinning. Then he laughed. He'd forgotten about Pat's vocabulary. "Well, it's good to see you. Glad you haven't changed."

"How's Kyle?"

"Okay, I guess." I only see him maybe once a year.

"Hmm." Pat rocked on her heels. "Guess he thinks you're fucking rubbish too."

"Come on Pat. You know I had nothing to do with that. I didn't even hang out with them."

Pat grunted. "Fine."

The three of them stood awkwardly, the ear-splitting chorus of an overly nasal country song kicking in. Lisa broke the tension.

"I have to drive Pat home. She came here with me." Lisa squeezed him tighter as if to reassure him that she wasn't fantasising about running away forever with Pat. Or to reassure herself.

"Oh. Yeah. Sure." Josh pulled his arm away. "I'll talk to you later?"

"Mmhmm," Lisa nodded. She grabbed Pat's arm and pulled her out of the bar. Pat was relieved to no longer have to endure the assault on her ears.

Lisa hopped into the cab of her truck and slammed the door. "Go ahead, say it."

Pat raised her eyebrow. "Say what?"

"Whatever you were going to say."

For once, Pat found herself at a loss for words. She might not have been pleased at what had just happened, but none of it had been unexpected.

"Alright. I never want to hear *Jim-Bob and the Cousinfuckers* again. I thought country music was bad before." Pat glanced at Lisa from the corner of her eye.

Lisa slapped her arm. "Not that. Though it was a little loud."

"Well, I'm known for my tact and decorum, so you're going to have to be more specific."

Lisa scoffed and hit her again.

"Let me rephrase," Pat continued. "What are you hoping I'll say?" The moon's glow filtered through the salt-crusted windows. Its pale blue light made Lisa look much sadder than she had only moments prior.

"That I should grow some balls and dump him." Lisa sighed.

"Those are two very different things, but I'm glad I could be your safe person. I fully support your gender journey." Pat put a finger to her chin. "If you're lucky, Josh will be into men as well."

"Shut the hell up, Pat!" Lisa laughed. It didn't mask the tears rolling down her face. "Why am I doing this to myself?"

"Doing what?" Pat felt like she should hug her, but the truck made it awkward. "Agonising over hurting a man's feelings? I've yet to meet a woman who hasn't" Pat put her hand on her knee instead. *Wrong move! Wrong move!*

But Lisa didn't flinch away. She only put her hand on Pat's and started the truck. "You don't seem to worry about it."

"Yes, well most people agree that I'm a monster."

Lisa's laugh was a little more genuine this time. It was easier to focus on Pat's glaring misandry than her own inadequacies. But really, what was she going to do? Stringing him along wasn't fair to him. Leaving wasn't fair to him. Being angry at him for being in this situation also wasn't fair to him.

Lisa wished she could be more like Pat. Pat would just say *fuck him* and leave. But Pat never cared about what people thought of her.

They were half way out of town when Pat disturbed her thoughts.

"So, er, I parked the lorry at your place, right?"

"Oh shit." Lisa shook the cobwebs out of her head. "I'll turn around."

"Eh. Don't worry about it. Just drop me off. I've got a flatbed I use for deliveries I can drive for now. We're almost there. You can pick me up later."

"You're sure?"

"Yeah. Be careful on this corner. It gets pretty slippy out here."

Lisa nodded and slowed down. "What am I gonna do, Pat?"

Her tone made it clear that Lisa wanted real advice this time, not deflection. "Does he know you used to date women?"

"*A* woman, Pat. I never got the chance to date more than one. And no. Would it make it easier if I told him?"

Pat took a deep breath. "He probably would have freaked out a lot more when he saw us if he did."

Lisa's palms went clammy. "What do you mean?"

"He looked at me as if I were there to steal his girl. Like Willow."

"I thought you said nothing happened."

"I said she kissed me once." Pat ran her fingers through her hair. "But that was enough for Northton."

The noise from the road was the only sound for a few more kilometres.

"Hey Pat?"

"Mmh?"

"How come you never brought anyone home?"

"What do you mean?" Pat leaned her head against the window.

"I brought plenty of boyfriends around. And Phaedra. I never met any of your girlfriends. You never mentioned them."

Pat took a deep breath. *That's because you were there. Because it crushed me seeing you with someone every time. Getting off while you were in the next room wasn't an option.* "I'm just a private person. You know that."

"I told you all about my love life."

"And I learned more about penises than I ever needed to know."

Lisa turned and shot her a smile before returning her attention to the road. "Will you tell me about one of them?"

Pat hesitated. *It's okay, you're friends,* she thought. Pat rolled her shoulders and relaxed. "The last one I was with before you got posted, her name was Josie. Her mom was Cree, she was really proud of that. I used to go watch her ribbon dances." Pat stared up at the ceiling. "She tasted like a peach daiquiri." Her fingers skimmed over her lips, like they remembered the flavour. Lisa remembered *that* conversation and felt a sudden flood of warmth.

"Oh." Lisa flushed. "Wow."

Pat frowned. "What?"

"Just, I dunno." Lisa's mouth opened and closed several times. "The way you described her. Not a word about what she looked like."

Pat thought about it. "I suppose not. I'd never really thought about it before."

Lisa looked over at Pat. "Looks don't matter to you?"

"What do you mean by *matter*?"

"Like, you don't notice what people look like?"

"I mean, yeah, I do." Pat blew out her cheeks. She'd looked at Lisa plenty. Hopefully without her noticing. "It's just, if someone asks me about someone and I tell them what they look like, I might as well show them a picture."

"I guess that's fair." Lisa hummed about it for a few moments before adding, "I told you what my boyfriends looked like."

"You did. Once. Then you never told me again." Pat nudged Lisa. "Because it didn't matter. You were either attracted to them or you weren't."

"What are you attracted to, then?" Lisa's eyebrows angled into a tent.

"Oh no," Pat protested. "We aren't doing that."

"Why not?"

"Because then you'll be pointing out every woman that looks anything even remotely close to what I say."

"Yes, but that's *fun,* Pat," Lisa whinged. "I miss having fun."

"You're in the wrong town for that."

"Please?" Lisa pouted.

"I don't point out every bloke holding a fish."

"Why would I care about fish?" Lisa grimaced.

"I haven't the foggiest. But every profile of every person you've dated had a picture of him holding a fish. Sometimes more than one."

Lisa tilted her head. "How do you know that?"

"I checked?" Pat curled her lip.

"You checked the profile of every guy I dated?"

"Yes."

"Why?"

Pat shrugged. "Lotta creeps out there."

Lisa's heart nearly exploded. All she wanted to do right now was pull over and throw herself at Pat. But she couldn't. Because Pat was her friend. Lisa inhaled several times to calm herself.

"You're not angry, are you?" Pat looked worried.

"No." Lisa took a final cleansing breath to wash the desire out of her system. She needed to change the subject.

"So, tits or ass?"

Pat frowned. "What?"

"What are you into? Share with me, goddammit."

"Yes?"

"You're into everything?"

"All women are beautiful."

Lisa rolled her eyes. "Wilma Perkins."

"Wilma Perkins was smoking hot back in 1968. Then she had Tyler's dad and joined the church."

Lisa narrowed her eyes.

"I saw a photo book at one of Tyler's birthday parties."

"He invited you?"

"Oh God no. I wandered in and no-one stopped me." Pat grinned. Her teeth shone a cool blue in the LED dashboard lights.

"I can't believe you never told me about any of this."

"When was I supposed to tell you?" Pat turned her hands. "You didn't know any of these people."

"I guess not."

Another few moments passed in silence.

"Pat?"

Pat turned to look at Lisa. She couldn't read the emotion, but her face seemed strained.

"It's been really nice catching up with you."

Pat inhaled sharply. It *was* nice. And as much as she didn't want to admit it, Pat had been lonely. For years. Yes, she had her *events*, but it wasn't the same as having Lisa's presence around every day. Her house felt empty.

If she were normal, Pat would pursue Lisa in a heartbeat. And then the town would talk and she would lose her job through some made-up excuse. Pat couldn't do that to her. And after what had just happened at Boots? Lisa wasn't ready for the repercussions of being queer in Northton.

God, she was stupid.

No, not stupid. Foolish.

Pat exhaled. "I missed this too." She stared out the window, dreaming of what could have been.

"My driveway is just up ahead. It's a bit of a blind corner, so you'll have to slow down."

Lisa downshifted. The truck wobbled to the left. Ahead lay the remains of a red Chevy, wrapped around a tree.

"Good thing I slowed down," Lisa muttered. She parked the truck and put the hazards on.

Pat stuffed her hands in her pockets and went to inspect the truck. Lisa dug around the glovebox for her Maglite.

"Er, Lisa?"

"Yeah?"

"Maybe don't look?"

"Relax, Pat. I'm a cop. I see all sorts of things."

Pat shrugged and stepped back from the truck. The block had been pushed clean into the cabin by a black spruce tree. The tree didn't seem fazed at all.

At first, Lisa only saw the truck, its paint camouflaging the frozen pool of blood and the body, reduced to ground chuck held loosely together by a crimson-soaked jacket.

"How the..."

"I told you not to look."

"Knock it off, Pat, I'm fine." Lisa shone her Maglite over the body. "It's like it went through a meat grinder." Lisa looked over at Pat. "That doesn't happen in a crash like this."

Lisa pulled out her phone and snapped a pic of the plates, but there was no need. She'd pulled this truck over yesterday.

"It's Caleb's." Pat called from the front of the truck.

"You recognise the truck? I thought you didn't go into town."

"Nope. I recognise his head. It's over here."

Lisa trudged through the ice crusted snowbank toward the tree. Pat was about to point at the head when she heard a sound from the cabin of the truck. Ice blue eyes stared at her through the shattered windshield. Pat hadn't seen those eyes in eighteen years. Her chance *had* been wasted and whatever ridiculous dream she might have had with Lisa became even more impossible than it already was.

five

How the hell does *that* happen?" Lisa took some more pictures.

"I don't know enough about physics to comment." Pat pried open the passenger door.

Lisa turned toward the creaking aluminium. "What are you doing? It's not a crime scene, but still." Then she saw what Pat had seen. A girl, slight, with matted black hair and brilliant blue eyes. Her face had blood smeared all over it and she stared, confused at the carnage around her.

"Oh shit." Lisa rushed over to help Pat with the door. After a few tugs, the bent hinge snapped and the door swung free. The girl sat, staring.

"My name is Lisa. I'm a police officer. Can you tell me your name?"

The girl blinked and looked at Pat as if she might have the answer.

Lisa shone the Maglite in the girl's eyes. She winced and shut them tight. Lisa turned to Pat. "I thought maybe drugs, but her pupils are just fine."

"There's a dent in the dashboard and it doesn't look like the airbag went off. She probably just hit her head wrong."

Lisa inspected the dash. There was a large split in the vinyl and yellow foam padding bulged out. The girl watched with curiosity, but didn't move out of the way. "We should get her out of the car now in case the airbag does go off."

"She can stay with me tonight."

"What?" Lisa spun around and caught Pat with the beam. Pat shielded her eyes. "Sorry!" She turned off her Maglite.

"Look, we're far enough out that the only ambulance is going to be a helicopter. I don't want to pay for that and she probably doesn't want to pay for it either. Aside from her head, she doesn't look hurt. Check her for ID and then we'll figure out the rest in the morning."

Lisa thought about it. The town had a pharmacist and a medicentre that wouldn't open until nine. The nearest hospital would be another hour away. And it's not like they would do anything except keep her under surveillance.

"You've got First Aid, right?"

Pat rolled her eyes. "Of course I do. There's a kit in the shop, one in the lorry and another one in the house. I promise I'll phone you if there's any brain haemorrhaging."

Lisa shoved her. "You're not qualified to do that."

"We had to trepan a guy on a rig I worked at years ago." Lisa looked sceptical. Pat raised one hand and put the other on her chest. "I swear to God, I'm not lying. *I* had to do it too, because the rest of the crew were cringeling milksops playing at being men."

Lisa narrowed her eyes. "One of these days, I'm going to make you tell me every little thing that you've done since I got here."

Pat flashed a smile. "I look forward to it."

They heard a scuffle. The girl had gotten out of the truck on her own. She stared at them like a lost child. Pat and Lisa exchanged glances.

"Help me get her cleaned up and then come see me when you have time to drive me into town to pick up the lorry. She'll probably know who she is by then. If not, I can drive her to a proper doctor."

Lisa fidgeted with the button on her Maglite. That sounded reasonable enough. "Yeah." She took off her coat and draped it around the girl's shoulders. "Let's do that."

Once they passed the thick brush Pat kept as an unkempt privacy hedge, Lisa saw the house – a simple two-story A-frame, quaint and warm-looking. The design seemed out of place for this area. Most people who owned land would build the largest McMansion they could afford. More unusual were the three other A-frames next to it, huddled around a circular driveway like a tiny village.

"How many people live here?" Lisa asked.

"Just me. Why?"

"There are four houses."

"Oh, yeah, no." Pat guided the girl around a patch of ice and jutted her chin toward the A-frame on the left. "That one's the house."

"What are those other ones?"

"That's a garage. It's hard to tell because the door is facing away from us. The other one's the wood shop and the last one's kind of a guest space. There's a jacuzzi in that one if you ever want to use it."

"Kind of? How many guests do you have that they need their own house? With a hot tub?"

Pat raised an eyebrow as if Lisa was supposed to know what that meant, but they had reached the steps of the house and Pat didn't explain further.

For someone who was *domestically challenged,* as she put it, Pat's kitchen was breathtaking. White oak cabinetry lined the walls, pieced together so expertly that Lisa couldn't see the seams.

"Jesus, Pat. This is amazing. I had no idea you could do this."

Pat ran the water until it turned warm. She wet a clean cotton cloth and dabbed at the girl's face. "Thanks. It's just a shame I can't really use them."

Lisa held the girl's hair back. "What do you mean?"

The brown crusts of blood loosened and Pat gently wiped them away. "I still can't cook."

Pat couldn't, but Lisa could. Visions of herself in this kitchen, wearing an apron, Pat behind her, arms wrapped around her waist. Her breath hot against the downy hairs at the back of her neck. Lisa pushed the thoughts away, lovely as they were. She didn't need those distractions right now. She took a deep breath. "Do you have a brush?"

"Er..." Pat ran a hand over her buzzcut hair. "There might be one in the closet over there." Pat pointed to a set of folding doors.

Lisa rummaged around and found a basket with old makeup - which she knew Pat never wore, soaps and several toothbrush cases. Different women's names were written in black marker on each. *Wow,* she thought. *That guest house must get a lot of use.* A pang of jealousy caused the muscles in her neck to tighten followed by a rush of excitement thinking of Pat in various states of undress. *Really Lisa? You have a jealousy kink now?* She shook the thoughts out of her head. Then she found one labelled *Phaedra. You don't have a right to feel this way,* she reminded herself. She put it back and found a hairbrush.

Lisa returned with the brush. "You have a lot of toothbrushes."

"Oh, yeah. Most of those are old. I should throw those away."

"One says *Phaedra.*"

Even Pat could hear the green in her voice.

"Yeah, her and Andi stay here on occasion when they're on holiday. I told you I made some pieces for them."

Lisa's heart did a small leap. She busied herself picking apart the mats before running the brush through the girl's hair. She hoped it would hide the mess of emotions. It did not.

"Is that… okay?"

Lisa continued detangling the girl's hair. "I don't know. I mean, of course it is. There's no reason why it shouldn't be." She refused to meet Pat's gaze.

It was clearly not okay, but Pat decided to let it be for now. She finished wiping the girl's face and hands. "Are you hungry?"

The girl shook her head.

"Alright then. Would you like to rest?"

The girl paused for a moment, considering. She nodded her head once and Pat led her upstairs.

Lisa ran her finger across the sturdy rectangular table in the dining room. It seemed to be made from a single solid slab of wood, but that couldn't be possible. Trees didn't grow that big.

Lisa turned when she heard Pat walking down the stairs. "How the hell did you make this?"

"Er, with wood and glue? Couple of bolts for the legs?"

"No, I mean, how did you get a piece of wood this big?"

"It's two pieces of wood." Pat held up two fingers.

"How? I don't see a seam."

Pat walked over to the table. She placed one hand on Lisa's waist and the other on her wrist. A fresh wave of heat flushed her cheeks. Pat dragged her finger across a spot on the wood. "You can see it right here. It was supposed to be for a client, but I couldn't send it out like that, so I kept it for here."

"I don't see it." Lisa doubted she could see straight right now anyway.

"Here, where the grain curves a bit inward and then cuts off." Pat traced her fingernail along a barely visible line.

"You line up the grain?"

"Yeah. That's how you're supposed to do it."

Lisa shook her head. "No wonder I've never seen you in town. No-one who lives there could afford this."

Pat gave a half-shrug. "You'd be surprised. A lot of money is tied up in farm land. Most of it's inherited and no-one has set foot on it in years. Or they're fighting over it in court."

"Huh. I guess I never thought about that."

Pat took a deep breath. "You want some tea? Or is it too late for you?"

The corner of Lisa's lip rose a hint. She wanted to stay here all night. "Yeah, I'll have some tea."

Pat returned with a teapot and poured Lisa a mug.

"Whaaaat?" Lisa grinned. "Is this my old RCMP mug?"

Pat smirked and nodded her head. "You left it when you got posted. I thought I'd hang on to it."

"You are far too sweet." Lisa took the mug from Pat and leaned over to kiss her on the cheek. Pat blushed.

Lisa's face drained, the reality of what she was doing hitting her a moment too late to stop herself. "That must be why all the girls are into you," she added, hoping it would suffice as cover.

Pat took a seat. Lisa followed suit and hid behind her mug of tea for a few moments to let her emotions simmer down.

"So, Caleb. How much do you know about him?"

Lisa knew almost nothing about Caleb. Just the occasional anecdote from Tyler or Josh, as well as some much less positive ones from Pat and Walter.

"The only thing I know about him that wasn't from telling him to get off Walter's property for soliciting underage women is hockey stories from Tyler and Josh. I was told never to arrest him unless I caught him, and I'm quoting Tyler here, *with his dick in her*. Otherwise, his family would tie us up in court for years."

"That sounds about right."

"So, of course, he never got charged." Lisa blew on her tea.

"That also sounds about right."

The gruesome spectacle outside was definitely a *person* but not one she could relate to especially well. Lisa thought that she should feel something more, but she simply *didn't*. Her lack of emotion wasn't lost on Pat.

"Police training kicking in?" Pat looked up at her from behind her mug.

Lisa winced. "I'm feeling guilty that I'm not upset. Weird that I'm not feeling much of anything when there's a whole person that I know out there."

"That's been happening a lot lately, huh?"

"What do you mean?" Wrinkles formed at the edges of Lisa's eyes.

Pat considered what she should say before she set her mug down again. She picked it back up, cradling it in both hands, as though it might protect her. Her head shook slightly. "You're really gonna make me say it?"

Lisa glared. "Is this about Josh?"

"No. Not about Josh. But it says a lot that you're getting defensive about a guy you're miserable with."

"I'm not miserable! And Josh is a great guy! He brings me flowers! He remembers things! He listens when I talk!" *And you're trying to dump him*, Lisa thought.

Pat stared at her tea, letting Lisa come to terms with how she had just done what Pat had said she would do. Lisa's mouth hung open.

Pat looked back up at Lisa. God, she was beautiful. Those coffee brown eyes. That errant curl of auburn hair. That crease line when she smiled that never truly disappeared. And regardless of what happened, she was more off limits than ever.

Pat had almost forgotten what she was doing when Lisa's half-formed ideas coalesced. Her eyes dropped to the table. "It's not about Josh, is it?"

Pat inhaled slowly. "Probably not."

"Does that mean? Am I…not into men?" Lisa couldn't bring herself to say *lesbian.* Why did you never tell me?!" Lisa waved her hands frantically.

Pat laughed low. "What? It's not like there's a mark on your forehead. We can't sniff each other out." Her face turned sympathetic. "And anyway, I have no idea. You might be. You might not be. All I can say is that you never acted the way you did around Phaedra with any of the men you brought around."

Or you. Lisa thought.

Pat sipped her tea and set it down, no longer needing it as a shield. "You haven't acted that way with any of the guys you've dated since then either, have you?"

Lisa groaned and slumped against the table, nearly dumping her tea. Pat reached across and moved it before she did. "I thought you said it was because dating women is different?"

"Yeah, sure. But you were only with Phaedra for a couple months and you're still chasing that high from over a decade ago."

"Maybe it's because it only *lasted* two months. There wasn't enough time for the infatuation to wear off."

Pat shrugged. "Maybe." She took an audible sip of tea.

Lisa pursed her lips. "Say it."

"Were you ever that infatuated with men?"

"Goddammit Pat. I can't be a lesbian."

"Okay." Pat took another sip of tea.

Lisa glared before giving up, melting into the matching maple chair. She never could win against

Pat's verbal judo. "What am I gonna do?" she whinged.

"Well, I became a quasi-hermit living near a town I hate. I don't recommend that option."

"I mean about Josh."

Pat sighed. "If we were anywhere else, I'd say tell him the truth and let him find happiness." Pat tilted her head in the direction of Northton. "But you live here and if Josh is anything like I remember, he trades gossip like Pokémon cards. He'll out you before sunset."

"He's not like that!" Lisa protested.

Pat shook her head. "He doesn't mean it maliciously. He's just part of the community."

Lisa frowned.

"You didn't tell him about Phaedra." Pat flipped her hand.

"No." Lisa hung her head.

"Because you didn't want the entire town to know."

Lisa raised her eyebrows in agreement. Josh really did love this town, and secrets didn't ever stay secret for long. "I am so screwed." Lisa whimpered. "What do I do?"

"Now you see why I left." Pat tilted her mug.

Lisa felt a pair of eyes on her from the staircase. She turned to see the girl and her ice-blue eyes drilling into her. Her brushed black hair hung straight and partially obscured her face. Lisa flinched.

"Ah shit, I'm sorry, were we being too loud?" Pat rushed over to make sure the girl was okay.

"You're sure you shouldn't bring her to the hospital? Everyone's going to find out she's here when they come to deal with the, uh..." Lisa motioned toward the accident. It hit her again that there was still a body frozen to the top of the truck.

Pat rolled her eyes. "People have been talking about me for as long as I've been here." She paused. "For as long as they've *known* I've been living here."

"That's the other thing. How pissed are they going to be now that they know you've been here the whole time?" Lisa took a sip of her tea. It was lukewarm, but she didn't care.

"They were upset that I was here twenty years ago. Nothing's changed."

"That's not going to cause problems for you?"

Pat shrugged. "They're angry if I'm here. They're angry if I stay out of their way. I owe them nowt."

"What about me?"

Pat took a few breaths. "That's fair, I suppose. But I also didn't know you were here until you phoned me out of the blue. Which reminds me," Pat tapped her finger on the oak table. "You called Phaedra to get my number. Why do I think that it wasn't just to get my expert advice on dating men."

"Oh, I totally forgot about that," Lisa rubbed her forehead. "You remember a girl named Willow?"

An unreadable expression crossed Pat's face. "Yes."

Lisa glanced over at the girl. She stayed on the stairs, watching intently. Not like she had anything better to do, she supposed. "Some of the guys remembered her too. They filled me in on what happened."

"What *did* happen, Lisa?" Pat moved her tapping finger from the table to her mug.

Lisa inhaled sharply and blew out her cheeks. "Someone vandalised her grave."

Pat screwed her eyes shut and gave the barest hint of a nod.

Lisa shrank in her chair. "Bill thinks it was some goth kids from the city. I don't think it was targeted."

Pat chewed at the inside of her cheek. Lisa looked over to the stair. The girl had gone.

Pat pointed at the stairs. "I should probably get to bed. I'm gonna have to phone Fred first thing if he's to get out here tomorrow and deal with the body."

Lisa couldn't help but feel rejected. Like she was being pushed out. But what was she expecting? The clock read 11:53 and they both had to work tomorrow. She had used the same excuse on Josh several hours ago – before she went to Boots with Pat and then drove her home. Lisa sighed. Now wasn't the time to deal with these feelings. "I forgot you knew Fred."

"He'll be close to eighty by now. I don't want to make him work too hard. Corinne would kill me if he hurt himself on the job." Pat swirled her tea, but it was too cold to drink now.

"I've never met Corinne."

"She was a funny old lady. Used to tell fortunes at the farmer's market." Pat stared up at the ceiling, a faint smile tugging at her lips. "Wilma got pissy about it being witchcraft once and Corinne made a big show and put a curse on her. Haven't seen her since and Wilma's still convinced she's cursed."

"She sounds like someone I'd want to be friends with." Lisa moved toward the door and slipped on her boots. Pat turned on the outside lights.

"Thanks, Pat." Lisa stared at her like there was more to say. She didn't know what it was, but she knew it was there.

"For what?"

Lisa gave a half-shrug. "For being you." She took Pat's hands. "I really missed you."

Pat squeezed and let Lisa slip away. *You're treading a dangerous line,* she scolded herself and turned toward the stairs. She had naïvely hoped this complication would never resurface. Pat steeled herself. None of this was fair. Not to her. Not to Lisa and not to the girl who had just upended everything.

six

She awoke, warm in a tiny room. Blackout curtains drawn, though she could make out a sliver of aggressively yellow sunlight filtering through. A plush tan rug covered the floor and a lone dresser stood in the corner. Old cedar wood panelling covered the walls and a full-body mirror pane had been clipped to the back of the door. Comfortable, but not fancy.

She pulled her fingers out from under the blankets. Waxy. With a dull grey hue to it. Did her hands always look like this? She couldn't remember. Two women had taken her from a truck. They had washed her face and hands. The pretty one had brushed her hair. The other looked like a man, but she couldn't stop herself from staring.

Pat knocked gently on the door. "Hey, it's me. How are you feeling?" The door swished across the carpet. "I have, er... a smoothie for you." Pat placed the cup with a large straw on the dresser. "I know you said you weren't hungry last night, but you should probably eat something this morning."

The girl turned, blinking the sleep from her eyes. Buried in the down-filled comforter, she appeared even more slight than she had when they took her in.

"Thank you" she whispered. Her tongue still felt strange. Like she hadn't used it in a long time.

Pat sat on the edge of the bed. "There's gonna be someone here to deal with the mess outside later today."

The girl inhaled deeply. Hunger gnawed at her belly. "That girl?"

Pat shook her head. "Lisa? No. Lisa's a friend though. You don't have to worry about her."

The girl nodded. Her neck felt stiff. "She's pretty."

Pat smiled and pointed to the smoothie on the dresser. "She is. You should probably eat. It'll bring your strength up. I'm sure you'll remember soon." She stood and stepped quietly toward the door. "I have to do some work in the wood shop, but if you want to have a shower, the lav's to the right."

The girl waited until Pat closed the door before she got up. She slipped out of bed and padded over to a floor length mirror on the wall. She looked awful. Skin that looked bruised and blue, yellowed, sallow eyes. And she had a headache. One of them had said something about hitting her head. Or maybe she was hungry.

She ran her fingers up her arms. Her skin felt cool. She felt slight, like she could turn sideways and dissolve into the shadows. Her stomach growled.

The smoothie smelled delicious. She put the straw to her lips and gulped voraciously. It disappeared far too quickly. She would have to remember to ask for more when Pat returned.

The stained wood washroom door at the end of the hall opened into a black void. Something flashed in her brain. Not a memory, a feeling. Was she afraid of the dark?

Her fingers skimmed along the wall for the light switch. The abrupt flash seared her eyes and she raced to shut it off again. Her heart slowed in the darkness. It wasn't that bad once she was on the other side of the door. Like stepping into a cold lake in the summer. As long as the door stayed open, the ambient sunlight from the hallway would be enough.

Dirt and blood mixed and swirled down the drain. She relaxed into the hot water easing her stiff muscles. She couldn't remember ever being this sore. She couldn't remember anything aside from waking up terrified, walking downstairs and seeing Pat and Lisa talking.

She stepped out of the shower, significantly cleaner. Her skin looked a lot better too. More colour. The mirror showed the same slight girl as before, but without the grey. She decided it was a good look. Thick black hair, tiny breasts and ribs clearly visible.

She wondered who this body belonged to. Who would inhabit a body like this? It looked meek and compliant. Afraid to stand up for herself. Was that who she was?

She waved her hand at the girl in the mirror. The girl waved back. This was her. Her body. She leaned over the sink staring deep into her reflection, trying to pull whatever memories she could from the iridescent blue eyes staring back at her. She still came back with nothing.

Could she decide who she wanted to be now? Or would this body impose its will on her? Like a fate that she could never outrun. And what would happen once she *did* remember? Would she still be able to choose or would she succumb to whatever life had been chosen for her?

Where did this train of thought come from? Why was this so important? She probably had a family. A boyfriend. People who were worried about her. The thought of attachments caused a twist in her stomach she didn't appreciate.

"You should probably eat more." Pat placed another smoothie on the counter

She jumped back, baring her teeth, but Pat only chuckled.

"It's okay. I'll bring you whatever you need. Here are some clothes for now." Pat held out a neatly folded plaid button up and some jeans, along with a sports bra and underwear.

"Sorry if they're the wrong size. I'm a little bigger than you are." Pat looked at the floor.

The girl took them. "Thank you." Words still felt strange in her mouth, but they came easier than before.

"You're welcome." Pat stood awkwardly. She pointed her thumb behind her. "I've got a bit more work to finish up. I put your bedding in the wash, though. Feel free to explore the house." Pat gestured her hands openly. "This isn't a film. There are no forbidden rooms or anything." Pat laughed awkwardly at her own joke.

The girl nodded and turned back to the washroom with her pile of clothes. She pulled her arms through the soft flannel. It hung ridiculously off her small shoulders, like a child trying on her dad's clothes.

The girl wrapped her arms across her chest, losing herself in the warmth of the shirt. Did she know Pat from before? She must, otherwise, why would she be so nice to her?

Or more likely, it was just a feeling of hopefulness. Just because she *wanted* Pat to know who she was didn't mean she did.

The girl lifted the sleeve of her shirt to her nose and inhaled deeply, closing her eyes. Did she remember this smell? No images came to mind. She liked it though. It smelled comforting, but that's all she could determine. She couldn't even name the scent.

She inhaled again and a tiny thrill ignited in her heart. She must be someone to Pat if her scent was making her feel like this. She just hoped she wouldn't be disappointed when she discovered their connection. If there even was one.

She lifted the straw to her lips, drinking deeply. She finished this one almost as quickly as she had the last. Whatever was in them, she decided she could live off of it.

She followed the carpet downstairs. She might not remember much, but the house had an *old* feeling to it. Though the carpeting wasn't worn. It must be new.

The kitchen also appeared to be mostly unused. The only modern appliance would be the expensive-looking blender on the counter.

The cabinets were gorgeous. Expertly joined. She could barely make out the edges. She recognised it as oak. Strange that she remembered wood, but almost nothing else.

Mahogany hardwood made up the kitchen floor, along with solid marble counters, a lighter colour. The cleanliness and lack of clutter would feel sterile in any other space, but the size and all of the natural materials made the house feel alive.

Heavy drapes blocked most of the sunlight. She wondered if Pat had done that for her sake. Her eyes seemed awfully sensitive. She tried to remember if Pat might be a nurse, but nothing came to her. She would have to ask when Pat returned.

A light wood also made up the table - maple or birch. She sat and ran her fingers along the edges of the matching chairs. Butter soft. Pat said something about a wood shop. Did she make this?

The door opening interrupted her admiration.

"Oh hey, you're still up!" Pat had a generous smile. The girl shifted in her seat and smiled back.

"Feeling any better?"

She nodded vigorously. "Um," the girl sucked her lip. "Do you have any more..."

"Smoothie? Yeah, plenty." Pat grinned and pulled a jug out of the fridge.

"What's in it? It's amazing, but I can't remember tasting anything like that before."

"Do you remember strawberries?" Pat called from the kitchen.

The girl pictured the red seedy fruit in her mind, but this tasted a lot sweeter than she remembered. "I guess not," she confessed.

Pat smiled, handing her another glass with a straw. "They grow wild out back," she thumbed behind her. "It's a completely different flavour than the ones you get in the shops."

"Will you show me?" The girl shrunk back, embarrassed at how quickly she had blurted out the strangely intimate request.

Pat's eyes crinkled when she smiled and the girl's heart did a tiny leap. "I'd love to." She shifted her stance. "But, er, they're not in season. There's still a bit of snow on the ground." Pat pointed to the jug. "These are from last year. I have a bunch in the freezer."

The girl bit her lip.

"It's okay. I suppose you didn't know." Pat raced to explain. "I need to go meet with Fred. He phoned me and said he was going to head over soon."

The mention of another person brought forth a twinge of envy. Not that Pat might be with someone, but that she knew people. Who was Fred? A husband? No, there wasn't enough stuff in the house for more than one person. A boyfriend maybe?

Pat saw the expression on her face change but misinterpreted it. "It's alright, we'll go later if you're still around. And if the deer don't eat them all first."

"Do I know Fred?" There. That was a safe question, she thought. She could escape accusations of being envious of a person she'd just met. Unless they *did* know each other.

"Maybe?" she guessed. "I've sort of kept my head low for the past few years. I don't really know anyone that well anymore."

"Oh. What do you do?" The girl tried to hide the disappointment in her voice.

"I make furniture. Cabinets, mostly. I sell it online. I don't really go into town. Not this one anyway."

The girl felt a rush of heat imagining Pat's forearms coated in sawdust. *Am I attracted to women?* She didn't remember, but she did have a gnawing feeling of something about it being *wrong*. Why did she feel that way? Who had told her it was wrong?

It didn't matter. Her body had decided for her. She could feel her pulse quicken, along with the light-headedness that accompanied it. The flush in her cheeks. The feeling of too much saliva in her mouth. She swallowed thickly, catching herself staring.

Her gums itched.

"Are you alright?" Pat's eyebrows knitted together.

She realised her mouth hung open. "Uh, yeah," she stammered. "Sorry, I think I need to brush my teeth."

"Yeah, no worries. I left a toothbrush out for you. It's the blue one." Pat pointed upstairs. "Anyway, I still need to meet with Fred when he gets here. He's dealing with the body."

"What?"

Pat tilted her head. "We found you in a wreck. You crashed at the end of my driveway."

"Was I driving?"

Pat shook her head. "A man. Do you remember him?"

"No?" She seemed unsure.

"He, er, didn't make it."

"Oh." The girl felt like she should be upset at this, but she couldn't remember anyone. Pat didn't seem as upset as she expected either.

"Anyway..." Pat pointed at the door.

The girl nodded.

The door clicked shut and she made her way back to the bathroom. Two toothbrushes stood in a cup. She took the blue one and began brushing. She remembered how to do that, at least.

She jerked her head back when she found blood on the brush. She must be brushing too hard. Her mouth still itched. Maybe she was allergic to strawberries? That was too bad. Those smoothies were really good.

She leaned over the sink and pulled her lip back. Blood welled up between her teeth. *What is going on?*

The itch morphed into a dull pain. The girl in the mirror was as shocked as she was when her canines lengthened. She leapt backward, covering her mouth, wide eyed in horror.

The girl slammed the washroom door shut, locking it just in case Pat came walking in.

"What is happening?" she whispered to herself. She dared to look in the mirror again, fingering her teeth. All normal except for the descended canines. The pain had gone away, as had the itch. The girl tilted her head this way and that, trying to get a better view. She knew she couldn't remember much, but she was certain she never had *these* before.

She ran the tap and cupped some water into her mouth, hoping the cold would make them shrink. It was a stupid idea. She knew it was stupid. With the blood rinsed away, all she got were slightly cleaner canines.

She took a few calming breaths. What was she going to do? Brilliant blue eyes stared back at her. They looked like the eyes of someone smart. Maybe she was smart. Maybe she could figure this out. If she kept her mouth closed, no-one would know. No-one would see them.

But she had already spoken with Pat. Pat would expect her to speak again. How would she react when she saw she had taken in a girl with fangs? Where would she go? She didn't know anyone else. Maybe

Lisa? But Lisa was friends with Pat. Pat would tell her everything.

The girl opened her mouth as wide as she could, trying to see how much her lips could hide. What angle would she need to keep her head at so they wouldn't be seen? She practiced saying a few words, keeping her mouth tight and narrow. The words sounded funny with her teeth in the way.

What choice did she have, though? If she mumbled when she spoke and kept her head low, she might get away with hiding them for a little while longer. Hopefully long enough to figure out who she was.

And then the pain started again. The girl clapped her hand over her mouth. They couldn't get longer, could they?

But just as quickly as they had appeared, her canines retracted. She gingerly ran her fingers over her teeth. They came away clean. The blood had gone. All she could do was to hope that never happened again.

seven

Pat heard the distant rumble of a motor long before she saw it. The trees grew thick here – pines, firs and spruce, mostly. It made navigating this stretch of road a lot more challenging to the locals who were used to being able to see all the way to the horizon. Especially at night.

Pat could have bulldozed the trees. Grown something. Made money. But she didn't want to. Pat owned this section outright. Her bills were few. Her verdant green square in a patchwork of yellow canola and blue flax was of more value to her than that.

Even in the city, where diversity is more common, gender non-conformity tends to attract stares. Pat expected it – ever since they had shaved her head at fourteen. She wore her defiance like a crown, but like all crowns, it had become heavy. And Pat had needed a break. A long, private one. In the country, surrounded by trees.

The rumble grew louder. Then, the arhythmic ping of gravel hitting the undercarriage. A shiny black SUV appeared – classier than the old hearse Fred used to drive. She stepped back from the road, the early spring breeze pricking at her exposed skin. The SUV slowed down, approaching the patch of ice cautiously before rolling to a stop. Pat cocked an eyebrow against the edge of her toque, but she didn't approach.

Fred rounded the vehicle and smiled. "I know you're there, Pat." He smiled.

"Fred!" Pat stepped out from behind the brush.

Fred opened his arms.

Pat fell into his embrace. "Corinne still keeps you around?"

Fred laughed. "You know how it goes. Are you alone?"

Pat shook her head. "Lisa and I pulled her from the wreck. She's inside. Probably terrified." Pat tapped the toe of her boot against the ground. "I wasn't sure that was going to happen. It doesn't fit with the rules."

"Corinne knows the rules better."

"If there are any. I swear she just makes them up sometimes."

"She's still angry with me about that." Fred muttered. "You know," he donned his heavy silicone gloves. "I don't think I've been out here since you figured out how to put that abandoned Bronco back together."

Pat bobbed her head. "It's in pieces again. Redoing the electrical." She pointed to the body. "How's the funeral home? I thought you would have retired by now."

Fred shrugged. "Corinne has a plan."

"Does she?" Pat leaned against the mass of crumpled metal. "She doesn't tell me that either."

Fred chuckled. "You know how she is. It's not much I have to deal with though. One or two bodies a month. Usually this sort of thing." He pointed to what was left of Caleb. "He'll go straight to the cremator."

Fred did not seem particularly shocked or upset that this local son's body was here. Repeated exposure to death must dull the emotions. Either that, or Fred was really good at hiding them.

Pat shifted awkwardly in the snow. "Need a hand?"

"There's gloves in the back." Fred unzipped a body bag."

The sun beat down from clear blue skies in macabre oblivion to the gruesome task beneath it. A large group of crows gathered in the trees, observing. Listening. Pat eyed them cautiously. Fred had gotten here just in time. Another few minutes and those *birds* would have been all over Caleb.

"You ever think about offering sky burials?" Pat placed Caleb's head in the bag.

Fred hummed. "You're not the first person to ask that. I looked into it once, but it isn't legal here. You'd have to fly the corpse to Nepal."

"Hmm," Pat mused. "That would probably defeat the purpose then."

Fred nodded, pulling the remainder of the body into the bag. Pat zipped it up and helped him load it onto the back of the SUV. She glanced over at the red Chevy. The flock of crows had already descended onto the hood to claim their share.

"You want to come in for tea or something? I remember Corinne made you give up coffee." Pat removed her gloves and handed them to Fred.

Fred stalled, bobbing his head.

"No-one comes this way. And Caleb isn't going anywhere." Pat jutted her chin toward the truck.

"Alright. It's not like there's much to be done. There won't be an autopsy. And in any case, it's pretty obvious what happened."

"More obvious to some than others."

Fred nodded.

Pat trudged through the slush and puddles. "Be careful, there are still some icy patches."

Fred showed her the spikes strapped to the bottom of his boots. "It's okay. Corinne made me get these." The grim reality of Corinne's concern wasn't lost on Pat, but she wasn't about to confront that now.

Pat put on a kettle and Fred looked around. "Beautiful furniture. Looks like trade school paid off."

"Yeah," Pat called from the kitchen. "It's what I've been doing out here." She noticed he didn't mention anything about her absence. Pat had always appreciated Fred's ability to keep his mouth shut.

"If I were younger, I'd get you to make me something."

"Whatever you want, Fred." Pat placed a trivet on the table. "I never did get to thank you. I know you could have lost your license over it. Or worse."

"Pft." Fred waved her off. "Out here? No-one cares about that."

Willow's parents had insisted on no embalming or cremation. In theory, it was forbidden due to a risk of disease transfer, but Fred had let Pat spend time alone with her anyway. Fred seemed as unfazed with rules as with death when it came to mourning.

The kettle whistled and Pat stood to retrieve it. "Out of curiosity, was it Willow's parents who asked about the sky burial?"

"You won't tell anyone?" Fred ran his fingers over the edge of the table.

Pat returned and set the teapot on the trivet. "You know I won't."

Fred nodded. "I can't imagine what those kids would have found when they tried to dig her up." He'd seen a lot, but decomposition after this long wouldn't have been pretty or even recognisable. It certainly didn't look like the movies.

"Did they investigate?"

Fred nodded. "I told Bill the same thing. Any remains would be indistinguishable from the dirt pile."

"And they believed you?"

"Between that and the cost of forensics? Yeah, they did." Pat held out the teapot. Fred lifted his mug.

"Lisa wants me to go for coffee." Pat knew that Fred would understand the implication. She would have to show her face again. The town would gossip. They would ask questions. They would speculate.

"You're worried about Lisa." Fred blew on his tea. Perceptive as ever.

Pat nodded. She filled her own cup. "She's with Josh, though. I'm hoping that mitigates things."

Fred gave a half shrug. "Willow was with Caleb."

Pat snorted a laugh. "I'll always be the town monster, won't I?"

"Someone had to be, once Corinne decided she'd had enough. And some people are okay with monsters."

"Too few."

Fred set down his mug. "There are more of them than you think."

Pat raised an eyebrow. "Do you have a secret list of monster lovers somewhere?"

Fred laughed and looked away. "No. They find people to tell. People who don't judge." He looked Pat in the eye. "People who don't talk."

"I only know of one."

Fred raised an eyebrow. "She doesn't know?"

Pat shook her head. "I'm an idiot, aren't I?"

"Corinne said you'd need to speak with her."

"Really?" Pat blew out her cheeks. "After refusing to talk with me for all this time, *now* she wants to meet?"

"I wouldn't get your hopes up. I doubt she'll answer all your questions." Fred blew on his tea. "She never answers mine."

"She hasn't told you when, then?"

Fred shook his head.

They heard a movement upstairs.

"Is that the girl?"

Pat nodded.

"You didn't consider the hospital?"

"You'll see why in a moment."

The girl padded down the stairs. She looked significantly healthier than she had yesterday. Raven back hair, straight and glossy. Her blue eyes practically sparkled, even in the dim early spring light. The colour had returned to her cheeks and she smiled easily.

"Hey!" Pat waved. "Feeling any better?"

The girl nodded.

"Do you want some tea?"

She couldn't remember tea, but it seemed like they were enjoying it. "Yeah." Her voice came easier.

Fred pulled out a chair for her. She sat, feet not quite touching the ground.

"I suppose I did make these a little high," Pat joked. "This is Fred." Fred smiled. Pat went back into the kitchen to find another mug.

"How much do you remember?" Fred took another sip of tea.

The girl shook her head. "Not much. Pat said I was in the truck that crashed outside."

"Do you remember the man you were with?"

The girl shook her head.

"Well, we just packed him up. They'll come to get the truck in a day or so." Fred wrapped his hands closer around the mug. "If you remember before we take care of him, let me know and I'll let you see him." He flicked his eyes up to meet hers. "If you want to."

The girl nodded. She felt like she *should* want to, but there was hesitation in Fred's voice. Was the man next to her in the truck bad? Had he hurt her somehow?

"What was his name?" she asked.

Pat returned with the girl's mug. "Caleb."

The girl looked at the bottom of the mug as if it held the answer. She found none. The only names she knew were *Pat* and *Lisa* and now *Fred*. Fred seemed nice. Handsome, but old.

"What have you been up to since you woke?"

The girl looked at Pat. "Mostly sleeping. I've explored the house a little bit. I don't remember any of it. I don't think I was ever here before."

"Maybe once." Fred muttered.

"Should I go into town?" The girl asked. Fred and Pat exchanged glances.

Fred shook his head. "That might bring more trouble than it's worth right now."

The girl seemed disappointed.

"Maybe bundle up, go for a walk in the woods. Try and remember the names of some different trees." Fred finished the last of his tea.

"That's not a bad idea." Pat agreed. "More tea?"

Fred held out his mug. "You've got a creek that runs through your property, correct?"

Pat nodded.

"Different trees there. Ones that like more water. Green alders. Rowans. A few cottonwood, I imagine."

"Probably." Pat shrugged. "I haven't spent much time there."

"Might be time to visit."

The girl looked between Fred and Pat. There seemed to be something going on here that she didn't quite understand.

"Would Corinne tell me that, at least? How is she?" Pat sipped her tea.

Fred held his closer. "I think she has to. She's running out of time."

Pat nodded. "I'm surprised she's let her illness go on this long. They haven't commented?"

Fred laughed. "Oh, no. Most of them have forgotten she exists. Except for maybe Wilma."

Pat stared pointedly. "She doesn't like being around people?"

"*You* don't like being around people. You two are a lot alike, actually."

"I don't know about that." Pat muttered.

"Find out for yourself. She said you should come by tomorrow. She promised to fill you in on some details."

"Not all the details?"

Fred stared at his tea and breathed a laugh. "You know that's not her style. She has reasons. Reasons you should know."

"It's going to depend on whether Lisa comes by to pick me up. My lorry is at her place."

Fred smirked. Crease lines nearly obscured his eyes. "You should know by now how to be discreet."

Pat sighed.

"Anyway, I should get going."

Pat nodded. "I assume I don't have to…"

"You don't have to assume anything, Pat. I won't say a word." Fred stood. Pat moved toward the door and handed him his coat.

"Even to Corinne?"

Fred shook his head. "Corinne already knows. That's why she wants you to come by so quickly."

"Did Lisa…?"

"No. Intuition, maybe?" Fred shrugged. "I don't know how she does it either."

Pat opened the door. "Thanks for stopping by, Fred. It was nice to catch up.

"Likewise. And uh," Fred pawed at the back of his neck. "Make sure she eats enough. Corinne said you never did."

"I'm a shit cook, Fred. But she's been loving the strawberry smoothies."

"I'm sure she has." Fred put his toque on. "Corinne said something about making those wrong."

"Corinne should stop snooping." Pat pursed her lips.

"Neither you nor I will ever be able to stop that." Fred grinned and shut the door.

Pat shoved her hands in her pockets and exhaled loudly. "I'll be out in the wood shop."

eight

The door stuck. The girl shoved it with her shoulder, stumbling into the wood shop. Pat turned her head briefly to acknowledge her presence and then returned to the bandsaw.

The girl found a clear spot on the tool bench and hoisted herself up, waiting for Pat to finish. While Pat focused on the machine, the girl allowed herself to admire the way she deftly manoeuvred the slab of wood along the cutting blade. Even though sawdust coated her like a blanket, hovering just above her skin in the tiny hairs of her forearms, the girl could make out each flex. Each liquid movement.

Maybe I do like women? she wondered. For all she knew, she could have a husband and three kids waiting for her somewhere at home. She caught herself curling her lip at the idea.

What about men? Yes, she decided. She did find men attractive. Quite attractive. A boyfriend somewhere then? Or perhaps she was a free spirit. Never settling down, taking lovers where and when she wanted? That seemed more appealing. *But Pat looked very much like a man.*

She wondered how ridiculous these ideas would seem when she recovered her memories. Would she find the idea of questioning her sexuality appalling if she turned out to have deep religious beliefs? Would it cause a crisis of faith?

The squeal of the motor stopped. Pat flicked off the dust fan and the metallic scrape of the blade slowed into silence. Pat removed her industrial yellow ear protection and coiled them around her neck. She smiled, running thick fingers across her chestnut brown buzz cut, showering the floor with sawdust.

"Hey." She took a few steps toward the girl and then leaned awkwardly against the table saw. She reminded the girl of an awkward teenager, though she couldn't picture any specific teenager in her head.

"Hey." The girl smiled. "You look like you know what you're doing."

Pat grinned and dropped her head. "I suppose. I haven't had anyone watch me work in a long time." She looked at the half-finished cabinetry behind her. "Clients seem to like it, though."

"How much does this all cost?"

Pat laughed. "More than I could afford if I wasn't building it myself."

"What would you do if you had enough money that you could afford it?" The girl tilted her head and swung her feet.

Pat smirked. These seemed like first date questions, but she felt willing to play. "Exactly what I'm doing right now." She crossed her arms. "I don't need a lot of money. I'm happy doing what I'm doing."

The girl raised an eyebrow.

"Actually, that's not true," Pat corrected herself. "I'd buy a new motorcycle. I can't find parts for my 94 V-Star anymore."

"Really?" The girl bit her lip. "Will you take me for a ride?"

Pat raised an eyebrow. "There's still snow on the ground. Not much, but still."

The girl looked disappointed.

"Once it melts. If you're still around," Pat offered.

The girl wondered if Pat wanted her to still be around. She hoped she did. Joy spread across her face. "You *do* seem like the type to own a motorcycle."

Pat shuffled her feet. "And what type is that?"

"You're a woodworker? With a buzz cut?" The girl looked up at Pat from under her eyelashes.

"I don't want my hair to get in the way of the saw." Pat shrugged. She knew she was making the girl squirm, but she always had enjoyed that.

"I didn't see any men's clothes, so I'm guessing you don't have a boyfriend either."

"Are you saying that I'm into women?" Pat locked eyes with the girl and took a step forward. "That's quite the accusation."

"I didn't *say* that." The girl sat up straight. "It was something that I *noticed*."

"What's the difference between men's clothes and the clothes I'm wearing?" Pat was having fun twisting the knife.

The girl bit the inside of her cheek. "They're cleaner. And they don't smell like men."

"What do men smell like?" Pat took another step.

"Not like you." The girl flushed. "There are no men's bathroom products either."

"What if," Pat took another step. "What if I make my boyfriend use my soap? " She took another step.

"And he doesn't shave." She reached out and rested her thick fingers on the girl's thighs.

The girl stopped kicking her legs.

"What if I keep him on a leash and my boyfriend calls me *mistress*?"

Pat's scent filled her senses. Wood resin and lye. The girl wondered if she made her own soap. Underneath that, something else. Strawberries and chocolate cream?

"Do you?" she asked, voice cracking.

A wicked glint appeared in the curve of Pat's smile. "No," she gave a scarce shake of her head. "I'm into women."

The girl searched Pat's eyes, a stunning olive and gold-flecked hazel. "I don't know if I am," she confessed.

Pat unflexed her fingers. "I can't give you that answer."

"It's just," the girl let her hands fall. "What if I have a boyfriend?"

"What if you have a girlfriend? Would that make you feel better?" Pat took a step back. She knew this game and she played it expertly.

The girl abhorred the sudden loss of her warmth. Why had she only been concerned about a potential boyfriend? "Have you been with girls who have boyfriends?"

Pat found her pockets and stuffed her hands inside. She nodded. "Most of them do. Husbands too."

"Why?" The girl's looked confused. "I mean, why would they...?"

"Oh, lots of reasons." Pat pawed at the back of her neck. "Some are only curious. Some like both. Some loathe their men, but still find themselves stuck with one."

"Do those ones leave them for you?"

Pat shook her head. "Not usually. If they leave, most of the time they'll find another one."

"That doesn't bother you?" The girl felt a wave of sympathy. She reached out her hand, but put it down again.

"Why would it bother me?"

The girl wasn't sure. She felt like it would bother her. "You don't feel used? Like you're not good enough for them?"

Pat tilted her head, contemplating. "Let's say that to them, men are like meat and potatoes. I'm candy. Everyone loves sweets, but they can't live off of them." Pat continued. "I know they're temporary. I don't expect them to stay."

The girl stared at her knees. "You don't want them to stay?"

Pat sighed. "What I want has nothing to do with it. This isn't my place." Pat stretched out her arms. "This isn't my world. It's theirs. Men get women. It doesn't matter what *they* do. *I'm* the monster, not them."

"That's not always true, though, is it?" The girl swayed her feet again. "There are gay couples."

Pat laughed to herself. She had a tendency to rant and this girl didn't know any better. The few people in Pat's life knew to steer clear of certain topics.

"And Shrek is a film about a troll who gets his happy ever after. He's still a troll, and now she is too. Most people don't want to be a monster, though – even if they're attracted to Shrek." Pat drew circles in the dust with her boot. "They're the exception, not the rule. I'm not going to put my faith in an exception."

"But there *are* still monsters" The girl focussed on her knees bobbing as she kicked her feet. "They don't disappear because they're not as common."

Pat sat with that a moment. She gave a curt nod. "What about you? Are you a monster?"

"I..." she stammered. "I don't know."

"Hmm." Pat took a step forward again. "That's just it, isn't it?" Another step. "It's one thing to talk about monsters. To tell yourself that monsters are *good.* That monsters *deserve love*. That monsters are *just like us*. It's a very different thing to *be* a monster."

Pat locked eyes. A strand of black hair fell over her face.

"To *be* a monster means you have to live it. Live with the knowledge that no matter what those well-meaning people might think of you, no matter how well you behave, no matter how useful you are, how pretty, how well-dressed, there will always be those who want you to leave. Or die. They're not picky."

The way Pat's eyes reflected the brutalities inflicted on her made the girl flush. Pat hadn't mentioned any of it, yet the girl could imagine every insult. Every broken nose. Every boot to the ribs. Something in the way Pat stood told her she had repaid it tenfold.

Pat placed her hands back on the girl's thighs. This time they opened to accommodate her. "And some days," she continued, "those people are the loudest. And those friends you thought had your back? They flinch when they think their kid might turn out like you. They disappear when the pitchforks and torches come out. They're only protecting themselves, after all.

You can't fault them for that. Because you're not a person, you're a political issue. They're not *evil*. It's just the economy."

Pat curled her muscled fingers against her thigh. *Rage?* thė girl thought? It didn't feel like rage. Or bitterness. She said it with *pride*. Pat knew her place. She chose to be who she was. And she had accepted the consequences.

Not accepted, *relished*. The world's vitriol was a badge. One that declared her refusal to play at being a pretty, pretty princess.

"Sometimes," she continued, "even the monsters themselves will join in. They think to themselves, *If I rat out the other monsters, they'll accept me. I'll be one of the good ones. I'll get to live like them."*

Pat leaned in. The girl's breath hitched. "And after all that," Pat's eyes hooded and dropped to the girl's lips, parted and aching. "The worst monsters are the ones who still choose to act like one. The ones who know they're monsters and know the consequences and still refuse to be anything but. It's a hard choice to make. Few people want to be one of *those* monsters."

The girl's heartbeat faltered. She didn't think she was gay, but something about Pat drew her in. Her intensity. Her confidence. Her aura screamed *predator*, but she hadn't pounced, even though she could have. Common sense told her to leave, but her curiosity pinned her in place. She was enjoying treading this edge, knowing that she could fall at any moment. "Are you angry at them?"

Pat shook her head, not taking her eyes from her mouth. "No," she spoke barely above a whisper. "They are who they are. I'm not a hero. I happily take the blame. If I didn't, I wouldn't get what I wanted as often."

"What do you want?" The girl knew full well what Pat wanted. She wanted Pat to get what she wanted.

Pat arched her neck skirting her lips a hair's width from the girl's. Her breath cascaded across her teeth. She smelled like her. Her soap. Her shop. Her clothes. Hers.

For now.

The corner of her lip turned up, eyes fixed on the girl's pulse point throbbing like a hummingbird as she thought. Weighing the consequences. What if? Was an imaginary boyfriend worth angering to be with a monster? What did her body tell her? Pat knew, but would *she* figure it out?

The girl's lips crashed into Pat. Short fingers and small hands grasping at the back of her neck, pulling Pat into her. She broke the kiss, her eyes dark and frantic, searching for any sign that she had made a mistake, but Pat gave none.

Her tongue burst across her lips. Pat opened wider. She loved this part. The part where they realised just how hungry they were. How starved they had been. And Pat would provide whatever they wanted. Like a buffet with a time limit. And they always ate like the plate would be yanked away at any moment. Pat savoured that *want.*

And she always reciprocated. She dug deep. Because she knew exactly what would come next. A remembered boyfriend. A husband would interrupt. It was never their fault. It was Pat who had done the damage. It was her role to take the blame.

And so, she grabbed hold of the opportunity while it presented itself. The future may be certain, but it was not *now*. *Now* was only the girl and the girl's tongue and the girl's mouth. A delightful cornucopia of violent flesh.

The girl pulled her forward and Pat lost her balance. Her hands slammed against the tool rack behind her, caging the girl. Several carving knives fell and clattered against the bench. A container of finishing nails tinkled against the concrete floor.

Pat withdrew, chest heaving, lips kiss-swollen and mouth agape. An angry scratch blossomed on her forearm. Beads of red appeared and coalesced into a line. Then a trickle.

Pat brought her arm to her mouth, licking the blood away. The girl captured the small red smear remaining on her upper lip. A frisson travelled the length of her neck. Was she some sort of sadist? Why was the sight of Pat licking away blood doing this to her?

She didn't have long to ponder. Pat's teeth collided with her lips. The taste of blood spread across her tongue. Smoke and sweat and resin and salt and a candy sweetness that she had never imagined before. She didn't remember much, but she was almost certain blood didn't taste like this. Her pupils dilated, painting Pat with a supersaturated halo.

She felt Pat's fingers slip under the hem of her overlarge T-shirt. She felt the tips graze along her ribs. Thumb the loose elastic of the ill-fitting sports bra. Heard her whisper *is this alright?* Felt the crush of lips against her neck when she nodded.

But all she could think about was her taste. The tease of residual blood on her lips was both too much and not enough. She wanted it. All of it. It had been like a memory, inaccessible. On the tip of her tongue.

But her body remembered, even if she didn't. Her body arched into her touch. Shuddered against the press of her fingers. Writhed in the ghost of her breath.

Even if she did have a memory, she would have put it all in a box and kicked it under the bed for this. She would have forgotten her life for a few brief moments. She understood with glacier-fed clarity why those girls would risk it all to be with Pat. She understood why Pat didn't mind playing the monster if this was the reward.

But monsters get moments, not happy endings.

Her teeth itched. Panic stabbed at her heart. The girl tried to ignore it. Maybe her teeth wouldn't grow. Maybe it had been a hallucination.

Pat had been talking about lesbians. Or at least, women who loved women. Pat didn't know she was a literal monster. What would she do when she found out?

And then the pain started. The girl could feel her canines press against her lip. Her hand sped to conceal her mouth and she slipped off the tool bench. She ran back into the house, expecting Pat to call after her. Pat did not.

The girl threw herself onto the bed, saltwater streaming across her face. Tears trailed down her elongated fangs. She knew exactly what she must have looked like to Pat – another curious girl who couldn't handle her. Who got scared that someone might find out. That Pat hadn't even acted surprised made it hurt even more.

How would Pat react if she knew the truth? What did she know about *real* monsters? Would all her big talk evaporate? Would Pat cast her aside as was the monsters' due? Or would Pat wrap her muscled arms around her? Protect her?

The girl heard footsteps approach the door. They paused and then retreated. The girl threw off the covers and ran to catch her, but when she opened the door, Pat was gone.

A smoothie stood in the middle of the hallway with a note.

I know.

nine

The house had an eerie ordinariness to it. Off-white clapboard siding on a matchbox style split level, surrounded by darker wood trim. Painted yearly, though Fred must pay someone to do it at his age.

The sodium bulbs on the streetlights still hadn't been upgraded to the newer LEDs. They bathed the cracked and potholed streets in monochromatic yellow. Pat avoided them, slipping through the shadow until she stood at the door, hands jammed firmly in her pockets. The door opened.

"Corinne said you'd be here," Fred smiled.

"That's why I didn't ring the doorbell." Pat walked in and used her feet to pry off her boots.

"I'll leave you two alone. There's a hockey game on."

"We both know the Flames will lose again," Pat grinned. She had missed teasing Fred.

"We know a lot of things and do them anyway," Fred called from the living room, overstuffed with a lifetime of warm-looking furniture and mismatched tchotchkes.

Pat made her way downstairs and opened the door, allowing a thin sliver of light to pierce the room. The scent of pear and elderflower hung thickly.

A hand grasped her throat, hammering the door shut with her body. The sliver of light disappeared.

"We both know you aren't into women," Pat rasped. "But if you've changed your mind, at least buy me dinner first."

The hand disappeared.

"Also, it stinks in here. You should let the sun in."

"You're a fool." Corinne's voice came at her like someone had adjusted the balance on a stereo midsentence.

"Only because you won't tell me anything."

"If I did, you'd only be a more dangerous fool."

The spark of a lighter illuminated the darkness for a brief moment. An incorporeal lit cigarette punctuated Corinne's words.

Pat sighed. "No need to take out your bitterness on me."

"No?" Corinne raised her hands as if laying out evidence in a courtroom. "Your fascination with trying to subvert the curse made you waste your only chance on the first straight girl who kissed you!"

"She wasn't the first. And straight girls don't kiss like that."

"Hmm." Corinne let her hands fall. "Marginally interested then. It doesn't matter, we're fucked now. And we're never breaking that curse."

Pat rolled her eyes. "I'm trying to make the best of my situation. *You're* the one who thinks I want to subvert a curse so old no-one knows the words. If it even *is* a curse. You're the one into the witchy shit, not me."

Corinne narrowed her eyes. "The *witchy shit* is why I know so much and you're still hiding in your little peasant cabins in the middle of nowhere."

Pat laughed to herself at the way Corrine's faded Slavic accent still underscored the *t* in *shit*. "Have you even been out there?"

"Frequently." Corinne crossed her arms. "You're currently working on a piece for Anastasia. With your talent for building things, you could have made a place worth living instead of that hovel."

"Do you enjoy spying on me?" Pat crossed her arms.

"Please," Corinne waved the accusation away. "You'd spy on me if you could."

"I would not. I have no interest in seeing you and Fred doing…whatever it is straight people do."

Corinne laughed dismissively. "At least we don't need whips and chains to get off. You should try it sometime."

Pat stuck her tongue out in disgust.

"Yes, yes. I know. It's an absolute waste that the only one of us who could, won't." Corrinne looked away.

"I've been called *a waste* before. I don't know why everyone thinks my only purpose is to ride dick."

"Not when you dress like that." Corinne swept her disapproving gaze across Pat. "You were supposed to end our suffering."

"Suffering." Pat rolled her eyes. "You're doing fine. And the only one who believes in this curse is you. Or did you find anything beyond the same scrap of paper you've been hanging on to for centuries?"

"Parchment. Paper is too fragile." Corinne's refusal to elaborate communicated everything she needed to know.

"It doesn't matter anyway because she's back. Which means I definitely wasted my chance and I can't, even if I wanted to. So, my apologies. Not your chosen one."

Corinne scoffed. "It has nothing to do with being *chosen*. You're where the witch saw the end of the line."

"You're making shit up now. You're as bad as Wilma."

Corinne scowled at the comparison before regaining her composure. "No matter. Now we have your daughter to deal with."

"Is this why you've finally decided to speak with me?"

"Partly. There are other things you need to know before Fred runs out of time and you haven't bothered to learn them." Corinne lowered her gaze for a fraction of a second. The loss of Fred would hit hard, even if she didn't want to admit it.

Pat felt a twinge of sympathy. "It wouldn't have worked and you know it. Fred knew it too. But I'm still sorry."

Her jaw tensed. Corinne refused to look at her. "I know. I've seen it."

"I could have seen it too, if you'd told me how. But you refuse to tell me about your crows. You refuse to tell me about seeing ahead. You conveniently *forgot* to mention anything about pheromones or biting men and watched me make a fool of myself." Corinne had always excelled at making Pat feel like a petulant child.

"Well, for one, it was funny. But also, you haven't proven that you're capable of knowing everything yet. You turned an eighteen-year-old, for fuck's sake!"

"I was sixteen when you bit me!"

"Exactly!" Corinne threw up her hands. "Look at how *you* turned out. The first thing you did was run off to stalk four construction workers.

"Because you hadn't told me anything!"

"Watching them argue about why the hot new receptionist was following them," Corinne laughed, wiping a tear away. "I'll never forget that."

"You're an arsehole." Pat wasn't sure why she felt so offended that they saw her as blonde with fake tits, a BBL and a spray tan. "I had no idea they were hallucinating."

"And then you tore them limb from limb." Corinne stifled her giggles. "The looks on their faces!"

"They deserved it," Pat mumbled

"And then you *bit* them."

"Also deserved it." Pat held up a finger. "But let's not forget who got off watching the whole thing like a pitiful cuckhold. And who drained them like a pack of Capri Suns after."

"Because you *wouldn't.* And then we had to run."

Pat scoffed. "The only reason you dragged me across the ocean is because you wanted to know why I didn't immediately turn them into ground beef. Don't think I don't remember the months spent poking and prodding."

"We're not talking about me. And you're missing the point. I had to clean up your mess."

"I'm *your* mess."

"Still trying to distract from the point. You're going to be cleaning up hers when she learns what she can do."

"I still don't know what *I* can do."

"Nor do I. By the time you figure it out, you've matured enough to use it properly." Corinne tipped her hand. "That's how this works."

"And who told you that? This isn't a film. There's no dark council in an underground gothic cathedral. No-one rules over us." Pat rolled her eyes.

"*Who told you that*?" Corinne mocked. "No-one. It's one more thing you figure out."

A few moments passed in the dark. Pat huffed. "You haven't spoken to me in twenty years and you asked me here for a reason. What is it?"

"Finally." Corinne exhaled. A lamp flicked on, filling the room with a smoky orange glow. Corinne moved toward a small table with an imposing elegance. She gestured toward a decanter.

Pat pulled out a chair and slouched, legs spread – a stark contrast to Corinne's crossed ankles and rigid posture. Her black hair cascaded in ringlets about her heart-shaped face, marred only by the curled lip at Pat's uncouth demeanour.

"Oh, come now," Pat smirked. "It's not like you didn't know this about me back then."

"I thought you were a man."

"Until you didn't feel the urge to tear my head off?"

"I still should have. After making me waste my one chance on *you*." Corinne muttered. "Now we're in this mess." She lifted the decanter and filled Pat's cup.

"It's not *my* fault you used that much venom."

"Now *I'm* the bad one because I took pity on you." Corinne made her best attempt to look wounded.

Pat held her breath a moment. "You only used that much because you were hoping to get yourself off on me before I died."

Corinne grunted. "A woman has needs."

"I accommodate all sorts of women."

"I prefer the real thing, thank you very much."

Pat smirked. "Straps have come a long way since you were turned. Say the word if you're ever curious." Corinne curled her lip in disgust.

Pat raised the glass to her nose and inhaled deeply. "Marissa?"

"Like I said, I prefer the real thing." Corinne lifted her glass and Pat clinked it graciously.

Corinne mirrored her and placed the glass on the cloth-covered table. She set her hands on her knee.

"You know I'm running out of time."

"Fred mentioned that."

"And you're too stupid…"

"*You* mentioned that." Pat set her glass down and wiped her lip with the back of her hand. Corinne made a face.

"Which means if I don't tell you *some* things, you'll end up making bigos."

Pat let her head fall to the side. "You could tell me how to see ahead. Then I'd know what *not* to do."

"You have no idea the consequences." Corinne drew her tongue across her lips. "I do. I've seen them. You would ignore what you saw and do what you wanted anyway. You always have."

Pat gave a half shrug.

"Your little experiment is going to kill us all. And there aren't many of us left."

"You know many are there?"

"Here? On this side of the world?" Corinne lifted three fingers. "You, me and the one you just made." She took another sip. "The ones that come to your *parties* are all back in Europe. There might be a few others elsewhere, but I haven't heard of them."

"One came out from Tunisia once, but that's the only other one I know of." Pat took another sip. "Even if you only get one, you'd think there would be more."

Corinne sighed. "You're not the only one who's wasted it."

"Nor you, apparently," Pat interrupted

"Yes, well." Corinne tapped her foot.

"Are you saying I'm not as bad as you thought?"

Corinne shook her head, locks waving in time. "God no. But surely you can do maths. New ones require too much supervision. Especially in this day and age." She tilted her glass toward Pat. "As you're about to find out."

Pat rolled her eyes again, certain this time that Corinne saw it.

"Once Fred is gone, I'll need to hibernate or move. Either way, you'll be on your own."

"I'm already on my own," Pat huffed. "You've refused to see me for decades."

"Decades are meaningless." Corinne stared at her glass, taking several deep breaths. She stood and opened a small drawer, removing a set of handcuffs.

"Kinky. I thought you weren't into that."

Corinne ignored the comment and cuffed Pat's hands together. "Try it."

Pat tried to slip through them, but the shadow wouldn't accept her.

Corinne produced a key and released her. "It doesn't burn or kill, but silver *will* prevent you from doing anything magical."

"You learn that by accident? From Fred?" Pat waggled her eyebrows.

Corinne stared pointedly. "I know because silver is what they used to restrain *my* mother."

Pat's expression dropped. "I'm sorry."

Corinne grunted. "Fire was how they finished her off. It's the only thing permanent." She stared at the ground for a few moments. "About two-hundred years ago, I believe."

Pat chewed the inside of her cheek for a few moments. "So, you figured out how to kill yourself."

"Don't be a bałwan," Corinne snarled. "I apologise - an even bigger bałwan."

"No-one is hunting vampires anymore. Not since you fed Bram a bunch of bullshit."

"God, I wanted to bite him so badly." Corinne stared off into the darkness.

Pat grinned.

"But," she sighed. "That's the curse." She turned to stare at Pat. "The one you think you're getting around. Thinking you're better than everyone else because you don't like men."

Pat pulled her head back and grit her teeth. "The only reason I *didn't* die after those bastards beat the shit out of me was because you thought you could get a quick man-snack and no-one would notice. So, you'll forgive me if I don't feel bad for you."

Corinne glowered angrily.

"Boo-hoo," Pat mocked. *"I can't bite the person I want to fuck because their blood will make me violent and I'll kill them*. Fucking spare me," she spat. "At least they're not threatening to marry you off. Rape you. Force you to bear and raise their disgusting children." Pat grimaced. "At least you're *free*."

"Hardly." Corinne looked away. "And times have changed."

"The fuck would you know about it? You've never been thrown on the streets because you got caught with a girl. You've never had to pretend to be a man so you could get a job. You've never been beaten to death because you refuse to fuck them. If anyone has a reason to hate men, it's me."

Pat shook with rage. "But between you and Fred? I'd still take Fred. He was the only one who ever did anything for me. He's the one who taught me how to rebuild the Bronco. Who got me to finish school. Who bailed me out when I got in trouble."

"And he was stupid enough to let you bite the first girl that you thought would stay with you forever. Based on what? Two weeks and a kiss?"

"Three." Pat mumbled.

"And now we're dealing with the consequences." Corinne pointed her finger. "Because you know as well as I do that she'll leave you for a nice fat cock as soon as she's able."

Pat narrowed her eyes. "Do you enjoy being cruel?"

"Very much so, yes." Corinne took another sip.

Pat sulked.

"Oh, don't be like that." Corinne pouted. "I promise you that I'll make it up to you when I leave." She grinned, the blood running garishly between her teeth. "I have plans."

"Am I going to have to clean up after these plans?" Pat stared up at her from under her frown.

"Consider it payback."

Pat pursed her lips and turned her head.

"I promise, it'll be worth it."

Pat didn't budge.

Corinne tapped the table with her fingernail. "Have I ever broken a promise to you?"

"Fine," Pat acquiesced. "Now, how come she can't remember who she is?"

"Because you bit her after she died. You know what we are."

Pat took a sip and recited dutifully. "Cursed vessels for blood magic."

"And while you may have given her a dose of venom sufficient to turn her, there was no blood sacrifice. Death is awaiting payment. She needs blood." Corinne tilted her glass toward Pat. "It still worked, though I haven't figured out how exactly." Corinne took another sip.

"How was I supposed to give her blood? She was dead." Pat raised her hands in exasperation.

"She's not anymore. Now's your chance."

"But I did. Plenty!"

Corinne shook her head. "Not any blood. *Your* blood. From the vein. That's what normally happens. You wake up angry, bite the first thing you can see and voilà!" Corinne spread her hands as if she had performed a magic trick.

"Normally, it's the person that bit you first, but in this case, she woke up, crawled out of the dirt and bit

Caleb. Which," Corinne let her palms fall open, "was one of many fuckups in a whole cascade of them that led us to where we are now."

"Fuck." Pat breathed.

"Exactly." Corinne finished her glass and set it on the table.

"This is *your* fault. It could have been avoided if you'd told me how it worked in the first place."

"No, it's Fred's fault for letting you in there. I should have bitten him, but then I would have had to leave sooner."

"You seem to have managed your curse well enough." Pat smirked.

"Have I?" Corinne scoffed. "The only taste I'll get of my husband will be my last."

"You'll find a new one."

Corinne scowled. "You dare say that when you tried to find someone permanent? I should rip your throat out."

"I'm sorry." Pat sighed. "I really am. You know how I feel about Fred."

Corinne poured herself another glass and downed it in one go, setting it back on the table noisily. "If you make her aroused enough, she'll bite you."

"That shouldn't be difficult." Pat bobbed her head. "It's what venom does."

"And vampire blood makes you aggressive. Not as much as male blood, but there will be violence nonetheless."

"So what? I know all this," Pat said.

Corinne cleared her throat. "Think. Would you take an eighteen-year-old to one of your *parties*? You may know what it looks like, but *she* doesn't."

Pat ran her hand along her jaw. "Fred said I should take her down to the river."

"Fred also watches grown men chase a rubber disk around a sheet of ice for hours on end. He doesn't know anything.

"And you love him for it." The corner of Pat's lip curled upward.

"I do. I'll be sad when he's gone."

"Me too." Pat reached her hand across the table. Corinne took it.

"You should go. The shadows will be disappearing soon."

Pat nodded and stood to leave.

"One more thing." Corinne turned to look at her. She paused, considering how much to say.

"You'll thank me later."

What the hell is she planning? Pat thought to ask, but she knew Corinne wouldn't answer.

"Thanks mom."

Corinne smiled. Pat slipped away into the shadows.

ten

The sun had started to poke out from behind the trees when Pat returned. She heard nothing. The smoothie and the note had disappeared. Lisa wouldn't be awake for a few more hours, so there wouldn't be any harm in attempting this now.

She allowed herself a small smile and then knocked on the door. The girl appeared, red streaks still on her face.

Pat thrust a coat and toque toward her. "Let's go for a walk. Unless you'd rather stay here? I can pick up pizza later and we can watch T.V.?

The girl took the clothes and put them on. A walk would be good. She wasn't hungry right now, but it might put her in the mood for pizza later.

The brisk spring air felt good in her nostrils. The scent of melting decay and fresh shoots of some of the more eager plants made her smile.

Pat pointed to a wall of pine trees. "This way. Fred suggested I take you down to the river."

"Does Fred know who I am?" the girl asked.

"I think he has an idea. It's Corinne who knows everything."

"Have I met Corinne?" The girl found her legs to be on the short side and she raced to keep up. Pat noticed and slowed her pace.

"Not a lot of people have. At least, not willingly."

The girl frowned at the cryptic answer.

Pat laughed. "Corinne doesn't like a lot of people. She helps Fred during the embalming process, but that's about as much as she gets out. She has to be extremely careful."

"Is she sick?"

Pat bobbed her head back and forth. "That's one way to phrase it."

Sticks snapped and boots squelched in the mud. Patches of snow hung stubbornly in the shade of the trees. The creek burbled in the distance.

"She used to do fortune telling. Tarot. Palm reading. That sort of thing." Pat continued. "Some of the church got upset and someone died over it."

"Someone died!" The girl's eyebrows hit her hairline.

"Kind of. Smarter fortune tellers don't predict death, even if they see it. Corinne wasn't as tactful. But that happened years ago."

"How?"

Pat shrugged. "A heart attack and a woodchipper, but Corinne got blamed for causing it. All she did was predict it, but that was enough."

Pat knew that was a lie. For years, Corinne had been predicting death and then causing it. It was the only way she could get her taste of men without drawing too much attention to herself. She'd gotten carried away with this one and had to rent a woodchipper for her *heart attack* victim to fall into.

Pat continued. "She'll only do fortune telling now if she likes you."

"She sounds cool. I kind of want to meet her now."

"Oh," Pat smiled. "I'm sure she'd love you."

The girl blushed. She wanted to take Pat's hand, but she wrapped her arms around herself instead. Pat noticed and slipped her arm around the girl's shoulder, bringing her in for a quick squeeze before putting her hands back in her pocket. The girl blinked before tears could form. She couldn't understand why Pat was being so nice to her.

"Do you know who I am?" She asked finally.

Pat bit her lip. "I know who you were."

The girl eyed her sceptically. "What is that supposed to mean?"

"Who you *were* is not who you *are*. If I told you who you were, you wouldn't believe me."

The girl frowned, confused.

Pat cracked her neck. "It's alright. It'll make sense when you remember."

Finches and chickadees traded insults in the trees. Pat smiled when the sounds of the creek got louder. "Looks like it's finally warm enough that the ice melted."

Moments later, they could see it. Ice still clung to the edges, but the murky water rushed along the muddy creek bed. Bark-stripped branches collected in the eddies, along with discarded refuse that had come from further upstream. Pat steadied herself to pull it out.

"Don't fall in!" the girl warned.

Pat shot back a cocky grin. "I don't need rubbish in my creek!"

"Is this where you get your water from?"

Pat shook her head. "There's a spring closer to the house. I put in a system years ago."

"You seem very self-sufficient." The girl pulled her toque tighter, the humidity of the creek making the air cooler.

"I suppose. I don't get along with a lot of people." Pat shook off the icy water from the plastic bag she'd fished out of the creek.

"Did we get along?"

Pat breathed a laugh. "Yeah. Probably a little better than we should have."

The girl gave a frustrated growl. "Why won't you just tell me?"

Pat ignored the question. "Fred said it might help if I took you here."

"Did something happen here?"

Pat nodded.

"Something good?" The girl's eyes looked hopeful.

Pat inhaled. "It depends on your point of view. But some people simply can't let good things exist."

Pat leaned against a rowan tree. Desiccated berries bobbed in the breeze. "Do you know these trees?" Pat gestured around.

The girl looked up. "The one you're leaning against is a rowan."

Pat nodded. "And that one?"

The girl smiled and pointed at each tree. "Ash, cottonwood, alder, fir."

Pat grinned. "You remember some things just fine."

The girl blushed as if it were a compliment.

"What about that one?" Pat pointed at a bend in the creek about a hundred metres away.

"I can't tell from here."

"Well, let's go then." Pat turned and headed toward the tree. The girl ran to catch up.

The bend seemed to be made just for this tree, almost like it stood on a magical peninsula jutting into the water. A large twisting trunk supported thin grey branches that overhung the creek and bent down to kiss the water flowing beneath.

Pat sat, nestled in the division of three great branches near the base.

"It's a Willow," the girl said.

Pat leaned back, satisfied. "It is." She turned to stare off at a lone crow perched high in a dead birch looking their way. "I left you a note. I said that I knew."

The girl stared at the ground, remembering the note. Remembering the relief she felt that she might not be alone. Then the thought that Pat clearly wasn't talking about her teeth. She was certain that Pat didn't know what she thought she did. "Do you know that I'm a… lesbian?" It was the only thing she thought made sense.

"You're not a lesbian," Pat laughed. "Though being with one is the reason we are where we are."

"What is it that you know then? Why are you being so evasive?" The girl pleaded.

Pat turned to stare in defiance at the crow. She may have fucked up biting her in the first place, but she had matured since then. Consent mattered, even if she *was* a monster. This girl wasn't just *food* anymore.

The crow twitched its head. *Or is it your feelings about Lisa showing back up in your life?* Pat glared at the crow. She would do this her way. She didn't need to make her aroused. Just hungry.

Pat removed a small pocket knife from her jacket. She unfolded it carefully and put the blade to her wrist. The slice made the girl flinch. A moment later, the scent of smoke, resin and candy perfumed the air. Her mouth watered. Her teeth itched. She couldn't look away from the thick rivulets of blood tracing the curve of her forearm.

Pat's stare locked her in place. There would be no escaping it this time. She knew. Pat knew she was a monster.

The dull ache began. Her canines slid free. There was too much blood this time for her to resist. Pat held her arm out and the girl launched forward, lapping at her wrist. The taste burst across her tongue, filling her mouth. Why did she taste so good?

Pat grabbed the girl's hair, jerking her head up to meet her eyes. The blood had disappeared, as had the cut that had caused it to flow. She nearly cried in disappointment, but Pat only smiled wider. "I told you I knew."

"Are you going to kill me?" The girl's canines still protruded.

"I couldn't if I tried," Pat laughed. "At least, not with what I have on me."

The girl's eyebrows knit together.

The cawing from the trees mocked her. The girl still wouldn't bite. It wasn't enough blood. The crow fluttered over to a closer tree. Pat growled. She hated when Corinne was right. "You really want to watch this?"

The crow shook its feathers.

"Pervert." Pat took a deep breath. "Fine. Have it your way."

Pat released her grip and pulled her lip back, exposing her teeth. Her canines lengthened effortlessly, with none of the pain the girl had experienced. "You'll be able to control it a bit better. Once you remember."

Pat sneered. The girl's heart stopped. She stumbled backwards, eyes locked on Pat and her teeth.

And then she disappeared, as if the shadows in the trees drank her up.

The dark coalesced around her and lunged. The shock of pain flashing at her neck provoked a scream but it only came out as a low whimper. The muscles in her arm slackened, a warmth spreading through her body. It felt like someone had replaced her blood with hot glitter.

A pathetic convulsion. Her body tried to fight the venom pouring into her like a sparkler igniting her nerve endings. Her vision doubled. Tripled. The movement of the branches in the wind seemed to flow like the air was made of oil.

Warmth pooled between her legs. All she wanted was Pat. For her to take her. Fuck her. Drink her until she fell.

But Pat stopped. She withdrew her fangs, wiping the blood from her mouth. Why? What had she done? She *needed* her.

The girl took a desperate step after her, arms grasping, drugged and clumsy. An awful void filled the pit of her stomach. The want for her touch morphed into desire to consume.

Pat flexed and unflexed her fingers. Her heart raced. Speeding the aggression of vampire blood through her body. Fun at her parties, but in this situation, it felt *wrong*. Pat eyed the trees, focusing her anger on that fucking crow, mocking her with its beady eyes. She could catch it. She could slip into shadow right now and take it before it could get away. "How would you like that, Corinne?" she hissed.

The girl stumbled forward, catching Pat's neck before she could take out her frustrations on the crow. Thick arms wrapped around her. She drank like a newborn from Pat's vein. Candy filled her mouth. She had never felt so relieved.

And then the memory hit.

Pat had known her.

She had kissed her. Here, in the crook of this Willow. *She* was Willow. That's why they were here.

"Are your parents from here?" Pat threw a rock across the long grass, brown from the recent drought. Kyle stared up at the clouds.

"Yeah, why?" Willow tucked an errant curl behind her ear.

Pat gave a half shrug. "They named you Willow. There aren't any willows around here."

"That's not true." Kyle didn't turn. He spoke directly to the sky. "There's at least one on your property. Down by the creek."

"Right." Pat threw another rock.

"Can I see it?" Willow smiled and then ducked her head.

"Yeah, sure." Pat grinned. "My place is a ways out though."

"We could drive out there tonight." Kyle rolled over and propped his head on his elbow. "You got your truck back."

"And my license." Pat flashed her new driver's license.

Willow bit at a fingernail. "Why did you wait so long to get it?"

"Didn't need it until now."

Willow frowned. "How were you getting into school then?"

"It's a secret." Pat leaned in, smiling. An adorable dimple formed.

Willow fought the urge to kiss it. She didn't even know if she *liked* women, but she liked Pat. Unlike her friends who had distanced themselves when she broke up with Caleb, Pat and Kyle had simply *let* her hang out with them. She had sat next to them, expecting at best, a separate, but parallel existence in an attempt to make it through these last two months of school. But any awkwardness she felt about it didn't seem to be shared by them. And Pat didn't seem to care that Willow constantly caught herself staring at her. *Maybe she doesn't notice?* A wave of insecurity tickled at the edge of her brain.

But that was ludicrous. It was just a little girl-crush. Pat was different, that was all. *Of course* she would be staring at her. *Everyone* stared at her.

"Yeah, I'll come."

Pat beamed. "Cool. I'll come by Kyle's house around eight."

And she did. All three of them on an ivory leather bench seat in Pat's 1977 Ford Bronco. The amber dashboard lights illuminated their smiles as they sang along to a John Denver 8-track. Willow couldn't ever remember having this much fun. She hadn't ever felt this carefree.

"How does your truck still look this new?" Willow yelled over the quadriphonic sound system.

Pat turned the 8-track off. "I don't give a shit about hockey boys, so I spend most of my time in the garage."

"It's true," Kyle confirmed. "If she didn't spend so much time on this truck, I wouldn't have anywhere to hang out and study."

Kyle, with his hunched narrow shoulders and brown curls, long enough to obscure his vision. He hid behind them, as if he could blot out the entirety of the teenage experience if he only stayed still long enough for it to pass him by.

"Becca thinks you're cute." Willow brushed the locks away from his eyes.

"Are you talking to me or to Kyle? 'Cause, no thanks." Pat sneered, but the corner of her lip still curled upward.

"Double no thanks." Kyle shot Pat a look.

Pat laughed. "This one's going to university. That's why he needs to study so hard. Getting someone pregnant at prom isn't in the cards for him."

Kyle made a disgusted face. Pat laughed harder. Willow felt left out of the joke.

"My parents can't afford tuition. I need scholarships." Kyle bobbed his head sheepishly.

Pat sneered. "We can't all have dads that own car dealerships."

"Or dump them." Kyle laughed.

Willow bit her fingernails anticipating the question. *Why would you leave such a catch? What's wrong with you?* But it never came.

Pat turned the music back on and they continued the rest of the way with the windows down. The flinty smell of gravel roads and cottonwood resin filled the cabin.

Three large willow trunks twisted upward from the same set of roots. Willow and Kyle leaned against the outside while Pat nestled comfortably where they joined, throwing rocks aimlessly into the creek.

"So why *did* you dump Caleb?" Kyle asked, finally.

Willow glanced over at him. She didn't need a lecture from Kyle of all people about how she was ruining her life.

"Lay off, Kyle." Pat threw another rock.

"Oh, come on." Kyle whipped Pat playfully with a fallen willow branch. "It's not every day I get dirt on the douchiest person in this town."

"He's worse than his brother with gossip," Pat explained.

"Yeah, but at least my gossip is *true*. Josh makes shit up."

Willow relaxed. She thought everyone loved Caleb.

"Like, does he have a micropenis or something?" Kyle grinned.

"I don't want to think about Caleb's dick, thanks." Pat shoved him. Willow laughed.

"I wanted to go to college. Caleb wanted me to stay here." Willow drew in the dirt with a stick. "He didn't like the idea of me moving away. My parents think it's your fault." She glanced at Pat and then returned to her drawing.

Pat huffed and shook her head. "Of course, your parents know who I am. I can't even piss at school without Vanessa convinced it's because I'm desperate to see her pancake arse. Fuck, I hate this town."

"Why did you move here, then?"

"Some minor trouble back home." Pat threw another rock.

It didn't sound like minor trouble. "Are you moving back after school?" Willow had a sudden hope that they might be able to go to college together. Her parents would never be able to afford tuition abroad, though.

Pat shrugged. "There are twats in cities too. There's more to do, so it's easier to avoid them, but they always find you eventually. Maybe I'll just hide out here forever."

Willow adjusted her legs. "My parents want to send me to conversion therapy this summer."

Pat laughed. "Oh my god. How much lesbian porn did they find on your computer?"

She had said it like a joke. Like a slice-of-life foible that happened to everyone. Judgement or mockery of who Willow may or may not find attractive was absent. Willow could only feel relief. And regret that she had wasted years fitting in with the popular kids.

"None!"

Pat raised an eyebrow.

"Fine. One picture of Demi Moore, I swear." Willow raised her hands defensively.

"Yeah, well even Kyle would drop his boxers for Demi Moore." Pat threw a pebble at Kyle. It stuck in his hair.

"You wear boxers, not me. I have more taste than that." Kyle stood up and dusted himself off. "I'm getting cold. I'm gonna get the blankets from the truck."

Pat nodded and threw another rock. "Hardly seems fair to punish you for something you didn't do."

"Not sure what I'm going to do there." Willow gave an exaggerated huff. "Yep, I agree with you. Not gay. I doubt they'll send me home after."

Pat dug around for another rock, but didn't say anything.

"What's it like?"

"What do you mean?"

"Being gay?"

Pat blew out her cheeks.

"I'm sorry. Is that rude to ask?" Willow bit her fingernail again.

Pat threw her rock. "Nah. It's..." she sighed. "I don't know. It's how I am. I can't compare it to something I'm not. I've never *not* been me."

"Have you ever kissed anyone before?"

Pat raised an eyebrow. She had done a lot more than kiss with the exchange student. Enough that Pat had been kicked out of her house and Camille had been sent back to Toulouse. But that had been before here. Before she had died.

"I'm not going to out your friends."

Willow's eyes popped. "What!"

"It's fine. Everyone gets curious. Then they come to me." Pat looked at the dirt. "Sometimes I let them. Sometimes I don't. It depends."

Willow tilted her head. "On what?"

"Whether or not I want to."

"Do you want to kiss me?" Willow hadn't known she'd had the courage to say that out loud.

"Try it and find out." Pat's hazel eyes caught the moonlight at just the right moment. She removed her hoodie and her scent slammed into Willow like a train. *She smells like chocolate and strawberry cream.*

Something about her felt amazing. Everything got fuzzy and all Willow wanted to do was to get close to her. Her lips parted, waiting for Pat to take the chance, but she refused. If Willow wanted this, she would have to do it herself.

And she did.

Her lips pressed against Pat. She might have looked like a boy, but this wasn't the same experience at all. No stubble. The softness of her face. The plush yield of her lips. She inhaled, taking Willows' breath with her.

The rustle of branches made her snap back to reality. Tyler emerged, wearing his red and white varsity jacket, as if anyone knew where Northton high school was. Or cared. His wispy brown hair clung to his face in the humidity of the creek. "Found them."

Another rustle. Caleb, several centimetres taller and kilos heavier ran at them like an enraged freight train. Willow scrambled up and bolted.

Pat turned and saw Caleb rush past. She got to her feet in time to stop Tyler from giving chase.

Caleb reached out and caught the hem of Willow's t-shirt. She jerked back and fell. Caleb climbed on top of her and tore at her jeans, red faced, yelling *fucking dyke*. She remembered how sore her throat was from screaming.

She remembered the dull crack when Pat's fist connected with Caleb's jaw. She remembered the blood pouring from Pat's mouth. She remembered Tyler lying on the ground, his knee a gaping wound.

She remembered Caleb's gun.

She remembered how close Pat was to him when it went off.

She remembered how it had flown into the creek, along with two of Caleb's fingers.

She remembered her hand around his throat, pinning him against the willow tree, her mouth hanging open, threatening to bite his face.

"Pat!"

Kyle appeared with blankets. "What the fuck?"

Pat dropped him and growled "Get the fuck off my property."

They walked back to the house. Kyle cleaned her cuts while Pat fumed, pacing back and forth.

"Are you sure he didn't hit you?" Willow was in shock. Pat had been standing in front of the barrel. She had seen it.

Pat lifted her shirt up to assure her she wasn't harmed. "It's alright. You're in shock."

"His fingers…"

Pat stared and waved it off. "His gun misfired. It's what happens when you try to replace the barrel of a cheap Cabela but don't know what you're doing." Pat paced around the room. "He won't try that again. Or maybe he will. He's fucking stupid."

The trip back did not feel nearly as jovial as the trip there. She dropped Kyle off first.

Pat brought the truck to a stop outside her door. "I'm sorry."

Willow looked at her, but didn't say anything. What could she say?

Pat took a couple of deep breaths. "You want to know what being gay is like?"

Willow picked at the stitching in the leather seat in silence for a few moments. "Why not just be with men then?"

Pat looked at her like she was stupid. "You don't think I would if I could?"

"Why can't you?"

Pat thought for a moment. "The same reason you can't marry Caleb. Even though you invite a world of trouble, you just can't make yourself."

Willow stared out the window. She turned to look at Pat. She wanted to kiss her again, to drown in the terrible violence of her mouth. But the aftermath of what happened the last time made her stomach lurch. She jumped out of the Bronco and ran to the door.

She called for her parents. There was no answer. They hadn't seen Pat's truck. A bit of relief. The last thing she wanted to do was to explain what had happened.

But alone, her heart raced and her thoughts spiralled. What had she done? What would Pat think? Where did Caleb get the gun? Would he come after her again?

She sent a text to her mother asking when they'd be home. Willow spent half an hour obsessively looking at the single crack along the screen of her red Nokia 1110. The pixelated envelope never appeared. Panic started to set in.

Willow opened the liquor cabinet. *Alcohol is a depressant,* she thought. She'd had drinks at parties before. Never enough to throw up, but enough to take the edge off. Willow poured herself a shot of vodka. It burned. Then she poured another.

Twenty minutes passed rocking herself on the sofa, feeling like bugs crawled along her skin. Willow wiped at her arm. Her fingers came away moist, even though the thermostat read 16°C. The hyperventilating wouldn't stop.

Pills. Her mother had anxiety pills. Those would be appropriate, right? After what had just happened?

Willow took two and curled up in her bedroom.

It was the last thing she remembered.

Willow withdrew her fangs from Pat's neck and looked down at the wound she'd caused. The puncture holes closed. Soon, even the redness faded. She looked up at Pat from under her eyelashes.

"What happened after the pills?"

Pat tucked a strand of hair behind her ear, still cradling her in her lap. "You died."

Obvious as it was, Willow still felt the shock of the statement. As if someone had just told her *you shouldn't be here. This place isn't for you anymore.*

"Why am I here, then?"

Pat took a deep breath. "Fred let me see you in the morgue."

Willow scrambled her legs. "What did you do to me?"

Pat didn't let go of her wrists. "I – I know. I shouldn't have. You're right. I've been kicking myself for it since then."

Willow scoffed. "And Caleb? That was him in the truck. Did *you* do that?" Her last memory had been of him coming at her with a gun and yet part of her still felt bad for breaking off the engagement. He didn't deserve to die.

"You killed him."

"I don't remember that" Willow struggled, trying to flail her arms. The aggression from drinking so much vampire blood caused her muscles to spasm.

"Probably because you had just woken up."

"You said I died!"

"You did. They buried you. It's why I was avoiding telling you anything." Pat tried to look her in the eye, but she evaded her gaze.

Hot tears formed and spilled across her cheeks. "How long ago?"

"Almost twenty years."

"Jesus," she mumbled.

"He probably wouldn't approve," Pat joked, but it fell flat. Pat inhaled sharply. "Listen. I know you're angry right now."

"No, just confused," Willow argued. "Alright, maybe a little angry. A lot angry." She felt the urge to claw and bite, but Pat still held her wrists. "Why did you let me stay buried for that long?"

Pat sighed. "What was I going to do? Dig you up? I promise, I'll explain as much as I can, now that you're… you."

"Such as?" Willow glared.

"To start, I wasn't certain that was going to work. I thought I was saving your life." She paused for a moment. "I suppose I did, only it didn't turn out the way I thought it would."

"And you let them bury me?" Deep furrows marred Willow's face.

"What was I supposed to do? Tell the town to hold off on burying a corpse until we're sure it won't reanimate? And also, the foreign kid the town hates bit it because she's not just a dyke, she's also a vampire?"

Pat tried her best to look sympathetic. "I know this is a lot. A lot of time has passed. Your parents don't live here anymore. You probably hate me, but you're still welcome to stay here." She tried to blurt out as much relevant information before Willow stormed off.

"Why?"

"I did this to you. I can't take it back. I'm trying to be responsible."

"Are you? You turn me into a monster to what? Play hero twenty years later?"

Pat leaned against the tree, loosening her grip on Willow's wrists. "I was turned after my coworkers beat the shit out of me. I pretended to be a man to get a job after my parents kicked me out. They decided to show me how much they didn't like that."

"Okay?" Willow flicked her head, impatient for the point.

"I was angry too. I didn't ask for it." Pat looked toward the creek. "But I didn't ask to have shit parents. Or be born a girl. Or a lesbian. At least now I can be who I am - without worrying about what these cornfed lackwits will do to me."

"But I'm not a lesbian. I was born *normal,*" Willow protested through clenched teeth.

Pat winced. "There's nothing you hid? Is that why you killed yourself?"

"I didn't kill myself!" The lines on her forehead deepened. "It was an accident!"

"Right." Pat nodded. "We all overdose on benzos when things are great."

Willow glowered.

Pat took a few deep breaths. Willow didn't try to pull away. Pat took that as a good sign. "Fine, you're normal. Whatever. You don't *have* to act like a monster."

"What do you mean?" A note of fear could be detected in her voice.

"You can live as normal as you want. Learn to control yourself and live your life. You don't *need* to drink blood."

Willow narrowed her eyes. Her lips moved to form a question, but she didn't know what to ask.

"This isn't a film. We don't die without it. It's more of a…" Pat bobbed her head, trying to avoid calling it a curse. *Curse* would make it sound bad, even if that's what Corinne thought it was. "More of a blood sacrifice." It didn't sound better.

Willow only stared, more confused. Pat's ham-fisted explanations weren't helping.

"You can't do vampire things without drinking blood. The more you drink, the greater the sacrifice, the greater your abilities." Pat thought that would cover the basics without causing her too much annoyance.

"What vampire things?"

"I mean, I don't know *all* the things. I'm not that old."

Willow decided not to ask how old she was. "What can you do then?"

Pat looked up at the trees. The crow stared back at her. *Yes, I remember. Not too much.*

"I have venom, obviously. I don't think you ever lose that," Pat pointed to her teeth. "You'll heal a lot quicker – provided you get enough blood."

Willow waited, but Pat just watched her face. "Does your blood count?"

"Vampire blood is a little different, but yes. It mostly makes you aggressive."

That made sense. She could feel her aggression starting to wane as she metabolised it. "Can you let go of me? I promise I won't attack you."

Pat released her wrists.

"Is there a vampire school that I go to now? Some giant is going to show up with a letter and a broom?"

Pat cringed.

"What?"

"I forgot you've been dead a while. That series turned out to be pretty problematic."

Pat looked up at the crow. "There aren't many of us. There's no school. No-one teaches you. You can hang out with me until you decide you don't need me anymore."

"How do I learn what I can and can't do then?" Willow frowned.

"You live a long time and figure it out. By the time you've discovered something you can do, you're mature enough to do it." Pat kept glancing up at the crow. "At least, that's how it was explained to me."

So, you're not going to tell me anything?

"I can show you. You can figure it out from there." Pat slipped into a shadow, materialising behind her.

Willow spun around to face her. "That's how you got into town without a truck!"

Pat nodded, grinning. "That's how I'll get us pizza too."

"I can't decide if that's the worst or the best use of a super power."

"Blood magic," Pat corrected. Willow seeing just a hint that not everything was terrible helped her breathe a bit easier.

Willow still felt angry, but she would need some time to process this. "Whatever. If you get us pizzas, I'll see what's on T.V."

Pat gestured vaguely. "T.V. has changed a lot since you died. Cable doesn't really exist anymore. And it's a little early for pizza."

Willow bit her lip. "I'll figure it out."

Pat scratched at the back of her head. Willow was being manipulative. The memory of how she had felt all those years ago wasn't what she needed right now. The crow fluttered and yelled its disapproval.

"I have to head out." Pat pointed toward the house. "Lisa should be coming by to pick me up soon. We'll do pizza tonight, okay?"

Willow nodded.

The shadows at the edge of the woods swirled and coalesced just in time for Pat to see Lisa's truck turning into her driveway. Her heart did a flip.

Fuck, she thought. *I am so fucking screwed.*

eleven

Lisa had been certain on the drive over that she would be able to tell Pat she was breaking up with Josh. And then she saw Pat.

And then Pat waved, forearms illuminated in the early spring light.

And then Pat smiled, and the world got twenty times brighter.

Lisa rested her head on the steering wheel.

What was she going to do after? Be single and moon over Pat, who had never shown an ounce of interest in her in that way? God, she was an idiot.

Pat opened the door and hopped in, reaching behind her and fastening her seatbelt. She smiled again, pulling the sunshine directly into her truck. *Dammit! Why is even watching her putting on a seatbelt too much?*

"Hey! Thanks for picking me up."

Lisa wished Pat would pick her up. She had no doubt she was physically capable. She could probably toss her directly…

"Are you alright?" Pat interrupted her thoughts.

"Uh," Lisa blinked. "Yeah, just spacing out. Period cramps." *Jesus, Lisa. Really? You've got at least another week.*

Pat unbuckled herself. "Hold on." She hopped out and sprinted toward the house. Even in heavy doek trousers, all of the best parts of her shone. Somehow, Pat made Carhartt's with too many pockets look obscene. She hadn't even dumped Josh yet and she was already behaving like this. Like her body *knew* she was available.

Pat got back in and handed her a Mason jar full of dried leaves.

Lisa took it, turning it over. "You're giving me a jar of weed? You know I'm a cop, right?"

"No," Pat laughed. "Raspberry leaves. Make a herb tea. They're good for cramps."

Lisa tilted her head. "Really?"

"I learned that from Willow's parents. Before… you know." Pat looked away.

"Right."

"There's a patch behind the house. I collect a bunch every spring." Pat looked back at her. "Let me know if you need more."

"I will." Lisa smiled. *Just friends* she reminded herself. "Thanks."

They pulled out of the driveway, narrowly avoiding the wreck. Lisa glanced at the hood.

"Fred picked him up yesterday," Pat explained. "Now we need to get Josh out here."

The mention of Josh caused a splinter of panic. Lisa took a deep breath.

"Speaking of which," Lisa cleared her throat, desperate to direct the topic of conversation away from Josh. "Tyler wants to talk to you about what happened."

"What? Why?"

Lisa shrugged. "No idea. Probably bored, to be honest."

"Sure, I suppose." Pat hadn't spoken to Tyler since she'd torn his knee open.

A few kilometres would pass before they hit pavement again. Pat relaxed against the door, staring at the sunlight splashing across Lisa's cheekbones. Lisa caught her looking.

"What?"

Pat turned away, a bashful grin on her face. "I just can't believe it's been this long."

"Why?" Lisa tucked a curl behind her ear. "Were you staring at the greys in my hair?"

"Yeah. I can't even remember what colour your hair was."

Lisa slapped her across the arm.

"How do you not have any greys yet? It's not fair."

Pat ran her hand over her scalp. "They're just hard to see behind all the sawdust."

"You don't even have any wrinkles. Maybe I need to be a hermit."

"The secret," Pat leaned her head toward Lisa, "is keeping men the fuck out of my life."

Lisa shook her head. "You haven't changed a bit."

"How's Josh?"

Goddammit. "I don't know. I haven't spoken to him since."

"He's not bad."

"Weren't you telling me I should leave him?"

"Well, yes," Pat leaned against the headrest. "But that doesn't mean he's bad. You could do worse. Like Tyler, for example."

Lisa made a face. "One, ew. Two, he's my boss."

"I was just saying."

"Why, though. Why say it?" Lisa twisted her head to glare at Pat. She turned to look back at the road before Pat could see her eyes moisten.

Pat stared up at the cloth ceiling vibrating with the gravel road. "I just want you to know that I didn't tell you to leave him because I don't like men. I don't care about that. I should have remembered that we're in Northton and your options are limited. I want to see you happy is all."

The tears threatening to burst forth surprised her, especially after the worst apology she'd ever heard. Lisa had to stare intently at the road to keep them at bay. But it was true. She wasn't happy. What would make her happy was maddeningly out of reach.

"What about you? How's your love life?"

Pat jerked her head. "Er."

"Don't *er*. You don't get to poke your fingers into mine without expecting some in return."

Pat chewed at the inside of her cheek.

Lisa narrowed her eyes. "Spill."

"There isn't really one." Pat sighed. "I don't know what it is. It's not serious and it sure as fuck isn't going anywhere. But I feel responsible for her." *There. That was accurate enough.* "Does that make sense?"

"So, like me and Josh."

"Huh? I don't get it."

"I – I feel bad about leaving because he didn't *do* anything. He's cute and sweet and..."

"He's *there*."

Lisa looked across the seat. Pat's eyes were sympathetic.

"I'm almost forty, Pat."

"Babies are also cute and sweet. I don't want a baby."

"If I cut him loose, where's he gonna go?"

Pat covered her face with her hands. "You are failing the Bechdel test so hard right now."

"What?"

"He's a grown man, Lisa."

"Who lives in Northton. Who's out there for him?"

Pat put a hand on Lisa's knee. It caused the same frisson as it had last time. "That's something *he* can take care of. You are too good for your own good."

"Fine. I'll leave Josh the day you leave whoever your current girlfriend is."

"Definitely not *girlfriend*."

"Fuckbuddy then. I don't know how these things work. I only dated one woman."

"Agreed. It's a deal."

Pat pulled her elbows over her head. She had no idea how that was going to work. Or what she even expected of Willow. Or what Willow expected of her. This was a conversation that needed to happen tonight before everything went pear shaped.

Lisa pulled the truck into her driveway. "I'm heading to the station right away. Do you want to follow me there? Get this thing over with?"

"Yeah, sure. That's the beauty of setting your own hours, right?" Pat flashed a smile. Lisa nearly melted. How could a woman possess that much confidence?

They parked beside each other at the detachment.

"That's new."

"Yeah, they renovated the building about ten years ago." Lisa held the door open.

"So genteel."

Lisa scoffed and signed them in.

The room went silent. Pat had been expecting it. She dealt with the discomfort the same way she always did - pure, unabashed bravado. "Tyler, where the fuck are you?"

Tyler ambled lazily out of his office and made a face when he saw who it was.

"Only *you* would saunter in here and yell *where the fuck are you* as a civilian."

Pat grinned and shrugged. Lisa tried and failed to hide her smile. Tyler walked back to his desk.

"See you in a bit," Pat waved to Lisa and followed after Tyler. She shut the door.

Tyler pressed the button on the tape recorder. "State your name."

"Why?"

Tyler pinched the bridge of his nose. "It's for the record, Pat."

Pat rolled her eyes. "What record? You need to record this?"

"Just..."

"Caleb crashed outside my house. Are you going to arrest me for growing suspicious trees a hundred years ago? Perhaps I caused the snow to melt as well."

Tyler stopped the tape recorder with an annoyed *click*. "No, Pat. No-one's arresting you."

"Then why the recorder?" Pat bounced her leg, waiting for the answer she already knew.

"Sherri's going to transcribe your statement."

Pat grinned. "Still making girls do your homework, eh? Haven't learned to write yet?" Pat knew that wasn't the reason. She could wait.

"I can write fine." Tyler flexed his fingers. "This is just faster."

"Hockey injury again?" Pat's eyes turned mean.

"You know, this is why you had trouble fitting in the first time." Tyler sneered.

Pat laughed. "Why? Because you nonces weren't used to someone willing to push back?"

Tyler picked up a pen and tapped it against his leg. "What are you doing out there, Pat?"

"Running a meth lab."

Tyler's eyebrows shot up.

"C'mon Tyler, you don't believe that. You've got a fentanyl problem here. Meth is passé."

"Seriously."

"Seriously, I make furniture and cabinets. It's about as boring as you can get aside from growing canola and fucking sheep."

"This is cattle ranching country," Tyler huffed.

"Look, I'm not here to judge," Pat leaned back and raised her hands.

Tyler looked out the window, annoyed.

"We thought that place had been abandoned." He clicked his pen.

"And you never bothered to check. Crack detective work there." Pat eyed his badge. "*Sherrif.*"

"Are you ever gonna drop your beef with us? That happened in high school."

Pat snorted. She knew Tyler hadn't let go of it, but she would play along. "I dunno, Tyler. You have kids?"

"You'd know, if you showed your face around here."

"Why would I do that? Answer the question."

"This is *my* office, Pat. *I* ask the questions." Tyler narrowed his eyes.

"Right." Pat cracked her knuckles. "Let's say Chloe turns out to fancy women."

"How do you…?"

"I ran into Marissa in the city," Pat lied.

Tyler tried to hold his expression neutral, but she caught a slight flinch.

Pat pointed at his face. "See? You bell-ends are exactly the same as you always were." She shook her head in disappointment. "The real question is whether you'll care more about her or your reputation."

"C'mon Pat, it's just not normal. You can't expect…"

"Neither is sheep-fucking. Or the shape of Corey Winter's dick, for that matter."

Tyler turned his head in disgust, but Pat continued. "You don't forget something like that. He could probably pick locks with it, if it didn't have that ninety-degree kink in it."

"Pat!"

"I'm serious." Pat was on a roll. Glee sparkled in her hazel eyes. "When you manky nobs took his trousers in P.E. and exposed the rest of us to *that*. Did you *know* that's what he was packing?"

"He's married, Pat."

"To what? A pencil sharpener?"

"Pat!"

"All I'm saying," Pat raised her hands defensively, "Is that I've never seen a dil look like that. It's just not *anyone*'s fetish."

"Jesus Christ, Pat." Tyler massaged his forehead.

"Wait. Are you getting all out of sorts because *you* look like that too?"

"Fucking hell, Pat!"

"This town is more inbred than I thought," she muttered.

"*This* is why you never fit in here!" Tyler erupted.

"Tyler," Pat grinned. "Mate." She leaned forward, elbows on her knees. "That's where you're all confused. You think your shitty little all-white community of pig-fuckers…"

"Cattle," Tyler interjected. Pat chuckled. She couldn't believe he kept walking right into it.

"You think we're all jealous of your community and that if we don't fit in, we're faggots or *cidiots* who don't know what *real* men are."

Tyler curled his lip.

Pat eyed the tape recorder. It was still off. "But two of you bumpkins couldn't even take me."

"You're a psychopath." Tyler lurched forward as if he was about to attack. Pat didn't flinch. "I saw what you did."

"Prove it." Pat spread her hands. "And take it easy on that knee."

Tyler snarled impotently.

"Not so tough without Caleb here leading the charge. You always did whatever he said, didn't you?" Pat's smile disturbed him.

"I saw that gun go off."

"You'd lost a lot of blood. You saw nowt." Pat spread her hands.

Tyler leaned back in his chair and pointed an angry finger. "That was your fault too."

"Please," Pat scoffed. "It's too late to do a dental imprint. If you'd reported it when it had happened, someone *might* have believed you, but not without an alcohol test. Which you would have failed." She tapped her tongue. "Lot of cheap vodka in your system."

"They would have. You'd hit me with your truck."

"You didn't even dent the Bronco. And you killed Willow." Pat stared icily.

"She killed herself, Pat." His face grew stony. They stared at each other for a full minute before Tyler decided to give up.

"Tell me about the girl."

Pat took a deep breath and sprawled out in the chair. "She has no memory."

"Name?"

"Nope. No ID either." Pat ran her hand over her buzzcut.

"And you're qualified to take care of her?" Tyler cocked an eyebrow.

"No law that says I can't."

"Look, Pat. It's suspicious, is all."

"Which part exactly?"

Tyler exhaled and glanced at the late winter snow squall gathering against the window panes before turning back to Pat. "The part where Caleb, who everyone knows you hated, ended up dismembered and frozen to a truck wrapped around a tree outside your house."

"I wasn't the only one who hated him." Pat sucked her teeth. "He should have worn a seatbelt."

"Caleb *always* wore his seatbelt," Tyler growled.

Pat raised her eyebrows dubiously. "Apparently not," she said under her breath.

Tyler frowned. "Preventing the girl from talking to us is suspicious."

"No, it's not." Pat laughed. "The only thing that's suspicious is why you need to talk to the victim of a shit driver. It's obvious what happened. Caleb found her who knows where, gave her a ride and then crashed. Probably while he was trying to force himself on her, too."

Tyler made a disgusted face, but Caleb had been known to take advantage of women before.

"I know what he does behind Boots."

"You're still preventing her from talking to us."

"She can talk to you any time you want. The only thing I'm preventing you from doing is coming on to my property."

Tyler set the pen down and exhaled.

"Why are you so adamant about proving Caleb's death was anything but the obvious?" Pat's tone turned curious.

Tyler turned to gaze out the window again. "He was a friend. One of us. You wouldn't understand." He turned to look at Pat. "You don't want to be part of the community, remember."

Pat chewed at the inside of her cheek and nodded slowly. "I might change my mind. It's looking marginally better without Caleb in it."

"That's an asshole thing to say, Pat." Tyler picked his pen back up and clicked it, knuckles white.

"Yeah, well, I'm not one to pretend shit people aren't shit. Not like you hypocrites, huddled around Willow's grave pretending like you didn't put her there."

Pat could hear Tyler struggling to keep his breathing under control. His nostrils twitched, itching to flare. She stood. "Are we done here, or do you want me to keep insulting you and your precious community?"

"I could just throw you in jail. Let you sit for a bit while I think up some charges," he threatened.

Pat bobbed her head. "You could," she agreed. "Try it. See what happens when Marissa learns you're getting transferred because you couldn't hold your temper. You're still with Marissa, right?"

"Fuck you, Pat."

"Tetchy," Pat laughed low. "Pass along my greetings when she lets you see Chloe."

"Get out." Tyler threw the pen down.

"Sure thing, sheriff. Bring a warrant if you want to set foot on my property when you come to collect the wreck."

Pat left Tyler's office. She made eye contact with Lisa on the way out.

"Phone me again, we'll get coffee."

Lisa nodded. Then she noticed Tyler's face. She quickly buried her head in her computer.

twelve

Something about being alone, surrounded by trees makes it easier to think. A forest reminds you of the ironclad rules of existence. New shoots bursting forth from the corpse of an ancient log that was once a shoot itself. The ground is rich with the scent of decay. Life paid for by death, without makeup or embalming fluid to cover it up.

Willow walked back to the house, alone. Like her namesake, only touching the water as it rushed past, tickling its branches while she remained frozen in time. Part of it, but now, outside of it as well. Admission paid in blood, a corporeal ghost.

A ghost that everyone believed had killed herself.

"Fuck her." She hissed quietly, as if someone might overhear. No wonder Pat had been so cagey about who she was. She'd almost had her convinced she was gay only to find out Pat had bitten her in a pathetic fit of loneliness.

That Willow had kissed Pat first was irrelevant. She had been manipulated.

She exhaled a cloud of vapour and zipped up the oversized quilted jacket. The winter chill clung to the woods, sheltered from an optimistic sun. "I bet I look ridiculous," she muttered.

How you looked had been important. She remembered that much. Her slight frame, black hair and blue eyes had made her stand out – the envy of all the other girls her age. She could have played Snow White in a play, if the high school had a drama class.

It did not.

Instead, Northton had an annual rodeo and a weekly farmers' market. She worked weekends at her parent's stall selling organic beeswax candles, incense and crystals. Tourists and boys trying to hit on her were the only ones who ever stopped by.

Unlike her mom and dad, she fit in. She made sure of it.

Her parents would say they were tolerant and in tune with nature. They lived sustainably. Cared for the environment and the next generation. The town would call them pompous and self-righteous. Ignorant of the work they really did and too stuck-up to bother finding out.

Willow chose the town. She gladly wore the gingham and cowboy boots. She went to the rodeos. She watched her boyfriend play hockey and even made an effort not to get lost in a book by the third period.

She went to youth group when her friends went – if they were doing something fun. The youth pastor, James, would tell the girls about keeping pure for their future husbands. He'd give the same talk to the boys, but then brag about his hot wife to titillate them.

The girls would pretend they weren't fucking the boys already and then ask his wife to buy them condoms so their parents wouldn't find out.

Willow may have been more like them than her parents, but it wasn't like she wasn't her own person either. It's just that interests that diverged from boys, hockey and Jesus were hidden away – acceptable only if you indulged at home, in the library, or online.

And that made her different. Unique. While other girls read Twilight, she'd moved on to Anne Rice. And when she'd finished that, she moved on to fanfic. She might have gotten into anime, had she been able to get it on a dial-up modem in rural Alberta.

Willow had known gay couples existed, but not in Northton. That was something city people did. Yet, in fanfic, she found story after story of every pairing imaginable, as if it were as common as breathing. Some of them weren't even people.

Her cheeks pinked remembering it. But those were private. Nobody here would understand it. And she wasn't even gay, just curious. Curiosity was normal for the smart girl.

The Smart Girl. She wondered what the town thought of her now. She hadn't exactly gone out on the best of terms. Nobody who commits suicide does. Even though that's not what had happened.

That was Pat's fault, too.

Pat – dropped here in grade ten. Her accent might have been charming, if not for the baggy Radiohead t-shirt, men's jeans and shaved head. She hadn't even tried to fit in.

Those who aren't fluent in the language of fashion can't understand. Her appearance wasn't a simple choice of expression. It was a call out. A direct challenge. And if you're new, you at least *try* to fit in. Pat didn't try. Pat didn't care.

Not true, Willow thought. Pat cared. Pat acted like she would be offended if no-one made fun of her. Not that anyone knew what to do with that. Not that she paid anyone enough attention to make harassing her sufficiently satisfying.

And then there was her mouth - a constant stream of words they were sure she had made up, but said with enough vitriol that it didn't matter. And Pat would parade around like she was above them all. Now she knew why, but at the time, it was so frustrating. And alluring. She wore the type of confidence that the boys with their swagger could only pretend to have. Willow wasn't gay, but Pat piqued her curiosity.

And then, out of nowhere, Pat hit Tyler with an old truck. She grinned like a maniac while she did it, too. Willow could picture every detail. The dimple on her cheek. The curl of her lip. Her gaze that never left the impotent teen, alternating between whimpering and swearing. She stared unblinking, like a predator. Like his suffering nourished her. The girls rushed to the town hockey star's defence, screaming at her. Calling her a psychopath while she laughed at them all, only proving their accusations. Why did that image cause her heart to race quicker? Why did it cause a flood of warmth to gather below her stomach?

Of course, she did nothing about it. What was she going to do? Chase after the town pariah like a cat in heat? Just to see? Just to become a pariah herself?

Oh, she thought about it. She thought about it plenty. How Pat's fingers would feel against her skin. How her lips would yield against the press of hers. The softness of those dimples against her cheek. Her boyishly handsome face with the gleam of a carnivore behind her hazel eyes.

Then, like a dream rudely interrupted, Caleb had asked her to marry him in front of the entire school cafeteria. His *boys* flanking him like some sort of celebrity. Girls with hearts in their eyes and hands clapped over their mouths.

Of course she had said *yes*. How could she do otherwise? How would that have played out? It would have ended the relationship immediately and she had no reason to do that. Caleb was the main character of the town high school and she had no experience beyond this town and these kids. The door to a cage she hadn't known she was in suddenly slammed shut - and Pat was on the other side of those bars.

Then the planning began.

Her friends swarmed like hens to a handful of corn, asking for details she didn't have. Hadn't she planned her wedding since birth? Since she'd dressed up in a torn princess costume and married the first confused boy she and her friends could catch? Didn't she have a colour scheme and a favourite flower? The names of her perfect children already picked out?

This was the grand achievement of her life. Why wasn't she ready?

"You'll need to lose at least five pounds."

"What?" Willow snapped to attention. That was her, in front of a tri-fold mirror with a half-zipped pile of white silk and organza draping off her shoulders and her future mother-in-law's lips in a tight line. Her own mother sat meekly in a corner with a calculator.

"Ten would be preferable, but if you want *that* in time for September, you'll need to see Charlene for Pilates." Her future mother-in-law turned to her mom.

"I'll give you the number for my dietician too and you can make arrangements.

Willow hadn't even known the town *had* a Pilates instructor, let alone a dietician. The reality of an entire life now decided for her felt like sky diving without a parachute and the reality of her future would come slamming into her at any moment.

She was barely eighteen.

She told her parents first. Arms wrapped around her, but the full weight of a mother's love absent. Her father had displayed more obvious disapproval. He understood that Caleb's parents would be upset enough to retaliate.

"Explain it to me." His face contorted in a way she had never seen. She hadn't been prepared for that. She had naïvely thought *I don't want to get married* would be enough.

"I-I'm not ready. I'm not even done with school!" She thought that should be sufficient, but the excuse sounded weak. "Caleb is the only person I've ever seriously dated," she added. Her father's face did not change.

"Sometimes, love at first sight really happens." Her mother squeezed. Her father nodded encouragingly. "It's normal to be nervous."

Willow bit her fingernails. "What if I find someone else at college? Caleb isn't going. That's four years, at least." College and an unspecified arts degree now felt like an escape instead of a foreign country to be explored.

"Did Caleb do something to you?" Her father's voice questioned low with concern. As if physical violence was the only believable reason his daughter would reject a boy like Caleb.

Willow shook her head.

"You don't love him?" Her mother fussed over Willow's hair. At least her mother seemed to understand that love was more than the absence of male missteps.

"What does that even mean, mom?" It felt strange coming out of her mouth. She had never questioned it before. She knew what love was, didn't she? But if she loved Caleb, why would she feel like this?

Her parents exchanged glances.

"I don't even know. Caleb is just *Caleb*. I don't want to just be a *wife* to a boy who inherited his dad's car dealerships and have babies." Willow escaped her mother's fussing and paced around the kitchen "If I get married right now, I won't even be my own person anymore! I want to be *more*!"

"Nothing is stopping you from being more." Her mother carded fingers through her hair. The comforting gesture only irritated her.

"Isn't there? He's not okay with me being gone that long. I don't know if I even want to come back here after I finish college."

Her father frowned. "What's wrong with here? *We* live here."

How strange that her father defended a place that treated him like a joke.

Her mother shot him a pointed look. He cowed away, but the anger remained. "Have you talked with Caleb about this?"

"Yes!" It came out louder than she had intended. Yelling wasn't something they ever did in this family.

"He says he'll have enough money for us both. But it's like he's not even listening! I don't care about money! He shouldn't even *have* a say in what I do with my life!" Willow leaned against the counter and dropped her head onto her chest. "He's just afraid I'll find someone else in college."

"Another boy, you mean." Her father gave her an odd look.

Willow didn't respond, but her eyeroll communicated everything he had already feared.

"Is this about that *Pat* girl?"

"What does *she* have to do with anything?" She hadn't ever spoken to Pat. Pat had never come over. And yet, Pat's existence alone was dangerous enough.

"Has she turned you into a..." her mother paused before she whispered "*lesbian?*"

"What? No!" Willow protested.

"Goddammit, I *knew* it when we found those pictures." Her father yelled at her mother and then turned to her. "No more computer time."

"I'm not gay!" Willow yelled. "Why do you care about Pat? I thought *you* of all people in this stupid town would be less homophobic!"

Willow stormed off to her room and attempted to slam the door. She had never done that before. The cheap hollow core doors didn't slam very well or provide the catharsis she needed. Mobile homes weren't built for teenage daughters.

Willow threw herself on the twin bed, a concerningly loud squeak, came from the mattress and the headboard slammed into the wall. She had never done that either. She had always been careful not to.

Willow. The smart girl. The pretty girl. The well-behaved only child of the local hippies. And she was about to blow up her life. And theirs.

If she went through with it, the town would gossip for *years* – not just about her, but her parents as well. She could practically taste the schadenfreude her classmates would feel, but wouldn't be able to spell. Or pronounce.

Willow groaned into her pillow. She couldn't do this to them. At least not without sleeping on it.

Willow scoffed at the memory. Back then, she wondered how Pat dealt with it. With constantly disappointing her parents and deliberately provoking Northton's ire. She had envied her freedom to be herself without ever second guessing whether it was acceptable or not. Now she knew the truth.

Willow was pouring skim milk over a bowl of her mother's home-made granola when her father walked in. His greying ponytail looked ridiculous with his male pattern baldness, but she wasn't going to tell him that, despite wanting to lash out after what had happened last night.

"Your mother and I talked about it after you went to your room."

Willow allowed herself a moment of relief. She expected him to say that they would support her decision to break off the engagement.

"We're sending you to a conversion therapy camp this summer. Caleb's mother has agreed to help pay for it."

It landed like a bomb. "A what?" Willow dropped her spoon.

"We know you've been struggling with..." he paused. "Inappropriate feelings around Pat. She's been a terrible influence at school." Her father stared at his feet, shaking his head.

"I told you, I'm not gay! I've never even talked to Pat!"

"It's only for two weeks."

Willow's face drained. She stared incredulously at her father for a few moments before leaving the table and marching out the door.

The speed at which her perception of her parents had changed gave her whiplash. Each hurried step only made her angrier, only cemented her half-baked idea on how to burn it all down. She stopped, hands gripping the nylon straps of her school bag so hard that it hurt and screamed at the early morning sky. It made her feel slightly less tiny and powerless, even if the only ones that heard it were the magpies.

She had made her decision. If they were going to treat her like a lesbian, she would find Pat. She didn't need to think on it anymore. She could learn not to care. If Pat could do it, so could she.

The stares when she sat with Pat and Kyle at lunch felt like knives. Each whisper. Each frown. Each mouth agape added to the growing ball of shame. With every passing moment, it became clearer that she had made a terrible mistake. But there would be no recovering from this, no turning back. Willow only prayed that the last two months of school would pass quickly.

But none of that venom came from Pat. She didn't even seem to notice. Nor did she comment when

Willow found them at recess. Or lunch the next day. Her presence simply *was*. As if she had materialised out of thin air with no past or connection to it.

Their conversation in the wood shop made a lot more sense now. Why should Pat mind? What was she to Pat? What were any of them to Pat? Why would she care what *food* thought of her?

Willow leaned her head back. That couldn't be completely true. Pat had been pretty certain that no-one wanted to be a monster. There must be something else Pat hadn't told her.

This isn't a film, Pat had said. What did that mean? Sunlight didn't bother her. And she had seen herself in a mirror. What else did she believe about vampires that wasn't true?

Willow brushed her hair out of her face. Pat may have locked her into a fate she hadn't chosen, like Caleb had tried to do – and she was still angry about that. But if the only consequence was a desire to drink blood? How upset could she be?

She wasn't going to thank her by any means. She hated not being given the choice. But it was an opportunity nonetheless. An opportunity she would seize.

Willow rummaged through the kitchen and found a pair of scissors. It should have been unfathomable to cut her hair – all the girls envied it. But she needed to change her appearance if she was going to be seen. She doubted people remembered what she looked like after twenty years, but one couldn't be too careful. Especially in a town that gossiped this much.

Great black hunks came away until she wore an uneven spiky mess. It looked like something Joan Jett would wear, but shittier. Maybe Pat could help her fix it.

And her hair wasn't her only unfinished business. She still had unexplored facets and unrealised desires to fulfil. She felt a growing surge of energy in her chest. The start of something new. A new life. A new *her.* Willow stared at herself in the mirror, standing on the precipice of her interrupted teenage rebellion. It was going to be glorious.

thirteen

The office phone flashed Bill's number.

"Christ, Bill, what now?" Tyler had been on edge ever since Pat had left his office. He didn't have any patience left for Bill's bullshit.

"There's something going on around the Soleil kid's grave again. I'm watching them now.

"Willow?"

"Yeah, that one." Bill sounded muffled. He must be away from the receiver, catching the reflection of something in the window.

"How close are you?"

"Tyler, I'm eighty-three, but the sun's still up. It's not a bag blowing in the wind."

"It was the last time."

"So back in 79, when your mom was in the hospital, me an' Wilma…"

"Goddammit, Bill, enough. I'm coming over."

Tyler slammed the receiver down before Bill could tell him about how his grandmother gave him a blowjob in the back of his dad's car again. The details got cruder with each retelling.

Tyler shoved his arms through his coat and slammed his muskrat hat over his ears. He glanced at his watch. 5:16 p.m. and getting darker. He was supposed to pick up Chloe at six.

"Fuck," he swore.

Tyler opened the door of the squad truck with a metallic creak and fired up the engine. He pulled out his phone and texted Marissa.

Three dots appeared and then disappeared. Marissa didn't respond. She didn't need to. There would be no way to argue out of it. Tyler would still go to the cemetery to check in on whatever Bill had seen and Marissa would still think he was a shit father.

Which was true. Tyler didn't know how *not* to be a shit father. He didn't know any fathers who *weren't* shit by Marissa's definition. They all worked to put food on the table and they all got yelled at for not spending enough time with their kids.

So, if Tyler had no chance of winning, he refused to play. He tossed his phone on the dashboard and flicked on the wipers. They stuck. Tyler swore under his breath and relaxed into the bucket seat while the window defrosted. He was going to be late anyway, so he might as well be really late.

Tyler ran his fingers through what was left of his hair, setting his hat on the passenger seat. Half of what he had lost, he attributed to the stress of his separation.

In the moment, it had come as a shock. Marissa's face, sallow and resigned, thrusting a few pieces of official-looking paper at him.

In retrospect, the marriage had been dead for a long time. They had sex maybe twice a year. Even then, she treated it like a chore. Tyler didn't feel appreciated. Loved even. He felt like a paycheque.

Ironic, he thought. In the years leading up to the separation, he had resented that feeling, and yet, to escape it, he had spent more and more time at work. Collecting more and more overtime. Providing more and more money. At the time, it was easier to tell himself that he was doing it for them instead of avoiding his family.

But Marissa made her own. Her job at the bank provided enough for her and Chloe to live on. Tyler hadn't been threatened by it. He still made more. He just hadn't thought he would become so *superfluous.* He thought that they would still have to depend on him. That they wanted to.

And now, he was literally *just a paycheque.* He sent child support every month and took Chloe when he could, which admittedly, wasn't often. Effectively, nothing had changed except where he slept. *Not true,* he thought – he had to do his laundry and cook for himself.

The sex she treated like a chore? Marissa had excised it from her body like you would a tumour. A simple cut. He wasn't needed. He never was. That was the worst part. He still craved it while she seemed relieved to never have to do it again. She hadn't even dated anyone since.

Either she had lied at the beginning of her relationship, or Tyler was so bad at sex that he had ruined it for her forever. Tyler believed the first one was more likely. She had never complained. She just stopped being interested.

The circle of defrosted glass slowly grew. He flicked on the wipers. This time, they moved, but all it did was smear a thin streak of water over the defrosted patch, instantly re-freezing. A classic example of rushing things and fucking it all up.

Was that the cause of his separation? Rushing into marriage right out of high school? He didn't think so. After all, who else was there to date in Northton? What else was there to experience? And they'd done the responsible thing and waited to have Chloe until he made Sergeant.

But what else was there?

Work. Until you retire. Then go fishing more often. Marissa wasn't content with that. Hell, *he* wasn't content with that, but at least he didn't complain about it. That's what you did. That was the deal. Marissa refused to accept that.

Marissa wanted more. What exactly that *more* was, she never told him. Maybe if she had had an affair, Tyler could have understood. But she didn't. He had even had her followed for weeks afterward. But all Marissa ever did was drop Chloe off at her older sister's house, go to work and come home.

What was the point of the separation then? Two houses. Two sets of laundry? Two sets of dishes? And a kid bouncing between them? How did she hate him this much and he hadn't seen it coming?

Pastor James had offered couples counselling, but Marissa had refused the moment the suggestion left his mouth. She was determined to be rid of him, regardless of how everyone would react.

Tyler hoped that the town gossip chain would push her back to him. It did not. He rented Pastor James's late mother's house hoping that a little space would make her see reason. Days passed. Then weeks. When Marissa did finally knock on his door, he had hoped to find regret. Reconciliation. He would be magnanimous and take her back.

Instead, her face had worn a different expression. The regret was there, but also anger and resignation. He never did have any talent at reading emotions.

"I'm pregnant," she said. It was more of an accusation. As if it was his fault.

"By who?" Tyler demanded. Marissa gave an odious sneer.

"By you." There was a note of disgust in her voice. "It was your birthday almost two months ago. Remember?"

"So…?" Tyler held that faint spark in his hands. Blowing on it just a touch. Maybe it would ignite their love anew.

"So, we'll need to revisit child support payments," Marissa said, as if it were the most obvious thing in the world and Tyler was an idiot for not knowing this. "I thought I'd do you the courtesy of giving you a heads-up first."

Tyler stared blankly. His ember of hope had been nothing more than a piece of glitter.

"You're welcome," Marissa backed out of the foyer and waited for Tyler to close the door.

"Uh. Thanks." Marissa turned and walked back to her truck. Tyler closed the door, stunned.

It wasn't the money. It was never the money. It was him. Marissa had rejected *him*. As a person.

Tyler opened the beige enamel fridge and pulled out a microwave dinner. He didn't even look at what kind. It didn't matter because they all tasted the same. It spun around, bathed in carmine light, filtered through the haze of dried tomato sauce. The microwave was so old that it rang a physical bell instead of beeping.

He tripped on the way to the table. Fettuccini alfredo flew through the air, landing wetly on the overbuilt oak table. Tyler swore at the pizza boxes and plastic trays overflowing the bin, mingling with the pile of laundry. If Marissa were here, she would nag him to clean up after himself. He sneered in defiance.

Tyler found the cleanest fork in the sink and set his dinner down on the tablecloth, now wearing a new stain. Pastor James had left his mother's furniture here and Tyler didn't feel like replacing it. If he did, that would mean he didn't expect Marissa to come back.

He scrolled social media while he ate. An *On This Day* picture from three years ago popped up. He had a lot more hair back then. He was thinner too. Marissa had somehow lost weight, even though she was now pregnant.

Tyler opened his photos app. Mostly fish. A few evidence photos. Chloe's first birthday. Some pictures Marissa had texted him while he was at work. It didn't mean anything. He wasn't a big picture guy. He hadn't even owned a camera until cell phones.

Tyler's eyes grew dry. It snapped him out of his awful reverie. The SUV had been running for at least thirty minutes and the windscreen was frost-free and dripping.

"Fuck."

Tyler drove the ten minutes to the cemetery. Nothing showed up in the headlights. Bill had probably spotted another plastic bag. Or they had moved on. Tyler clicked on his Maglite and swept the beam across the field. Nothing, except the stand of trees at the northeast corner and the snow-topped piles of dirt left over from when those goth kids had vandalised Willow's grave.

Pat had been more upset than he'd thought over that. He should have known she would blame them. It wasn't their fault Pat stood out so much. Pat *tried* to be as confrontational as possible. The clothes, the hair, the attitude. It all made her *ugly*. Nobody *wanted* to be ugly. Except Pat. She did it on purpose just to be an asshole. She didn't *want* to fit in. She'd admitted as much this afternoon. His adrenaline spiked thinking about her.

Tyler didn't understand what was so bad about this place. The biggest crime here was the occasional bar brawl or some kid joyriding on a quad. And yeah, they were gonna make fun of you if you stood out. That's how they kept the freaks out. That's how they made sure everyone fit in. Everyone had their place.

Even now, at his lowest point, this community took care of him. The separation hadn't even been public for half a day before Pastor James stepped up. Because he fit in. He knew his place. The town knew it too. Pat's problem was that she didn't understand small towns. They didn't bully her because she was different. It was because she thought she was better than everyone else.

And Pat refused to learn the lesson. She refused to tone it down.

Bill had made a half-assed attempt to fill the hole back in, but with the weather, he hadn't gotten far. At least he had covered the coffin.

Tyler scanned the site for footprints. Maybe there would be a boot he could match. At the very least, he could tell Bill he had tried and they were on the case.

The Maglite swept over the dirt pile, illuminating the name plaque. *Willow Marie Soleil.*

"Fuckin' hippie name." He felt a pang of guilt, but it had happened so long ago that he found it easy to brush aside. He mumbled "Sorry," to no-one in particular and resumed inspecting the dirt. He wasn't sure when he'd gotten so superstitious.

A slight impression in the frozen mud caught his eye – hard to see in the growing darkness and his light created too many shadows. Tyler pulled out his phone and snapped a picture. An icon spun around on his screen while the photo processed the low-light conditions.

A bird fluttered in the copse of trees in the corner, but it didn't call. Owl, or maybe a crow at this time of day. The sun had set and the gunmetal grey horizon only provided the barest outline. Tyler swept his beam across the trees and found them full. Hundreds of beady black crow eyes reflected back at him, mute and unblinking.

Tyler frowned and looked back at his phone. Five small toes and the pad of a foot.

"What the fuck?"

A jolt of panic. He drew his service revolver, steadying his aim with his torch hand. The beam swept along the trees again, reflecting the same stares of hundreds of silent crows.

"Fuck this spooky shit." Tyler marched back to his still-running SUV, angrier at his unmanly reaction to some harmless weirdness than the situation itself.

A silhouette outlined in the headlights blocked his return.

"Marissa?"

She didn't move.

"Fuck," Tyler gestured impotently, "Marissa. I'm sorry. I know I'm late. I texted you." Tyler re-holstered his pistol and turned off his Maglite.

Marissa stretched out her arms in exasperation. Was it exasperation? Tyler narrowed his eyes. It looked more like affection. That couldn't be. Marissa hated him. Had she changed her mind?

He stepped closer, entering her space. Marissa's arms slipped around his neck. After weeks of frozen meals, stale wallpaper and unwashed laundry, the smell of pears and elderflowers pushed him over the edge. He hadn't realised just how much he had missed this. Missed her.

"I'm so sorry," he burbled. He hadn't known he was crying. He could chastise himself for it later. "I don't know what I can do to make it up to you." He sniffed loudly and wiped the unmanliness from his face with his sleeve. "I'm willing to try."

Marissa slid her fingers across his half shaven jaw and around to the back of his neck. He leaned down to kiss her, but she turned her face to evade him.

Tyler tilted his head, confused. His throat exposed, Marissa launched herself forward, catching his trachea between her teeth. Tyler tried to scream, but his breath didn't reach his larynx.

His limbs fluttered – a bizarre, involuntary sensation he hadn't known before. His mind drifted away, like the muffled words of an AM radio station, just before you turn the knob too far. Their distant voices cling to you in that sticky almost-silence. The magical residue of a life ending before it all turns to static.

His fingers felt so far away. His heart rate slowed and spread warmly like an old quilt. He sunk into the earth. He flew along the wings of a crow. He became one with the universe. He finally understood the hippie shit.

fourteen

Lisa stared at her reflection, toothbrush whirring a lather across her teeth. She could psych herself up to let Josh go.

Then what?

Then what for both of them? It's not like she would find anyone else here. Was that such a bad thing? Or should she just wait it out and kill the relationship when she finally got that transfer she wanted? But now Pat was here and she didn't *want* to leave.

What would that look like?

If Pat didn't figure into the equation, she could endure the town gossips and steel herself to exist alone. God knows, she spent more time avoiding Josh than seeking him out. But now that she knew Pat was here?

How would that work - if she got what she wanted? She'd be the town dyke. *Her* town dyke. The thought filled Lisa with a warmth she hadn't expected - thumbing her nose at them all just to be hers.

Lisa groaned, flicking toothpaste all over the mirror. What the hell was wrong with her? She gave the mirror a quick wipe with a towel and headed to work.

Her reputation had been hard-won. The new kid, and a woman, thinking she could tell these people what to do because she had a shiny badge. She'd be throwing that all away if she got what she wanted. Not that she loved her job. She just followed her father into it. A rough-and-tumble daddy's girl that got more praise for being *one of the boys* than winning spelling bees.

But it felt like so much wasted time. So many years spent doing the wrong thing just to turn around and blow it all up. *Not blow it all up,* she thought. No-one would fire her. She'd just be making her life more difficult. *Which is why you haven't dumped Josh yet.* Lisa rolled her eyes at herself. *Stop being such a coward and do it already.* Her truck hit a pothole as if to emphasise the point.

The first thing she noticed was the crows. Hundreds of them. A black writhing legion over the dead grass in the cemetery. Then she saw Tyler's truck.

She pulled over and radioed Jacob.

"Officer McLeod, where are you right now?"

The radio hissed and popped. "I had to pick up coffee because I left my radio on my desk yesterday. Double double, right?"

Lisa rolled her eyes. "Did Tyler come in at all this morning?"

"No. Was he supposed to?"

"Get over to the cemetery."

Lisa hung up the receiver and checked her pistol before getting out of the car. The black wrought iron gate hung open. Sunlight glittered off of the patches of refrozen snow. Lisa checked the truck first. No sign of Tyler, except his cellphone still on the dash. Two missed messages, both from Marissa.

Her boots squelched against the saturated earth, like the dead objected to her presence. Bill would reseed after May long weekend, but for now, the earth was a dangerous mess of slippery vegetation and mud. No-one visited at this time of year.

The crows took no notice of her at first. Then, they scattered haphazardly in pockets as she approached, only to return once she had moved on - an ever-moving circle around her like a spotlight. Lisa prepared herself to find Tyler's body. A heart attack, perhaps. Or maybe a stroke. The separation had taken a lot out of him and he'd been eating cheap takeout since Marissa had left.

Lisa didn't dislike Tyler. He was a good boss. He had shown her the ropes. Been lenient when she messed up her first few reports. He brought coffee. Let her leave early when she needed. Work *felt* like family. Like a community. And that was everything here.

Communities had deaths, she reminded herself. Remember your training. Steel your stomach.

That worked until she came across a flap of scalp. A body, she could handle. A scrap of skin, waxy with wisps of hair attached, she could not. This wasn't at all like Caleb, frozen in the dark. Lisa vomited. The crows took no notice.

Jacob arrived and found Lisa sitting in her car, siren blaring to keep the crows away. He helped her put up police tape and then they called K division.

Marissa opened the door to find Lisa and Jacob. Two officers only showed up at your door with expressions like that for one reason. The late winter chill and the furnace blasting hot air through the door no longer mattered. She threw herself into Lisa's arms and cried, her faded pink terrycloth housecoat whipping around her ankles.

She pulled herself away, turning back into the house. The officers followed. Invitations were not required here. Jacob stood awkwardly, shifting on his feet. Lisa found a place on a sagging sofa with several worn and faded patches.

She locked eyes with Jacob and tilted her head toward the loveseat, raising her eyebrows. Jacob took the hint.

"How?" Marissa came into the living room with a pot of coffee. Red streaks still marked her face, but Marissa needed to be strong. For Chloe.

Lisa looked over at Jacob, sitting uncomfortably and fiddling with his hands. He nodded.

"We're still waiting on the autopsy."

"Don't bullshit me, Lisa." Marissa wiped her nose with the sleeve of her housecoat. "How'd he die?"

Lisa blew out her cheeks. "He was checking out a disturbance in the graveyard. It didn't look like a homicide." Marissa almost rolled her eyes. Homicides didn't happen in towns like Northton.

Marissa picked up Lisa's mug and filled it. "Heart attack?" That would be a relief, she supposed. It would have happened quickly. "Do I have to identify the body?"

"That's... not necessary." Lisa picked up her coffee and blew on it. No sugar had been offered and she wasn't about to ask.

Marissa eyed her sceptically.

"You don't want to see him like this, Marissa." Lisa did not look up.

"Just tell me what happened."

Jacob shook his head. "He's in pieces."

Lisa shot Jacob an angry stare. Marissa blanched and stumbled. Jacob sprang forward to catch her before she hurt herself. Coffee spilled everywhere.

"What the hell, Jacob?" Lisa hissed, running to the kitchen to grab a cloth.

"Sorry?" he half-whispered.

Lisa dabbed at the coffee before it stained the carpet more than it already was. "We think it might have been a wild animal." She took Marissa's hand.

"There aren't any around here." Marissa protested. "How could this happen?"

"Dogs maybe?" Jacob guessed. "Wolves wouldn't come this far into town. Coyotes couldn't do this."

"Jacob. Shut. Up." Lisa gritted her teeth. She turned back to Marissa. "We have K Division support coming this afternoon to get their opinion." Lisa took the mug from Marissa's shaking hands and placed it on the coffee table.

Chloe started crying in the other room. "Excuse me a moment," Marissa turned and left hurriedly.

Jacob looked over at Lisa. Lisa sighed. "Let's get his insurance paperwork filled out asap."

Jacob nodded. "I'll get Wilma and the church to put together some meals."

"Wilma is Tyler's grandmother," Lisa whispered. "Isn't that going to be awkward?"

Jacob shrugged. "That's just how things work around here."

Lisa nodded. She couldn't stand Wilma's holier-than-thou attitude, but if there was one thing she was good at, it was organising meals. And gossiping. Lisa had briefly been the victim of their nattering when she first got here.

According to Wilma, Lisa was a harlot. It took her weeks to figure out *why* Wilma had told everyone this. Lisa's advice to Sherri about buying her first vibrator had been overheard and Wilma had taken it from there. She firmly believed that vibrators were satanic and they ruined women for men. It didn't matter that it was the only way Lisa had been able to get off since Phaedra, but then again, Wilma wouldn't have approved of that either.

Lisa had briefly considered trying to convince Phaedra to move here. She could have started her own piercing studio. It would have been small, but rent here was affordable. Wilma's tongue had dissuaded her of that notion. There was no way in hell Phaedra would have changed herself to fit in. Nor would the town have changed to make room for her.

But Pat.

Pat refused to change. And apparently, refused to leave either. That blossom of warmth returned when she thought of it. She didn't understand how Pat could *not care*. How did she turn that off?

Marissa returned with Chloe on her hip. The chubby toddler looked at Lisa with Tyler's eyes before burying her head into Marissa's neck. Lisa felt a fresh wave of sadness knowing that she'd never see him again.

Not that they were close. Tyler acted like a young, old man. He worked, he went home. Occasionally went to drink with the boys or go fishing.

Tyler didn't do sports. He'd said he wrecked his knee playing hockey as a kid - not that uncommon around here. He'd go watch the local beer league games and occasionally spring for a night in the city for the farm team. She'd never known him to be a fanatic though. Not like some men who made their favourite sports team their entire personality.

Lisa knew about the separation. Everyone knew everything in this town. She didn't pry, or believe half of the rumours. It simply didn't work out. For some reason, Lisa found that a lot easier to accept than the rest of the town. Like nattering magpies, they pestered Marissa to take him back. It only made her angrier at Tyler.

Maybe that's why Tyler liked her. She never asked about Marissa. She knew that sometimes relationships failed because you didn't click anymore, no good guy or bad guy. It simply died. Like her and Josh.

No, she thought. Her and Josh died because Josh was the best option in a small town. And she hadn't worked up the nerve to tell him it was dead. What did it say about him that he hadn't noticed? Or was he content to have *anyone*?

Lisa snapped out of her self-loathing and looked from Chloe to Marissa. She was being so incredibly strong right now. She hoped that if she had kids, she would be able to be as strong for them. Though if her present cowardice was any indication, she had doubts she would be. She was too old for kids anyway.

"We'll get the paperwork filled out for you and make all the funeral arrangements." Lisa leaned forward, resting her elbows on her knees. "Jacob's gonna get Wilma and the church ladies to make some meals and bring them around. I'll get Josh to gather some people as well."

Jacob nodded.

Marissa wiped another tear away with the heel of her hand. Chloe sucked lazily on her pacifier, her eyes still half asleep. "Thank you," her voice faltered. "Sorry for being such a mess."

Lisa stood, followed quickly by Jacob. He shifted his feet restlessly.

"I'm here for you, Marissa." Lisa tilted her head. "Call me for *anything*. We all loved Tyler, and I promise we'll take care of you."

Pat killed the engine only to hear another crash coming from the end of her driveway.

"Jesus shitting fuck, what now?" She hopped out of the lorry and stomped through puddles of slush toward the noise. A blue Dodge crumpled around the rear bumper of the now twice-destroyed Chevy. The birds had fled and the only sound was the hiss and creak of the cooling engine block.

She recognised the truck. What was Marissa doing out here? Pat knocked on the window, jolting a dazed Marissa awake.

"Pat? Oh my God, what are you doing here?"

"Er, I live here." Pat kicked at the gravel in the snow. "Though it seems a lot of people are dropping by lately." She tilted her head toward the beat-up Chevy, both ends now ruined.

Marissa rolled down the window. "I thought you'd left."

"People keep telling me that." Pat pointed toward the house, though it wasn't visible due to the overgrowth. "What are *you* doing out here? This road doesn't go anywhere. At least, nowhere important."

Marissa blinked trying to focus her eyes. She must have a concussion. "I – I needed some air. I had to get out of the house. I got in the truck and drove."

What was she thinking? She could have been killed. She could have killed Chloe! She burst into sobs.

Pat put a hand on her shoulder. Marissa jerked to attention.

Pat stared with concern in her eyes. "Do you want to come in? Josh is supposed to come by later and pick up the wreck. He can give you a lift back."

Marissa nodded.

Pat penguin-walked over to the other side and pulled Chloe out from her car seat. Chloe appeared startled at first, but almost immediately fell asleep in Pat's arms.

Marissa shuffled around piles of melting snow to catch up to them.

"You're a natural with her. She usually screams when anyone but me picks her up." Marissa sniffed, her voice nasally from the crying.

Pat grinned.

"Even Tyler..." Marissa stared in horror, realising that Tyler was gone.

Pat cocked an eyebrow.

Marissa inhaled sharply. It would come out soon anyway. "It hasn't made the news yet, but Tyler is..." She forced herself to say it. "Gone."

"I'm so sorry." Pat wrapped her in a hug and Marissa melted into her arms. Chloe didn't stir.

Why did this seem so easy? She hadn't seen Pat in decades. It felt so familiar. Like she *should* be in Pat's arms. She must be in shock, still reeling from losing her husband. *Technically* her husband, she reminded herself. Her *late* husband.

But the worry about how she would deal with all of this, how she would tell Chloe that her father was never coming back, how she would manage the guilt all seemed to disappear in Pat's strong arms and intoxicating scent. She felt like a bowl of ice cream your parents bought you after getting stitches. She missed this, even though *this* had never happened before.

Of course it hadn't. She and Pat had never hugged. They had barely spoken in high school. Maybe she *did* have a concussion. Whatever it was, she didn't want Pat to let go. She pulled her tighter.

Pat returned from the kitchen with a pot of tea. "Sorry," Pat gave a bashful smile. "I'm not a good cook. And I don't have biscuits or sweets or anything."

"Thank you." Marissa accepted the mug. Chloe continued to sleep soundly in her car seat that Pat had gone back to retrieve. "She's never like this. You should run a daycare."

Pat rubbed at the back of her neck. "I don' know about that. Also, I live out here. I don't think you want to drive all the way out here every day."

Marissa stared at Chloe sleeping. "Maybe not. So, what *have* you been doing all these years out here?"

Pat knocked on the table. "Building furniture."

"You made this?" Marissa's eyes widened. Pat nodded. "This is amazing! I had no idea." Marissa ran her fingers along the table trying to find the seams.

"Yeah." Pat looked away. Marissa could tell she wasn't used to taking compliments.

Then again, Marissa thought, she probably hadn't received many in school. Pat always walked the hallways back straight and head high. As a kid, she assumed Pat didn't care what people said about her. As an adult, she knew better. Having no friends hurts, even if you don't show it. There is no such thing as a lone wolf.

"Are you out here by yourself?" Marissa blew on her tea. "Who lives in those other houses?"

Pat nodded. "I mean, there's the girl that I pulled out of that truck here right now, but mostly I live alone. The other houses are the garage and the wood shop." Pat did not feel like explaining the *other* one.

"Girl?"

"A couple days ago, from the wreck you just hit." Pat pointed in the direction of the ruined vehicles. "I found a girl with no ID, unconscious."

"Who is she?"

Pat shook her head. "Don't know. No memory."

Marissa raised her eyebrows. "And you're keeping her here?"

"I'm not *keeping* her. She can leave whenever she wants."

"That's awfully generous of you."

Pat shrugged. "I thought that's what you community types were all about."

Frown lines appeared on Marissa's forehead.

Pat bobbed her head to the side. "I'm sorry. I'm being hostile for no reason."

"I don't - I don't blame you." Marissa's eyes softened. "We were assholes to you, Pat. I'm sorry."

Pat blinked, holding her tea with both hands in front of herself like a shield. "Huh."

Marissa stared expectantly.

Pat looked away. "You're the only one who's apologised about that."

"I'm not surprised." Marissa said to herself, but Pat heard it. She waited for an explanation.

Marissa took a deep breath. "Tyler and I were separated."

Pat raised her eyebrows. "I ran into him. He wanted to pin that crash on me somehow."

"That sounds like him. He hasn't changed. The town hasn't changed. Everything is someone else's fault." Marissa threw up her hands. "Everything would be paradise if everyone just left them alone, like they'd be completely self-sufficient raising cattle. As if their taxes even cover the roads they drive on. I work at the bank. I've seen the bills," she muttered. Marissa took a sip of her tea like it was a shot of whiskey. "It's the constant resentment I can't deal with anymore. It's like a poison, just bubbling away under the surface, waiting to take someone down." Marissa met her eyes. "I can't be around it anymore, Pat."

Pat stared confused, suddenly wishing she'd made more of an effort to get to know her in high school. "I thought this was the place to raise your kids. Everyone looking out for them and all that?"

"Right, crime." Marissa huffed. "But it's not like anyone is going to build anything for us out here." She pointed at her swollen belly. "And if that's the case, I don't want Chloe and this one growing up with nothing but anger. They'll just get bored and drink themselves stupid like we did. And then get pregnant by the town hockey star who swears he would have gone pro if he hadn't wrecked his knee."

"This seems very specific."

Marissa looked away. "There's nothing here for them, Pat. We don't own land. There's no family farm or legacy they need to uphold. And now half of the kids are vaping fentanyl or some crap."

"I'm not gonna argue with that." Pat raised her hands in concession. "But I thought the plan was to get married and raise your kids together with your friends."

"Friends." Marissa laughed. "My younger sister left as soon as she could. And now she has a bigger group of friends with kids than I do." She fingered the rim of the mug. "To be honest, most of my friends haven't spoken to me much since I left Tyler. Even Vanessa."

Pat shrugged, but she stayed quiet. Marissa didn't need her to badmouth Tyler right now.

"I'm sorry." Marissa ran her fingers through Chloe's hair. "I don't want to shit on Northton. I'm just exhausted and I hate being pregnant. And now this."

"It's okay." Pat slipped her arm around Marissa.

For a moment, Marissa felt like everything would be alright. Pat speaking jolted her back to reality.

"Anyway, I should get back out there. Josh should be here soon." Pat took one last sip of her tea.

"Should I..."

"Nah, you stay here. I'll come get you when he's ready to take you home." Pat put on her coat and made for the door.

"Pat?"

Pat turned around and saw Marissa gazing at her with pure longing.

"It was good to see you again."

"Yeah," Pat shuffled her feet. "Yeah, it was good to see you too."

"Can you come visit sometime?" Marissa didn't know why she'd asked, but it seemed important at the moment.

Pat's face lit up. "Yeah, sure." She turned and closed the door before she embarrassed herself.

fifteen

The tow truck fishtailed before it came to a stop. Luckily, Josh was a somewhat better driver than either Caleb or Marissa and he managed to recover. The spot was clearly a hazard and if the entrance to Pat's driveway were on a more populated road, there would be more trucks piled up.

Josh flicked the switch that set his ambers flashing. Two trucks. He had only been told about the Chevy. The Dodge looked like Marissa's. He stepped out of the cab. Lucy followed, running a few circles in the mud.

Pat appeared as if out of thin air, though it wasn't surprising given the shrubs and weeds.

"Pat?"

Pat nodded, continuing her walk up the driveway. "Yep. Still live here. Even though everyone thinks I left."

Josh adjusted his red Flames snapback. "Why would I come out here? We all thought you'd left." He walked around the trucks to figure out how best to deal with them.

Pat slid and held on to the Chevy for balance. "Fair enough, I suppose."

"Looks like Fred's already been here." Josh removed his cap so it didn't fall in the muddy snow. A brown stain had frozen to the truck. Lucy ran over to lap at it.

"Lucy, no!" Josh scolded. Lucifer ignored him.

He reached for his collar, but Lucy evaded him, scampering over to Pat. Pat scratched his ears and Lucifer sat.

Josh shook his head and let it be. "So, this truck," Josh pointed to the Dodge. "That's Marissa's. I guess something else happened here."

"She's inside. I was hoping you could give her a lift back to town." Pat pointed back toward the house. "She's got Chloe with her."

He nodded. "I can do that. I'll need to make a couple trips though."

"Whatever, as long as it gets moved. I have furniture to deliver. I can barely get an empty lorry around it."

"You deliver furniture?" Josh narrowed his eyes. "How come we haven't seen you in town until the other day?"

"I *make* furniture," Pat said, a little too testily. "And no-one in this town has ever ordered any."

"Well, geeze." Josh gave an easy smile. "I know Marissa needs new furniture. And Dan retired. There hasn't been a place selling furniture here in six years."

"You're telling me no-one has bought a sofa in six years?"

Josh laughed. "No, but flat pack is garbage and when you factor in the shipping, it's an even worse deal."

Pat's expression remained unchanged.

"C'mon Pat. You know what happened to Tyler. She needs a hand," Josh pleaded quietly.

Pat sighed. "I literally just found out, and only because Marissa showed up. Town gossip doesn't usually make it this far out."

"Yeah, but…" Josh pawed at the back of his neck.

"And aren't they divorced? Why does she need my help?"

"Separated. And you know." Josh put his cap back on. "She's got Chloe. And the other one."

Pat nodded. She could admit that his concern for Marissa was admirable. "You were the only decent person in this town, Josh."

"Nah," Josh turned away. "You only remember the mean people."

"Like Caleb?"

Josh inhaled slowly and held his breath.

"It's okay," Pat waved it off. "I'm not going to force you to speak ill of the dead."

"Thanks, Pat." Josh blew out his cheeks.

"I have no problem doing that myself. He was the town bully and the rest of you arselings were too cowardly to do anything about it."

"Hey!"

"You were younger. I don't blame you."

"Thanks, I guess," Josh muttered.

"You can thank me by making sure no other kids go through what Willow did."

"Or you?" Josh smirked.

"I have my big girl pants on." Pat remained stone-faced.

"Fair enough." Josh looked for an anchor point he could use.

Pat straightened up and crossed her arms. "Do you need any help?"

Josh stood, shaking his head. "I'm gonna have to move Marissa's truck first. I'll take her back with me and then come by in the evening for the other one."

Pat nodded. "I'll go get them."

Ten minutes later, Pat carried Chloe, still sleeping in her car seat with Marissa holding on to her other arm for balance. Lucy danced around her heels.

"Hey Josh!" she called, waving.

"Hey Marissa. Looks like you had a little trouble."

Marissa nodded and grew quiet, remembering why the accident had happened in the first place.

"I told Pat you needed some new furniture. She said she'd make you some."

Pat raised her eyebrows at Josh, but managed to get her expression under control before Marissa turned to face her.

"Oh my God, Pat! Thank you!" She threw her arms around Pat. The scent of her neck gave her that fuzzy feeling again.

"I'm sorry!" Marissa let go and stepped back. "I didn't mean to choke you!"

Pat chuckled, embarrassed. "It's okay. Let's get you in the car. I'll come by later this week and see what I can do." She opened the door to the tow truck and buckled Chloe's car seat. She scowled at Josh once Marissa had turned away. Josh grinned in return.

"You know Jacob has Wilma and the church ladies organising a meal drive for Marissa, right? You should join them." Josh leaned on the lever and the winch squealed to life. A loud *pop* enunciated the separation of the front and rear bumpers.

"Wilma and the church ladies can fuck each other in the arse." Pat growled.

Josh continued, unfazed. "They might do that, but I'm sure they'd love to have you help."

"Help fucking them in the arse?" Pat's face scrunched up at the thought. "You need to be nice and relaxed for that and I'm pretty sure having me around would do the opposite. They never did like me."

Josh laughed. "Probably not that. I meant cooking."

Pat blinked. She had somehow forgotten the casual misogyny. "Well, I can't cook. Maybe you should help them and I'll take over driving your tow truck." Lucy's tail beat against her Carhartt's. "I'm sure you would love that, wouldn't you?" she said to the black Lab.

Josh kicked at the filthy slush. "Alright, I guess I deserved that."

"Yes, you did." Pat took a breath. At least he was being mature about it. Maybe Lisa had picked a good one. "Wilma's going to do nowt, you know that, right?"

"What do you mean?" Josh raised his shoulders.

"Wilma is Tyler's grandmother. She's not going to organise a meal drive for the woman who left him."

Josh curled his lip in shock. "What? She's not like that."

Pat pulled out her wallet and slapped a twenty-dollar bill on the crumpled aluminium, ringing with a hollow metal clang to emphasise her point. "If she organises a meal drive that isn't half-arsed and lasts more than a week, you owe me twenty."

Josh grinned and took the bill. "I think they'll surprise you. They're not as bad as you think." Josh tucked the bill into his front pocket. "You know that Lisa told me she's bi?"

Pat scrunched up her forehead. She'd given him too much credit. And she'd *told* Lisa not to say anything about that. She *knew* Josh had a big mouth. She'd have to ask Lisa about it later. "Lisa was my roommate. I know *far* more about Lisa than you do. Things that wouldn't be fit to print in Penthouse Letters."

Josh blanched. His reaction gave Pat a thrill. He opened his mouth to protest, but Pat interrupted.

"Honestly, why would I give a soggy shit about who Lisa fucks? Is this some sort of *I have a gay friend* thing?"

Josh's eyebrows met at the bridge of his nose. "You *do* have a gay friend. Lisa's gay. Well, *half* gay."

Pat winced, "That's... not how that works."

Josh shook his head defensively. "What I mean is, she's kinda going through the same thing you and Willow did."

"What?" Pat knew she didn't understand most men, but Josh's train of thought was on an entirely different track. And it wasn't even a train. More of a golf cart trying to waterski.

"She's gay in Northton. And she's doing fine."

Pat knew that Lisa was most certainly *not* doing fine and *of course* Josh wouldn't pick up on that. That needed to be its own conversation, though.

"And what if I hadn't known? You just outed her to me. Are you now going to out her to the whole town?"

"But that's the point. They aren't like that."

Pat rubbed her forehead. "Josh, I know you're trying to connect with me, but I don't have the patience to explain how fucking stupid what you said was."

Josh's brow furrowed in confusion.

Against her better judgement, she continued. "Is she dating a woman right now and they're all cool with it? Is there another queer couple here that no-one has driven out? Is that why you think they won't care?"

"What? No, *we're* dating." An ugly shock wriggled through him at the thought of Lisa dating someone else.

"Then you know naff all about how they'll react."

"But they won't, because we're dating."

Pat massaged her temples. She briefly considered explaining bi-erasure, but Josh's experience with queerness probably started and ended with *Chasing Amy*. She needed to de-escalate this before she bit him in frustration. Pat could examine why this conversation was aggravating her so much later., somewhere far away from Josh. "Yes. I know. I saw you at Boots. Remember?"

Josh tried to parse her tone, but couldn't. "Do you not approve?"

"Approve of what? I said I don't care who Lisa fucks. I *do* care if she's happy."

"Is…is she not happy?" Josh searched Pat's eyes for clues, but he knew he was bad at reading women. If he wasn't, asking Lisa to move in with him wouldn't have gone so poorly.

Pat stared blankly. Josh might be cute and sweet, but he was thick as treacle in January. No wonder Lisa worried about what he'd do when she dumped him. Pat needed to end this conversation *now*. "I'll see you this evening, Josh." She turned and walked back to the house. Lucy tried to follow, but Josh redirected him to the truck bed. He sulked, but stayed.

Josh tried to shrug it off by escaping into the cab of the tow truck. It ate at him anyway.

"Thanks, Josh," Marissa spoke quietly. Chloe stirred in the car seat between them.

"Yeah, Marissa." Josh shifted in his seat. "No problem." He signalled and turned to check for traffic. Not that there would be any on this road, but things had been odd lately. He sighed. "You know we'll take care of you, right?" He kept his eyes on the road. "Lisa always spoke so highly of Tyler. *Like a responsible big brother*, she said."

Marissa knew that she wouldn't exactly miss Tyler. Her concern was feeling responsible in some way for his death. If she had responded more forcefully, would he have ignored Bill and picked up Chloe for the evening? Even she knew such thoughts were futile and only causing her more grief. But to not feel anything made it worse. She decided it would be easier to focus on something else right now.

"How's Kyle?" Marissa adjusted Chloe's blanket. She hadn't seen Josh's older brother in years.

"Eh. Doing something at the university. I don't think he gets paid much, but he doesn't want to move back. I don't think he liked it here. He didn't fit in either. I don't really know."

Marissa kept her mouth shut. There had been rumours after what had happened between Willow and Pat, but she didn't know if Josh knew. Bringing them up would be cruel anyway.

"That girl," Marissa said after several minutes of silence, "There's something familiar about her. I can't get it out of my head."

Josh frowned. "What girl?"

"The one Pat took in. I saw her in the hallway when Pat was out talking with you." She gripped the handle of the car seat. "Something just feels off about her."

Josh blew out his cheeks. "It's probably just the stress." They crested the hill and the lights of the town came into view. "C'mon, I'll stop at A&W and grab you a coffee."

"I don't think that'll help my stress, Josh. But thank you." She sighed.

"Hot chocolate then." Josh grinned.

Marissa smiled and nodded. *Lisa was a lucky woman,* she thought.

sixteen

Pat stormed into the house, annoyed at men in general and Josh in particular. Willow's head peeked up from behind the sofa. She looked like a blue-eyed hedgehog.

Pat raised an eyebrow. Willow grinned sheepishly. "I don't know anything about cutting hair, but that was probably a good idea."

"I saw Marissa."

"Oh?" Pat removed her jacket and hung it up.

"It's so weird. Waking up and everyone you know is twenty years older. Except for you, of course."

Pat frowned. "She didn't recognise you?"

"No," Willow shook her head. "I'm a master of disguise."

Pat blew out her cheeks in relief. "Good. That would have made for an awkward conversation."

"What's got you all worked up?" Willow picked at the cloth at the back of the sofa.

She shook her head, as if men and misogyny and this whole fucking town was a cobweb stuck in her hair. "Josh got on my tits. And the town. They're as shitty as I remember."

"Josh seemed cute."

"Sure. If you're into that sort of thing." Pat sighed. Wouldn't that be the perfect solution? Willow could take Josh off of Lisa's hands? Everyone would have their happy ever after?

"I *am* into that sort of thing," Willow said a little too pointedly. "I told you, I'm not gay."

God, Pat was an idiot. Biting Willow in a moment of hormones and anger had fucked her life up in ways too innumerable to count. She hated it when Corinne was right.

"I don't care what you are. You can't go after him."

"Why not?"

"Well, for one, Lisa's dating him." Pat turned to hang up her toque.

"Lisa is cute too."

"I thought you said you weren't gay."

Willow shrugged. "I can be curious."

That caused a swell of jealousy. Thankfully Pat was facing the wall and she managed to get her face under control before she turned around. "We need to talk about some things."

"I thought you said I needed to figure things out on my own?"

"Look." Pat ran her hands over her face. "If I go fetch pizza right now, will you wait for a moment before trying to fuck everything with a pulse that crashes into my driveway?"

Willow stared. Those ice-blue eyes were so unnerving.

"Please?"

"Fine." Willow turned and slumped back down onto the sofa. She found the remote for the T.V. and flicked through the channels, but all of them were static. Pat had said something about cable not being a thing anymore. Willow turned it off.

She took a deep breath. If she was going to get out of here and start living, she would need to figure out what she could do. She'd seen Pat slip into shadows, maybe she could practice that?

The midday sun didn't provide much opportunity, but she found an old bookcase that had maybe a foot or so of shadow cast against the wall. Willow thrust her hand into it.

Nothing happened.

She tried it again. Still nothing.

Willow took a deep breath and exhaled in frustration. Maybe it was more of a mental thing? She could do that. She wished she'd paid more attention when her mother tried to teach her yoga.

Willow crossed her legs and walked through the steps to clear her mind. Acknowledge thoughts as they come. Say hello and then wave goodbye as they leave. Don't hold on to them. Don't get frustrated when they linger. Let them parade through your mind until the end. When the cleanup crew came and removed the glitter and debris, all that remained was Willow and the shadow.

Willow presented her arm to the shadow again. This time, she felt a slight tug. She opened her eyes to see the edges of her fingers blurred. She stayed there, watching for twenty minutes. Dry eyes from staring were her only reward.

Which is when Pat closed the door. The smell of warm cardboard and melted cheese filled the room.

"Trying to slip into the shadows?"

Willow turned her head, embarrassed. She wasn't sure why she should feel this way. Maybe because she had always been the best at school. Failing was new to her.

"I can feel it, but I can't slip into it like you can."

Pat looked at the wall and the foot-wide shadow against it. "Stand up."

Willow rose to her feet.

"Can you fit into that shadow?"

She looked at the book case. It came to her waist. There was no way she could completely cover herself with the shadow it cast.

Pat opened the pizza boxes and set them on the table. "I know you used to like plain cheese, so that's what I got."

Willow grabbed a slice and threw herself on the sofa. "How long has it actually been?"

Pat did a bit of maths in her head. "About eighteen years."

Willow bit into her pizza. "How old were you?"

"When I bit you or when I turned?"

"When you turned," Willow mumbled, mouth full of pizza.

"Sixteen."

"You don't look sixteen."

Pat brushed her hand across her scalp. "Stress will do that to you. I didn't have the greatest life."

"I'm sorry we treated you like that." Willow stared at the floor.

Pat gave a non-committal grunt. "It wasn't just you. My whole life was shit. You pissants were just the shit cherry on top of a shit sundae."

Willow looked up at her, waiting for more.

Pat took a deep breath, pausing to reflect on how best to explain her situation in as few words as possible. She didn't need Willow to be her therapist. "Religious family, oldest daughter, caught with a girl when I was fourteen. They shaved my head as punishment and then got mad when I kept shaving it. They told me to leave when I was sixteen. You heard the rest already."

Willow could admit that Pat had been dealt a terrible hand, but it still wasn't fair to make it her problem. "They didn't send you to conversion therapy?"

Pat shook her head. "Too many kids, not enough money. *Repent or leave* is cheaper."

Willow sat in silence for a few moments. It annoyed her that her struggles couldn't compare.

"Why exactly are you angry with me?" Pat walked into the kitchen to give Willow some time to reflect without hovering.

"I don't know," she admitted.

Pat returned carrying two glasses of water. "I can guess."

Willow eyed her sceptically.

"It makes you uncomfortable that a lesbian took interest in you." She set down the glasses on the table. "I did something to you without your consent. I get it. It was a shitty thing to do. I shouldn't have done it and I apologise."

Pat took a spot on the sofa with a bit more restraint than Willow had. "The only bright side is that my fuckup gave you another chance. Now you can do whatever you want. I'll help you however I can."

"I'm still mad at you."

"I can live with that."

Willow made a face and stared.

Pat put her pizza down. "It's not an excuse, but as pathetic as it sounds, you were the first girl to show interest in me since Camille that *wasn't* because of the pheromones and I didn't even get to see where it would end up and so I acted like an entitled arsehole. I really am sorry."

"Wait, the what? Pheromones?"

Pat stared at her for a moment. "Did you never wonder why I always wore long sleeves?"

"I always thought it was to hide how jacked you were." Willow smiled with a hint of a blush.

Pat rolled her eyes. "Your skin secretes a pheromone. It's a mild hallucinogen, UV sensitive, so it really only works on people in the dark."

"Is that why you smell like chocolate and strawberry ice cream?"

Pat frowned. "I smell like ice cream?" She lifted her arm to her nose and inhaled. "I don't…" She shook her head.

"You definitely do." Willow laughed.

"If you say so."

Willow resumed eating her pizza. Pat followed suit.

"You're going to have to explain more about these pheromones."

Pat finished her slice and reached for a napkin. "People hallucinate if they're exposed to your pheromones. Then they made up *compulsion* to explain why they invited you in."

"Does something stop you if you aren't invited in?" Willow looked confused.

"Yeah," Pat curled her lip. "Common decency."

"What?"

"It's *rude*."

"Are you serious?" Willow put down her half-eaten slice on the lid of the box.

"You *don't* think it's rude?"

"I mean, you *bite* people. I figured a little breaking and entering would be no big deal."

"I only bite people who want to be bitten, Willow."

Willow pulled her knees to her chest. "So, in the dark, when people are tired, they get a little too close to you and start seeing things and then they invite you in and ask to be bitten?"

"Something like that."

"And the venom?"

"Makes women, er..." Pat took another slice of pizza.

Willow raised her eyebrows. "What about men?"

"You don't bite men."

Willow frowned. "Why not?"

"Remember how you bit me and you got really tense and aggressive?"

"Yeah?"

"It's a lot worse with men. Testosterone, maybe? I don't really know. It's not like there are enough of us to run experiments on."

"Huh." Willow let her legs go and reached for another slice. "You don't find that weird?"

"Corinne thinks it's a curse, that we're cursed vessels for blood magic."

"Seems like it worked out in your favour."

"Did it?" Pat glanced over at Willow before going back to her pizza.

"You get to bite and have sex with the people you want, don't you?"

Pat put her pizza down and wiped her hands. "Sure. I guess. It's just sex."

"You can't just go into the city and find a lesbian who wants to be with you?"

"I've found plenty."

"Then what's the problem?"

Pat shifted to face Willow. "You're eighteen and you just turned, so go nuts and find out yourself. Fucking people who are hallucinating and suffering from blood loss is boring. It's more of a repayment for the blood you took."

"What about sex with other vampires?"

Pat wasn't about to give Willow a tour of her party space. "We're rare. And exactly three people in this town know I'm a vampire. You, Corinne and her husband."

"Is he also a vampire?"

Pat shook her head. "She hasn't bitten him."

"Why not?"

Pat sighed. She could tell from the way Willow said it that this was going to be a struggle. "I already told you, you can't."

"Yes, but you didn't explain why."

"He would die. There are no male vampires."

Willow eyed her sceptically. "That doesn't make sense."

Pat shrugged. "Vampires have always been women. Dracula and Edward only exist because it makes straight people feel less…" Pat rested a finger against her jaw. "Conflicted."

Willow stared, the muscles in her face tense.

"Think of it this way," Pat continued. "What would it do to your happy, happy marriage if you had a dream about a woman biting you? If in that dream, you felt desires you didn't know you had. You didn't just feel them, you *needed* them fulfilled? Desires so filthy, you'd never tell him because he can't even bring himself to go down on you. You can't remember the last time you didn't fake it. You remember *her*, though. Your dream woman. Your monster who made you scream so loudly your throat was still raw in the morning."

Pat settled back into the sofa, an upturned curl to her lip.

"Most women like dick, Pat." Willow glowered, head to the side.

"They do, don't they?" Pat smiled sweetly. "So, imagine what it does to you when you start to go to bed early every night? At first, you'd tell yourself that you're just tired. It has nothing to do with that dream. You like men. You like their muscles. The angles of their bones. Their strength. You feel protected and secure. Even a little bit afraid of them. But you still can't get her out of your head.

When she appears a second time, your heart flips. You've soaked the sheets before her venom has even touched your neck. You know you're not supposed to want this. But that night, you come so hard you can't deny it any longer. You're ready to run away with her the next time she returns.

But she never does.

You sink into a deep depression. You ignore your children. You stop eating. Your husband takes you to doctor after doctor. Eventually, you find one that you think might understand. You confess everything. They tell your husband.

But they change one detail. Because women don't *do* that. Women don't *want* that. The existence of monsters is more believable to them than women who want to fuck other women." Pat took another slice of pizza.

"I'm not questioning whether monsters exist." Willow had completely missed the point. "This sounds like your own personal vendetta. I'm sorry your life sucked, but we're not all lesbians and I'm going to bite men if I want."

Pat groaned and rubbed the palms of her hands into her forehead. She was not getting through to Willow at all. "Fine." She rolled her neck from side to side. "You want an idea of what it's going to feel like if you bite a man? Bite me."

Willow recoiled into the corner of the sofa. "You just dress like a man. And I already bit you."

Pat laughed. "You stopped as soon as you recovered your memory." She rested her head on the back of the sofa, exposing her neck. A finger travelled along her right carotid artery. Her lip curled upward. She knew Willow couldn't take her eyes off of it. The rush of blood just beneath, bloating the skin with every pulse.

"You don't need to hold back. I invited you. I can hear your mouth watering."

Willow tucked her legs in tighter. Her hand clapped over her mouth. She could smell Pat's blood. Resin. Smoke. Candy. How could she be so hungry after eating three slices of pizza?

She couldn't stop them. Her canines slid free, slipping against her fingers. There was no itch, no pain this time. Her mouth kept watering. She tried to swallow, but her throat stuck. Pat and her arrogant smirk. Her fucking neck the most delicious shade of pink, beckoning.

Willow launched herself into her throat. Pat's head snapped back, but her smirk remained. Sweet, sugary blood burst across her tastebuds, but it wasn't enough. She needed more.

She growled, pushing her away angrily, leaving a tear at her neck. A fountain flew from the wound, landing in thick splatters against the hardwood. Pat smiled serenely, like a stained-glass saint while the gash healed itself with unnatural speed.

Willow screamed in frustration. How *dare* she recover from that. How *dare* she taunt her. Rage sped through her veins. She leapt forward again.

Pat slipped like smoke through her fingers clawing at air. Willow yelped in shock when Pat's fangs sunk into her throat. Venom dripped through her like warm honey. Her raging heart sped it to her core. The flood of lust, devotion and anger, a game of fuck, marry, kill concentrated on one person.

Pat leaned against the wall, hands resting on her head. Eyes hooded and condescending. The spray of blood had soaked half her shirt. It clung immodestly to the swell of her breast.

Willow tried again. This time, Pat didn't move. Her teeth crashed against her mouth, canines piercing through her bottom lip. She grinned, wearing Willow's teeth like a pair of labrets.

She tore herself free, the lip reknitting itself. Willow plunged her tongue into Pat, a wanton kiss before the rage took over and she bit again. Pat wrapped a hand around her throat and ripped her free. "Be nice." She knew she couldn't. Her toxic blood would cause her to be aggressive for a few more minutes yet.

Willow growled, tearing at Pat's coveralls. They shredded like a paper medical gown. The exposed flesh only drove her lust further. She threw her head from side to side, snapping her fangs, but Pat refused to relax her grip. Willow clawed between her thighs.

Her fingers found her, slick and wanting.

"This shit turns you on, huh?" Willow choked out. "You're a sick fuck."

Pat's breath hitched. "You don't seem to be complaining."

Willow curled her fingers more violently than she thought would be pleasurable, but the noises Pat made dispelled that notion.

She screamed again in frustration, but with Pat's hand around her throat, she could only hiss. She wanted Pat to *hurt.* Willow jammed her fingers under her ribs, Pat's lung's pressing into her touch with every breath.

Pat grunted, but barely. Like a boxer who had been hit with an insufficient body blow. She angled her hips, grinding into Willow's hand. Willow pushed back, gypsum board cracking around Pat's silhouette. Pat only smiled arrogantly, daring her to continue.

Her breath hitched, muscles clenching around the pads of Willow's fingers when she released. Pat collapsed to the floor, knees shaking. Willow stood over her, the fog clearing. Her triumph turned to horror, suddenly aware of what she'd done. Blood smeared on the walls and sticky pools on the floor made the room look like a murder scene. But the only evidence of violence remaining on Pat were the four rapidly disappearing red marks her fingers had left.

Pat leaned her head back against the wall and looked up at her creation with smug satisfaction. "Male blood is ten times worse. Find me a man who could survive what you just did."

Willow turned and hurried to her room.

seventeen

Josh hooked the winch up to the frame of the red Chevy. Once the back end had been lifted up, Josh could see that the front wheel had completely twisted. There would be no salvaging this. And he'd be lucky if he could move it on a dirt road if the front end couldn't roll.

Pat appeared holding a slice of pizza.

"I might have to come back," he called.

"Why?"

Josh pointed to the bent wheel. "I can't use rollers on that. Not on this road."

"What do you need?"

Josh removed his ballcap and wiped his forehead. "The flatbed."

"I have one." Pat turned around and walked away.

"What?" Josh said to himself more than anything. Pat didn't answer.

Moments later, Josh heard the sound of a diesel engine roaring to life. Pat backed up a flatbed at full speed through the brown curtain of weeds using nothing but her rear-view mirrors. She rolled down the window. "Put the back end on here. I'll tie it to the post and then you pick up the front end."

"I didn't know you had one of those." Josh turned and walked back toward the tow truck to hide his shock at Pat's recklessness. "What happened to the Bronco?"

"You didn't know a lot. And I still have it. It's in the garage in pieces. I'm redoing the electrical."

It took about half an hour to manoeuvre the truck onto the flatbed. Pat rolled down the window again. "Hop in. We'll drop this off and then I'll give you a ride back here."

Josh opened the passenger door with a creak. The smell of old carpet hit his nose. He must have made a face because Pat protested.

"It hasn't been driven much all winter. Most people don't want big pieces delivered in the snow."

Josh nodded agreeably. "Marissa said you had some nice furniture in there."

"I don't know about that." Pat acted surprisingly humble. Josh had always known her to be bold and confident. Not that he had known her for long. "My place is pretty small."

"That's even more impressive then." Josh grinned. "Show me your workshop sometime?"

Pat eyed him suspiciously. "Lisa's not going to get jealous?"

Josh laughed. "No, Lisa's not like that."

Pat pursed her lips.

Josh crumpled like crepe paper. He always did wear his heart on his sleeve. "Actually, Lisa's not doing so hot right now. She's taking Tyler's passing about as well as Marissa." Josh removed his ballcap and played with the snaps. "Just kinda strange, you know? Two people dying so close together like that?"

"Were the rest of you this upset about Willow being dug up?"

Josh looked over at Pat, confused.

"Lisa was the only one who told me. From what I could tell, I was the only one who gave a fuck. Everyone else seemed to treat it like petty vandalism."

"I didn't really know Willow. I mean, I knew she broke off the engagement with Caleb and then, uh… hung out with you and Kyle for a bit, but she never came over. And her parents left soon after." Josh sat and watched Pat suck her teeth. Clearly, she was upset about his answer.

"I'll be honest," he continued. "I don't get you, Pat."

"Most people don't."

Josh ignored the retort. "You disappear for twenty years and then show back up just to judge us for something that we didn't even do?"

"You think I'm judging you?"

"Well yeah, kinda." Josh snapped and un-snapped his ballcap.

"Why do you care what I think?" Pat stole a quick glance before returning her eyes to the road. "I mean, you said it yourself. I've been gone for twenty years."

"We're a community, Pat. We look out for each other."

Pat laughed so loudly that Josh jumped. "As far as men go, I think you're ace. Dim, but still. I say this with no malice at all."

Josh looked apprehensive. "That doesn't sound like there's no malice." He wasn't one hundred percent certain what malice meant, but it sounded bad.

Pat ignored his comment. "*You're* in a community. You. Not me. If I was, people would know I was still here. Not a single person has bothered to knock on my door. No one in town even knows what I do."

"Yeah, but you never showed your face in town in all that time."

"Because I'm not part of your community. I don't belong to you. And yet, the first thing you did when you found out I was here was ask me to cook and make things for Marissa."

Josh shifted in his seat. "*I* want you to be part of the community."

"I'm sure you do." Pat paused. "It's really nice to have this fantasy of a town where everyone belongs and everyone helps one another." She looked over at him. "It's just not true though, is it? You punish people who stand out. Who are different. Who offend your bizarre values in some way."

"Geez Pat, we're not monsters."

Pat gripped the steering wheel tighter. "I'm the one who took that girl in. Tyler wanted me to dump her in a hospital and forget about her."

"I don't know what Tyler wanted. I wasn't there." Josh admitted.

A pothole bumped the truck a little too violently and Pat turned to check on the Chevy. It swayed a little, but remained in place.

"Where am I dropping this wreck?"

"Over at Mike's" Josh pointed. "Turn here."

Mike had already gone home when they arrived, but Josh had the key. He opened the gate and they lowered the truck with the winch. Josh locked up and hopped back in the cab.

"He gave you the key?"

"What am I going to steal?" Josh grinned. "Half his business comes from me. Community, remember?"

Pat's patience was running thin. "Does Lisa fit in?"

"I mean, yeah, I guess."

Pat nodded. Lisa wasn't for her. She might not be happy with Josh, but if she fit in here, *happy enough* would have to do, wouldn't it? Pat needed to put an end to her fantasies and walk away. Monsters don't get happy endings.

But Josh continued. "I dunno. Maybe not."

Pat raised an eyebrow.

"I think I might have messed things up asking her to move in with me. She doesn't really talk as much to me anymore. You're her friend. Did she say something?" Josh's face was pitiful.

What was she supposed to say to that? Lisa wasn't the effervescent twenty-something she knew when they were roommates, but who didn't change after this long?

Or maybe it *was* that she didn't fit in.

Pat must have taken too long because Josh added, "She's been trying to transfer out."

"Can you blame her? What's here for her?" Pat cursed herself. She probably should have thought before blurting that out.

Josh didn't respond.

"I'm sorry, I shouldn't have said anything. It's my own issues with this place getting in the way."

"Did you even try?"

"Try what?" Pat frowned.

"Try to fit in." That had been the wrong thing to say and Pat couldn't hold back any longer.

"You mean let some man jizz in me and then complain to his fishing buddies that I'm no longer fuckable after his fourth kid while I stay home, change nappies and do the laundry he can't be bothered to pick up? I'll pass, thanks."

Josh rolled his eyes. "No, but you don't have to be, I dunno, so *in your face* about it. We get it. You're different."

Pat looked over at Josh, eyeing him up and down. "Different how? I'm wearing the same thing you are." She ran a finger across her scalp. "I guess I have a bit more hair than you, but the cut's the same."

Josh pressed his lips together and snorted. "You know what I mean."

"Yeah, I do. That's the problem. Your excuses for treating me and Willow and who knows who else like rubbish only sound reasonable to you." Pat slowed the truck as they neared the slippy part. "You believe you're part of this wonderful community where everyone helps each other and looks out for each other because you fit in here. You don't see them act like arseholes to everyone else and when you do, there's always an excuse. They couldn't take a joke. They rubbed it in our faces. They don't understand small towns. You're not a community. You're a town clique, Josh. The only people who enjoy cliques are the people in it."

Josh sulked. He hadn't really thought of it that way and if he was being honest, he didn't really want to.

"Why are you here, Pat?"

"What do you mean?"

"If we're so awful, why are you here? Why didn't you leave? Why not move to the city?"

"I did leave."

"Why did you come back then?"

Pat sighed. "Not for your community. If I had, you would have seen me before now."

"That didn't answer my question."

"I liked my place. I wasn't going to let a bunch of pissant bumpkins kick me off of my own land."

The corner of Josh's mouth lifted a hint. "You're stubborn."

Pat breathed a laugh. "You could say that."

Josh played with his hat while Pat slowed the flatbed to a stop next to the tow truck.

"Listen," he said. "You're right. I hadn't thought about this place that way before. And I'm sorry we acted that way."

Pat huffed. First Marissa and now Josh. "You can't apologise for them. You weren't part of it."

"No, but I am anyway." He took a deep breath. "I really love this place and I want you to be a part of it."

Pat side-eyed him. "You're inviting me in?"

Josh nodded.

"You're sure you want to do that?"

"Look, I know that you think we suck."

Pat scoffed.

"And you're right. We do. And that's probably not gonna change overnight. But the only way it will is if someone like you sticks around."

Pat raised her eyebrows. "I'm not your lesbian hero, Josh. They're not gonna be throwing Pride parades this summer."

"No, but you're stubborn. You admitted as much."

Pat bobbed her head. "I thought you said I was too much. That I didn't try hard enough to fit in."

"Maybe I changed my mind. *I* like having you here. I think the community will too if you stay long enough."

Pat released a breath and bowed her head. "I don't think you know what you're asking, Josh."

"Maybe not, but I'm asking anyway. Give us another chance." Josh smiled hopefully.

"Alright. Just remember, you invited me."

Josh nodded and stepped out of the cab. He felt much better about this whole thing with Pat. Maybe they could shed the whole homophobic small-town image after all.

The tow truck roared to life and he rolled off the side of the road.

Josh punched in Lisa's number. It went to voicemail "Hey babe, I'm on my way home, just checking in."

A few moments later he got a text.

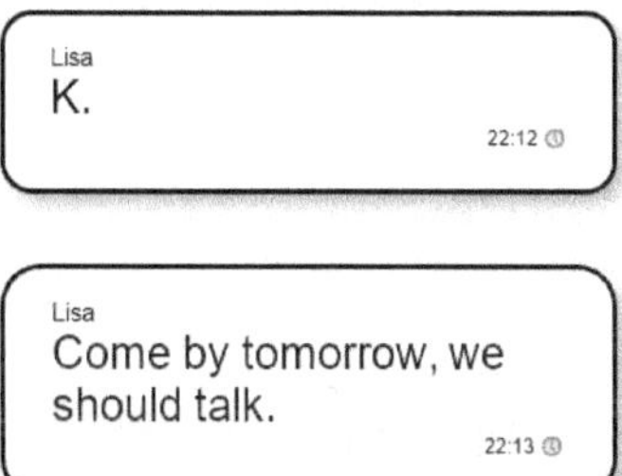

Josh tried not to let it bother him, but Pat's words had stung. He wouldn't describe Lisa as *aloof*, but he had always felt like Lucy after being cooped up in the house all day next to her. Not necessarily begging for attention, but Lisa had always been more reserved.

Josh had never met Lisa's ex-girlfriend, so he couldn't compare how she had acted around her. And now, like a noxious weed, he found himself pulling at the roots of doubt.

What if Lisa really was gay? What if the only reason she was with him was because she needed to fit in while she was here? Was he preventing her from being happy?

Even if it was true, he didn't know what he could do about it. He couldn't just walk in and say *I'm totally cool if you want to leave me for a woman.* That would be weird. It would also hurt.

Josh sighed and adjusted his ballcap. Why was he feeling so insecure about this? It wasn't like he and Lisa were *serious* serious. She didn't want him to move in, but she hadn't given him any reason to doubt her either. And it's not like he could talk to Mike or Jacob about any of this. He knew he'd run his mouth and out Lisa to them. Then Pat would be angry. Angry Pat was a lot to deal with.

He sighed and dialled Kyle's number.

"Hello?"

"Hey, Kyle."

"Josh? Are you okay? You sound awful. What happened?"

"Eh, nothing. Just checking in."

"You never call just to check in."

Josh sighed. "Somebody said something about me and Lisa and I can't get it out of my head."

"Wait, are you calling me for relationship advice?"

"I guess?"

"You know that I don't have a good track record on that, right?"

"Is that why you never bring anyone around?"

The line remained silent for a few moments. "No. You know that's not why."

"You hear that Caleb died?"

"Oh shit, really?"

"Yeah, car accident."

"Huh."

Josh frowned. "I thought you'd be more upset about it."

"Is anyone there upset about it?"

"What do you mean?"

"Just what I said. I'm sure the church ladies are sending plates over to his parents and all, but is anyone there really upset about it."

"I don't know. People are talking about it."

"That's not the same thing."

Josh sniffed and bit the inside of his cheek.

"Weren't you friends with him?"

"Yeah. In grade four."

"Tyler died too."

"Jesus. How is Marissa?"

"Not good."

"Listen, I gotta go right now, but tomorrow's Saturday. I'll come down, meet you at the river and we'll go fishing, alright?"

Josh nodded. "Yeah, let's do that."

He hung up. It didn't help with Lisa, but it would be nice to see Kyle again.

eighteen

Loose gravel crunched under the wheels. Josh hopped out of his truck and pulled his fishing gear from the bed. The river flowed quickly at this time of year – its energy pent up from being stuck in ice all winter.

Kyle waved from the edge, a rod already in his hand and a box of tackle at his feet. Lucy galloped over to him at a full tilt. He sniffed at his hands for a few moments before racing into the river.

Josh made his way down the hardscrabble slope. "Those are some fancy boots."

"Yeah, well. I don't get to use them too often in the city." Kyle spread his arms and Josh hugged his older brother.

"You're too clean to be a fisherman. You look like Eddie Bauer threw up all over you."

"Canadian Tire is more your speed?" Kyle shook his head. "I never did fit in here."

"I'm hearing that a lot lately." Josh rummaged through his tackle box and pulled out a hairy looking fly.

"From Lisa?"

"Nah." Josh attached it to the line. "But it wouldn't surprise me if she's thinking it."

"From who then?"

"Pat."

"As in, *Pat* Pat? The one that I hung out with all senior year?"

"That's the one."

Kyle checked his rod. "I would have thought for sure she'd leave."

"She did." Josh stood up and stretched. "I guess she was Lisa's roommate during cadet training."

The corner of Kyle's lip rose. "That's what has you nervous? That Lisa might be gay?"

Josh's eyes flicked around as though someone might be listening. "She's had a girlfriend before." Josh could tell Kyle. Kyle wouldn't tell a soul.

Kyle sighed. "I've never met Lisa. I *have* met Pat. Pat is almost *too* cautious when it comes to women." Kyle cast his line. It landed in the river with a satisfying splash and drifted along the current. "Pat isn't chasing your girl."

Josh cast his line and waited a few breaths to respond. "It's not Pat I'm worried about."

"You're worried about Lisa?"

Josh nodded.

"How long have you been together?"

Josh watched his bobber dip, but it didn't take. "A few years now. Maybe five?"

Kyle arched his eyebrow but didn't say anything.

"I asked. She said no." Josh reeled in his line.

"You know I don't know anything about women, right?" Kyle removed his tan fishing hat. The sun shone off of his bare head. "But even *I* know that your relationship probably isn't going anywhere."

Josh grunted and recast his line. "I just don't know where I went wrong. I buy the flowers. I remember the anniversaries. I take her out on date nights. I don't know what else I can do."

Kyle clapped his palm against his brother's shoulder. "Then it's probably not you."

Josh took a deep breath. "Is it over?"

"Maybe. I don't know." Kyle shrugged. "We've already discussed my qualifications with women."

That wasn't the answer Josh wanted. He wanted to be told what to do. How to fix things. He couldn't do any of that if he wasn't the problem.

"What about you, then? Are you seeing anyone?"

Kyle side-eyed him. "I'm not telling you. You have a big mouth."

"No, I don't." Josh grimaced.

Kyle rolled his eyes. "You're single handedly responsible for half the town's gossip. You always were."

Josh shoved him.

"If I tell you, you can't tell anyone else."

"Who counts as *anyone*?"

"Lisa. Pat. Mom and Dad. Lucifer."

"Leave Lucy out of this. Who's he going to tell?"

Kyle reeled in his line. "You'll use him as a loophole. When the whole town finds out, you'll tell me you were talking to the dog and someone happened to overhear."

"Okay, that only happened *once*."

"Which is why I'm including it *this* time."

"Fine. Now tell me."

Kyle took a few moments to compose himself, but Josh caught the upturn at his lips. "I'm engaged."

"What?!"

Kyle glanced over. Josh had dropped his fishing pole and was now scrambling to catch it before the current caught it. Lucy ran over to help.

Josh reeled in his line, now tangled around Lucy.

"How? When?"

"This summer. Morris asked me on a yacht in the Bahamas." Kyle couldn't help beaming.

"The professor you were working under?" Josh's eyes went wide. "Isn't he fifteen years older than you?"

"Sixteen, and yes."

"How come…"

"Because you have a big mouth."

Josh's big mouth hung open.

"You can't tell anyone."

"What about Mom and Dad?"

"*Especially* Mom and Dad."

"But," Josh tugged at the now irreparably tangled line. "You're not inviting them to the wedding?"

"No."

"But they're our parents!"

Kyle rewound his spool. He turned to look at Josh and then back at the river. "I notice you didn't ask *why*. You went straight for *they're our parents*."

Josh's shoulders slumped. "You sound like Pat."

"Maybe think about why that is."

Josh took a few deep breaths. He dug around inside the tackle box for some new line before finding a dry rock to sit on. "Sorry," he mumbled. "It feels like everyone lately hates this town that we all used to love. And nothing's changed." Josh waved his hands and let them fall down limply at his sides.

Kyle took a deep breath. He put down his rod and pulled a six pack out of the water. "I'm sorry. C'mere." He sat next to Josh and held out a beer.

Josh took it and examined the label. "Fancy."

Kyle ignored him. "I know you love Northton. A lot of people do. Nothing's changed."

Josh shrugged hopelessly. "I guess. Ever since I found out Pat was back, it's like no-one can see the good parts of it anymore."

Kyle blew out his cheeks. "Pat's… unbelievably traumatised. You think I had it bad? You have no idea the things she's been through."

"She could tell me," Josh started, but Kyle held up his hand.

"Why would she do that? She barely knows you. And you tell everyone everything."

Josh's mouth hung open, "But Lisa…"

"If she's friends with Lisa, she's in a very rare group 'cause Pat has only two settings – *ignore* and *attack.* And if she's attacking you, she likes you better than if she's ignoring you." Kyle shrugged. "I don't even think she *can* talk to anyone without mocking them to keep up a wall of plausible deniability. Maybe if she'd had a normal childhood, she'd be different, but she's not."

Josh stared at his beer. It had no more answers than he did.

"Look," Kyle paused to take a drink. "What you're going through is just your thirties. All your young dewy-eyed friends who got married and had kids are either bored, burnt out or getting divorced. Or they left. Northton wasn't the utopia they were told it was. But that's okay. Nowhere is."

"What about you?"

Kyle snorted a laugh. "I wasn't popular enough to be disillusioned. Neither was Pat."

"So, I should leave?"

Kyle looked at his brother with sympathy. He was sweet, but so stupid sometimes. "No, Josh. But, maybe think about what it would take for Northton to welcome Pat."

"I already tried." Josh slapped his knees. "She said she'd take my tow truck and I could help the church ladies cook." He left out the ass-fucking part.

Kyle laughed, shaking his head. "Do I even want to know what you asked her?"

Josh looked ashamed and shook his head. "Prolly not."

"Well, you're starting at the wrong end. Pat can get up and leave. Hell, *I* did. But there will be other people like me and Pat. If you use those community connections you're so good at maintaining to force Northton to be a little bit more progressive, Pat might come around."

"If I did, would you come back?"

Kyle looked sadly at his brother. "It's too late for that. There's nothing for me there."

"Pat came back."

Kyle stared at the river burbling away. He finished half of his beer before speaking again. "Pat has bigger balls than both of us combined. And if you *do* manage to make Northton carve out a space for her, it's going to take time. Pat has the patience to wait them out. I don't."

Josh wrapped his arm around Kyle. Kyle leaned into the hug.

Josh drove home in the dark. The automatic wipers started up before he even noticed the late winter rain. It didn't take long before it started freezing against the windscreen. Josh slowed down and cranked the defrost.

He caught a flash of white in the headlights and slowed to a crawl. A girl appeared standing in the ditches with a grin on her face. He pulled over and rolled the window down.

"Are you okay?"

"Great actually." The girl's short black hair stuck to her face, dripping. Brilliant blue eyes shone back at him. Lucy clambered into the back of the cab.

"You don't need help getting into town? Is your car nearby?"

The girl shook her head. "Just going for a walk."

"In the freezing rain?"

The girl nodded.

"Wearing that?"

The girl looked at her attire. An oversized T-shirt and baggy jeans probably wasn't the best choice, but she didn't feel cold.

"You're not on drugs, are you? I have a naloxone kit in the back."

"What? No."

"Okay, just making sure. I can give you a lift if you need a ride to Northton.

She thought about it. She could easily make it back to Pat's place through the shadows after practicing all afternoon, but now she had been seen. It would be suspicious if she didn't accept the ride.

"Yeah, sure."

Willow rounded the truck and hopped into the cab. She remembered Josh, Kyle's younger brother. Josh didn't seem to recognise her. He looked even better up close.

"Thanks." She slicked an uneven strand of hair back. Josh averted his eyes from the soaked cotton clinging to her slight curves.

"So where are you from?" Josh signalled and pulled back onto the road.

"The city. Just visiting Pat for a bit." Willow thought it would be best to cover a lie with a bit of truth.

"Oh? Is that girl still with her?"

Fuck. "Uh, no. She remembered who she was and left."

"Who was she?"

Willow shrugged.

"Well, if you're going to Pat's, I can take you there. She lives a ways out of Northton."

Willow shook her head. "We were going to meet in Northton."

"Oh yeah? Where at?"

Willow wracked her brain. "The coffee shop." She hoped one still existed.

"You mean A&W? That's the only place that serves coffee, aside from the gas station."

"Yeah. Sorry, I forget things sometimes."

Josh laughed. "Yeah, me too." He turned off the highway and onto the main road. "How do you know Pat?"

"I went to school with them." Willow looked out the window to see how much the town had changed. Stop lights were newer. Boots was the same. The houses looked more run down and the road lines were more faded with more potholes. Lines of asphalt sealant spiderwebbed across the street. The town definitely hadn't improved since she'd died.

"You mean in the city? I thought they went to different schools."

"They did. I went to school with Pat. Lisa hung out with us."

"Oh, so you do carpentry too?" Josh looked over at her. "Huh. I thought Pat would be the only woman doing that, but I guess not."

Willow grinned. She could see A&W a few blocks ahead. Almost in the clear.

"I'm sorry, I didn't ask your name."

"Rowan." *Good work, brain.*

"Nice to meet you, Rowan. I'm Josh. How long are you in town for?"

"A couple weeks at least. I'm between projects at the moment, so I thought I'd take some time for myself."

"That's cool." Josh pulled into the A&W parking lot. He turned and flashed a grin.

Willow blushed. "Thanks for the lift."

"Yeah, you're welcome." Josh turned to put the truck in gear, but he paused. "Actually, I have some things I need to talk with Pat about. I should go in and say *hi*."

"Uh," Willow stammered. "It's kind of a girls thing, you know."

"Oh, uh, yeah. Of course." Josh turned away.

"It was nice meeting you, though. Maybe I'll see you again sometime."

"Yeah," Josh felt his ears go red. "I'd like that."

Willow waited for Josh's truck to disappear before she slipped back into the shadows.

nineteen

Pat was making breakfast for herself in the kitchen when she caught the scent of cherry cola. Willow sunk her teeth into Pat. Pat turned her head to stare at her hanging off her shoulder muscle. Willow looked up at her with puppy dog eyes. Pat shook her head. She wasn't a stupid teenager foolish enough to believe Willow was doing anything beyond exploring herself anymore. She turned on the blender.

"You're no fun."

"I see you figured out how to use the shadows."

"Yes. Now I'm hungry."

"Yep. Doing that will make you hungry." Pat turned off the blender and poured two glasses. She handed one to Willow.

"These are so good. What's really in them?" Willow gulped greedily.

"Strawberries. I told you." Pat drank hers with a bit more restraint.

"There has to be more than that."

"Marissa's blood."

"What? When did you get that?"

"I have more in the freezer. I collected it when I found out she was pregnant."

Willow's eyes widened in horror.

"Remember? Monsters." Pat shrugged. "And pregnant women are *divine*."

Willow looked at her smoothie, now half empty. It was too good not to finish.

"I ran into Josh while I was practicing."

"He didn't see you, did he?"

Willow shook her head. "At least not in the middle of anything. He gave me a lift to Northton."

"Your pheromones probably got washed off in the rain." Pat sighed. "Fill me in. What did you tell him?"

"My name is Rowan and I'm living with you for a couple of weeks. The girl with the memory loss moved on and I know you and Lisa from school in the city."

Pat nodded. "Got it."

"That's it? No lecture?"

"What would I lecture you for? He invited you in, he didn't see you do anything strange and you covered your arse. Good job." Pat finished the last of her smoothie. She was determined not to be as condescending to her daughter as Corinne had been to her.

Willow smiled at the praise. "I think I'm getting the hang of this."

Pat raised an eyebrow. "Don't get cocky."

"He's still cute."

Pat shrugged. "Fuck him if you want."

"You're not going to get all weird about it?"

Pat rinsed out the blender and filled it with soapy water. "Why would I care? I meant what I said in the wood shop."

"I thought lesbians found men gross. That they hated it when their exes left them for men."

Pat ran her hands over her hair. "You're not an *ex* and I don't care who you or anyone fucks."

Willow finished her smoothie, loudly through the straw.

"It's not a moral failing to find men attractive. Just don't bite him."

"Just feels like you think you're more of a feminist because of it." Willow held out her empty glass to Pat.

"I said naff all about feminism. You fit in. I don't. I don't know why you'd think anyone should care about my opinion."

"You're like the one kid who likes black liquorice, then?"

Pat snatched the glass out of Willow's hand. "I will not tolerate liquorice slander."

"You mean *black* liquorice."

"Liquorice. Anything else isn't liquorice."

"So why do they call red liquorice *red liquorice*?"

"Red liquorice tastes like plastic and poverty," Pat grumbled. She put the glass in the dishwasher.

"Says the woman who just drank a pregnant woman's blood mixed with strawberries." Willow walked into the living room and hopped on the sofa.

"I also put some cinnamon in there." Pat took the other corner.

Willow turned and smiled. "And you said you couldn't cook."

Pat returned the smile and turned on the T.V. "Find a man and make him one of those. See what he says about your cooking skills."

"You told me I can't bite men." Her voice grew an edge.

"Do whatever you want. You already know what will happen."

Willow leaned against the counter and sulked.

"Lisa is going to come by for a bit tomorrow."

"Oh good, she's cute too."

Pat raised a sceptical eyebrow. She knew Willow was trying to make her jealous.

"What?" Willow grinned impishly.

"Calm your libido. You can't see her anymore."

"Why not?" Willow's smile turned into a pout.

"Because you told Josh that the girl with the memory loss is gone. Lisa has already seen you and Josh has a big mouth."

"Right. Pheromones?"

Pat shook her head. "That's not how those work. You'd have to be practically naked for those to have any effect at a distance of more than ten feet."

"I can do that." Willow grinned.

Pat threw a pillow at her. "You also have no control over what she'll hallucinate."

Willow opened her mouth to protest, but Pat interrupted.

"*And*, she'll be here during the day. Your tiny white arse will be standing naked in the cold and that's exactly what she'll see."

"You like my tiny white ass." Willow winked.

"All women are beautiful." Pat scrolled through the list of films.

"All of them?" Willow rolled her eyes. "Now who needs to calm their libido?"

Pat threw another pillow.

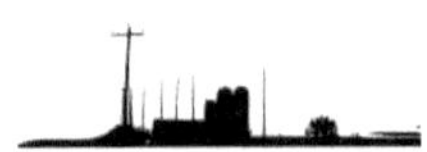

The ink ran out of Lisa's pen. She stared vacantly at the half-completed transfer request forms. Her high school notebooks had fewer doodles and she had been working on them for so long that Oatcake had fallen asleep on her lap. She had stopped purring half an hour ago.

Lisa grabbed the pages in a fit of resignation and crumpled them into a ball. Oatcake mewled. She knew exactly why she couldn't finish filling them out. How could she leave Northton if Pat was still here?

Yes, Pat hadn't reciprocated her feelings when she had embarrassed herself all those years ago, but she was young and naïve back then. The situation was different now, wasn't it? They weren't roommates anymore. She wouldn't be leaving for a job. And she was certain she'd caught Pat looking at her once or twice. Pretty certain.

That's just your imagination. It's just what you want to happen. Lisa ground the heel of her hand into her forehead. She was almost forty. The worst that could happen is Pat would say *no.* Then she would know for sure. If Pat rejected her, she could transfer out and never look back. No risk, no reward. She owed herself that much. Lisa grabbed her keys.

Her truck left the pavement and the loud rumble of the dirt road filled the cabin. She turned the radio up to compensate. Lisa needed to do this now before her sudden burst of courage dissipated into the aether.

Tyler's *life* should have been enough, but his death had given her the wakeup call she'd needed. Life was short. Too short to waste it on a man who did nothing for her, cute as he was.

Lisa rolled the word around in her mouth. *Cute*. Not *hot*. How could she have been this stupid? Dimples were cute. Puppies were cute. Tiny cupcakes were cute. She scoffed and shook her head in disbelief.

She should have known. Years ago. She'd *had* girl crushes as a kid. But she'd always dismissed them as *girl crushes*. She'd thought she'd wanted to *be* them, not be *with* them. How could Pat have had so much self-awareness at that age while she'd been so blind? How do you not know what you find attractive?

Lisa sighed, tapping nervously on the steering wheel. Even if she had no-one else until she left here, she knew one thing for certain – Josh was not for her. Josh could be sweet and kind and cute for someone else. She wished him luck.

At least she would the next time she saw him. And that's what she would tell Pat today. She needed the advice on exactly how to phrase it.

The other part was also up to Pat. She would either say *yes* or *no*. Either way, Lisa couldn't delude herself into believing that she didn't still have feelings for her anymore.

Lisa parked the truck. In the afternoon sun, tall grasses poked through the puddles of melting snow. Pat clearly didn't care about yard maintenance. Surrounded by trees and scrub, the small A-frame might be mistaken for a witch's cottage.

Pat
I'm in the garage.
09:21

Lisa
Which one is that?
09:22

Pat
On the left, behind the house.
09:22

Lisa put her phone in her jeans and walked the trail of trampled grasses to the garage. She found Pat underneath the frame of a truck, wires hanging everywhere.

"Do you not care about fires?" Lisa found a stack of wheels to sit on.

"Are you talking about the grass or the truck?"

"The grass. You look like you know what you're doing with the truck."

Pat poked her head out from under the frame and grinned. Lisa felt like she was about to combust and then they'd have another fire to worry about.

"How come you know how to do everything?" Pat wiped the grease off of her hands, forearm muscles rippling beneath her skin.

"Huh?"

Lisa kept her eyes on her face, but her boyish smile and wide hazel eyes weren't helping. "You somehow know how to do everything."

Pat shrugged. "Why would I give a fuck what people tell me I should know." Her cocky smirk made it hard for Lisa to concentrate. "Also, I can't cook, remember. Or mow the lawn, I suppose."

"And yet, you still had all those women after you." Lisa swung her feet and stared at the stained concrete. "Sounds like you did alright."

Pat nodded. "Perhaps."

"You ever going to settle down?" Lisa kicked herself. This was not where this conversation was supposed to go.

"If I find the right person."

"Describe for me this *right person.*" Lisa half-hoped that Pat would say *you,* but that only happened in movies.

Pat rolled her eyes. Only because she knew exactly who the right person was and it would never work. Not with who she was. Not with Willow being a complication. Lisa wouldn't live long enough for her to deal with all of that.

Lisa didn't press. "Did you hear about Tyler?"

Pat threw the J-cloth in the rubbish bin. "Yeah, from Marissa. Josh said you took it pretty hard."

"I may have bent the truth on that a little." Lisa stared at her knees.

"You didn't like Tyler?"

"Not that, I dunno." Lisa took a deep breath. "I was upset, sure. Especially with all the crows. That was..." Lisa raised her eyebrows. "I didn't feel like dealing with Josh that night and I made up an excuse," she confessed. "Does that make me a bad person?"

Pat ignored the question. "Crows?"

"Yeah, the cemetery was covered in crows."

"Strange." Pat turned around and busied herself with the wiring on the disassembled Bronco. *If Corinne is feeding on people openly, something is happening.* Pat needed to change the subject.

"How's Josh?"

Lisa's mouth dried, but she would say it anyway. She could do this. "I'm leaving him."

"Does he know that?"

"No."

"How are you feeling about it?" Pat forced her heartbeat to slow down. She kept her eyes focussed on the mass of tangled cords so Lisa wouldn't see her expression before she got it under control.

"Stressed? Guilty? Like I'm making a huge mistake?" Pat turned around. Lisa melted into her eyes. "Mostly though? Relief.

Pat picked at her work shirt. It suddenly felt too tight, even if it hung loosely off of her frame.

"No words?" Lisa swallowed thickly. "Didn't you say I should dump him and marry Phaedra?"

"No," Pat turned to look away. "You definitely should. I just..." Pat searched for any words that would smooth over this situation and weren't *please kiss me right now.* She rubbed her forehead, leaving a grease stain. "I'm really happy for you. I hope that you get everything you want." Pat stared, trying to communicate telepathically whatever it was she was supposed to say but didn't have the words for.

Lisa lowered her eyes, but the corner of her lip turned upward.

"What?" Pat fidgeted with the hem of her shirt.

"Come here." Lisa held out her hand. "You have grease on your forehead."

Pat trundled toward her, like an awkward teenage boy, a half-smile on her face. Lisa spread her legs so Pat could step closer. She leaned over and Lisa ran her thumb along Pat's face.

"You smell like an engine." Lisa bit her lip.

Pat felt her face flush. "That would be because I spent the last hour and a half under one."

The words felt too close, like they tumbled across Lisa's face. Fell across her upturned nose, the bow of her lip. Pat could hear her blood rush beneath the surface of her skin.

Lisa turned her head, but not in the direction Pat thought she would. She raised it up, eyes screwed shut, catching Pat's lip.

Pat's eyes opened wider than her mouth. *Fuck*, she thought. *The pheromones.*

Lisa jerked back and caught Pat staring at her in surprise. She clapped a hand over her mouth and rushed out of the garage, "I'm sorry," she yelled, jumping into her truck. The engine roared to life and Lisa backed out of the driveway. *You were supposed to tell her, not kiss her!*

Pat blinked once. Twice. The spring sun splashed across the garage, not a scrap of shadow in sight.

twenty

"Thanks for meeting me here." Josh warmed his hands on the heavy white ceramic mug.

"Yeah." Pat bit her tongue and stared at her coffee. Josh didn't know and she wasn't going to be the one to tell him. Her lips still burned where Lisa had kissed her. "What's up?"

"I, uh," Josh reached for a creamer and dipped the top into his coffee.

"Are you daft? What the fuck are you doing?" Pat wrinkled her nose.

Josh stared. "Putting cream in my coffee?"

"Aren't you supposed to peel the lid off the cup first?"

"Have you never done this?" Josh waited for the heat of his coffee to melt the glue and gave the plastic cup a gentle squeeze. A pool of white clouded into his coffee. He raised the open cup triumphantly.

Pat stared disapprovingly.

"What?"

Pat cleared her throat. "You took a creamer." She gestured toward the stack of tiny plastic cups in the bowl. "That every lurgy snot goblin who has ever sat in this booth has touched." Pat swept her hand across the restaurant. "And you dunked it in your coffee?"

Josh's face fell. His trick seemed a lot less impressive now. "I don't think everyone here would appreciate being called a *snot goblin*."

Someone sniffed loudly before blowing their nose into a napkin. Pat raised her eyebrow and tilted her head in the direction of the noise.

Josh exhaled and sank into the orange leatherette bench. "Are you ever impressed by anything?"

"Plenty." Pat sipped her coffee. "But I have a feeling that the things I'm impressed by aren't fit for polite conversation." Pat gnawed at the inside of her cheek, picturing the tiny elevens on Lisa's brow when she had kissed her. That image would remain clear as day for as long as she lived. Which would be a very long time.

What would be the harm? she thought. She knew damn well. It would be so *easy* to submit to her desires - to *both* of their desires, apparently. But her heart wouldn't be able to take it when Lisa learned the truth and recoiled in horror. Better to keep her walls up.

Josh cleared his throat. He knew better than to prod at that statement. "You and Lisa are so different. How did you even become friends?"

Pat drew her thumb along her jawline. "Different how?"

"You know?" Josh played with his fingertips. "You're so *open*, I guess. You don't hold back. Lisa's a lot more reserved."

Pat gave a blank stare remembering Lisa bursting into the kitchen asking about straps. This poor fool had no idea who Lisa was. Pat couldn't fathom how much of herself Lisa had been hiding trying to fit into this place. "How long have you been dating?"

Josh scratched at his stubble. "Five years, give or take?"

Pat wanted to shake her head. And then shake Josh. Tell him to run away and save himself. She tapped her fingernails against her coffee mug instead. "So, what did you want to talk to me about?"

"Right." Josh took a deep breath like he was trying to avoid the thing he'd asked her here for. "I…" He stared out the window for a little too long.

Pat slurped her coffee in the hopes it would prod him to get on with it.

"I know I can't apologise for how the town treated you. And Willow."

"And Kyle," Pat added.

"And Kyle." Josh nodded. "Did you know he's getting married?"

"Yeah, in Greece. I still have to find a plus-one."

"What? He invited you?" Josh leaned on the table.

Pat stared. "I got the invite months ago."

"He didn't invite me!" The restaurant turned to stare at Josh. "Sorry!" He raised his hand and slumped back into the booth.

Pat shook her head in dismissal. "You'll get yours later. If he'd sent it out earlier, you would have told your parents and he doesn't want to deal with them."

"Am I that bad?"

"Yes." Pat finished her coffee and set the mug at the end of the table.

"I still don't get it." Josh's lips formed a white line. He stared out the window.

"And you never will. Because you fit the conditions of your parent's love. Kyle doesn't *owe* them anything."

"They love him unconditionally."

"No, they're *supposed* to love him unconditionally. Just like you think this community accepts everyone unconditionally. They don't. It doesn't. That's why people who don't fit leave. That's just how it is."

"And yet, you're here." Josh nodded slowly. He looked back up at Pat. "Kyle said you have bigger balls than both of us combined."

Pat looked up at the fluorescent lights "I probably do, but I left my pack at home." She flicked her eyes toward Josh. "I don't really want to check, though. You can keep your trousers on."

"A...pack?"

Pat waved her hand. "Never mind, you wouldn't get it."

"No," Josh pressed. "I *want* to get it. I want to understand."

Pat waited until the server had refilled her coffee before she turned back to Josh. "A pack is something women wear. It fits in their pants and gives them the appearance of having a penis."

To his credit, Josh tried very hard to conceal the disgust on his face. The effect ended up closer to constipation. Pat made no effort to conceal her smirk.

"Why… Not *all* women wear those, do they?"

Pat stared into her coffee. "No, just the ones who want to look like they have a penis."

"Why would you want to look like you have a penis?" His voice rose at the end. Josh's expression still had not resolved itself. Pat was very entertained.

"What am I wearing right now?"

"A...pack?" Josh guessed.

"No, you apple-head. Look at me. What am I wearing."

"Uh, jeans? A work shirt?"

"And do you think I got these in the women's section with the lingerie and perfume?"

"No?" Josh still wasn't sure if he was answering correctly.

"Exactly. I got these in the men's wear section. A pack is just the same thing. I don't want to *be* a man, though some people who wear packs *do.* It's just another way to express yourself and to fuck with people's ideas about what women should or shouldn't look like."

"You really like to do that, don't you?"

"Do what?"

"Mess with people's heads."

"It's not about that." Pat massaged her neck. "You asked me a couple days ago about making this place better. I do that every day, just by existing. And just being myself generates so much pushback that it's hard to see it changing any time soon."

"Ah." Josh finished his coffee with a grin. "It's a good thing I asked you here then."

"Fucking finally." Pat rolled her eyes.

"Yes. Anyway. What if I helped?"

Pat narrowed her eyes. "Are you...are you coming out to me?"

"What?"

"Because if so, that would solve *so* many problems." Pat sighed and put her hand on her chest. "You have no idea."

"What are you talking about?" Josh blinked several times. "What problems?"

Pat propped her head up on the table. "What are you into? Bears? I'll bet it's bears."

"Bears?"

"No? Twinks then? A skinny wee thing in a crop top and short shorts?"

"What's a…twink?" Josh leaned forward, head askance.

"Please tell me you're not into the professor type, are you? Cause that screams *older brother issues* and Kyle would lose his shit."

"Kyle?"

"*Really?*" Pat winced. "Kyle is gonna kill me when I tell him. But I'm not here to judge."

"Pat!" The restaurant turned to look at Josh again. "I have no idea what you're talking about," he hissed.

"So… you're *not* coming out to me." Pat gave him the side-eye.

"I'm not gay."

"I've heard that before. Recently, too." Pat pointed her mug at Josh.

Josh narrowed his eyes. "What problems would that solve, exactly?"

"Doesn't matter," Pat waved dismissively. "What was this thing you needed to talk to me about before you *didn't* just come out to me?"

"I want to help."

"Help what?"

"Help make the town better. For people like you."

Pat ran her hand across her buzzcut. "This sounds like a cross between a political campaign and a charity pitch. I don't need your help."

"*You* don't. Kids like you might."

"You know, you can just say *queer*, right?" Pat's lips pressed together. "You don't have to say *like you*."

"Are you always this combative?"

"Yes. How long have you known me?"

"That's fair, I guess." Josh hummed while the server refilled his coffee.

"I'm sorry." Pat conceded. "What are you planning on doing?"

"So, I know it's small, but we have to start somewhere, right?"

"We?"

"I assumed you'd help."

"Help with what? I'm already at maximum lesbian. What else did you want me to do? Carry a labrys around?"

"A what?"

"A labrys. You know, one of those…" Pat waved the thought away. "Never mind, of course you wouldn't know what that is."

Josh opened his mouth to ask, but after learning about packs, he decided he'd absorbed enough queer culture for the day. "I was just going to hang a Pride flag outside the tow-truck garage."

"And you need help with that?"

"I have no idea where I'd get one."

Pat sat back in the booth. "That's…" she exhaled loudly. "Actually cool. Yeah, I'll help you. You're going to want more than one."

Josh frowned. "Why? Is there a sale or something if you get more?"

Pat sighed. "God, you're dim," she said more to herself than to Josh. "No. There's no sale." Someone will get offended and rip it down within a week.

"They wouldn't..." Josh started, but Pat interrupted.

"They sure as fuck would. To you, it might look like a harmless prank or *of course* no-one would trespass on private property because of a statement they didn't like." Pat turned to look at the restaurant crowd. "You see them like this – a bunch of harmless townsfolk who look out for each other.

We see them when they're bigoted monsters whose defences go into maximum overdrive the moment anyone suggests something change." Pat took another drink. "And if you hang that flag, you'll see them too."

Josh sat with Pat's words for a moment, nodding slowly. "Alright. I'll still do it."

"You're a good man, Josh."

Josh beamed.

Pat sighed and stood up. Lisa was going to break this man's heart. But she had to. Pat just hoped he wouldn't turn into one of those monsters after she did it. "Thanks for the coffee."

Pat walked back to her lorry, wishing the Bronco wasn't still in pieces, when she heard a cawing from the roof of the A&W. She shoved her hands in her pockets and turned.

"You have a lot of explaining to do."

The crow flew off and landed behind the dumpster. Pat followed, turning her head this way and that to make sure no-one saw her.

Corinne stood back straight and terrifying, even dressed in filthy rags. She couldn't stoop if she tried.

"I thought there were no homeless in Northton."

"Plenty of fentanyl addicts, though." Corinne waved her hand and several crows materialised to keep watch.

"You're still not fooling anyone."

Corinne smiled and flipped her hair. "You're just full of compliments today."

"What the fuck is going on. Why did you kill Tyler?"

"Oooh, I love it when you're confused." Corinne spoke in a baby voice and grabbed Pat by the cheeks. Pat didn't fight it. There was no point. "I thought you'd be happy. You hated him."

Pat grimaced. "You didn't do that for me."

"You're right. I've been dying to taste that one for a long time."

Pat stuck out her tongue. "Gross."

"You're the odd one, not me."

"Which is why I make a much more contented vampire then you will ever be."

"Do you know what we call killers who enjoy killing?" Corinne shifted her stance and held out her hand, palm up.

"Is this a morality lesson? From you?"

"We call them psychopaths. You're not supposed to enjoy being cursed."

"And yet," Pat bowed in mockery, "here I am."

Corinne made a face of disgust.

"Are you going to tell me why you've decided to show yourself outside your own home for the first time in decades, or do you want to continue telling me what a reprobate I am?" Pat pointed her head in the direction of the A&W. "Because if you're going to keep talking, I might as well get some more coffee."

"You need to check your mail."

Pat scoffed. "I thought email made that obsolete."

"Fred passed."

Pat sighed. She knew it was coming. So did Fred.

"Did you enjoy him at least?"

Corinne's look grew sombre. "Very much so. I know you like being crude to hide your feelings, but those are intimate details I won't be sharing with you."

"Why are you still here then?"

"I need to make an appearance at the funeral. Go check your mail."

"You could just tell me."

Corinne glowered. "I knew you'd say that, so I stole it from the post office." She handed Pat the envelope.

Pat glanced at it and looked back at Corinne. "A registered letter?"

"I couldn't give it to you. It came from the lawyer. It's his will."

"Wouldn't you inherit everything?"

Corinne shook her head. "I don't want it. You do." She put a hand on Pat's shoulder and looked her in the eye. "You are a disgusting creature with revolting tastes. But you're getting what you always wanted."

Pat rolled her eyes. "You're the shittiest faerie god mother ever."

"And that's the way you like it." Corinne wrapped her arms around Pat. Pat stiffened and then hugged back.

twenty-one

Lisa texted Josh to come over later tonight to have the talk. With previous boyfriends, she would do this in a public place. You never knew how they would take the news and you didn't want to end up as a statistic.

But Josh.

Lisa sighed. Josh deserved something a little more private. He deserved some dignity - as much dignity as could be had with something like this.

She hated that he had been the perfect boyfriend. Hated more that he had been her longest relationship by far. And hated even more that she couldn't be what he deserved.

Because she was into women. She poured herself a glass of wine. *That* had been a revelation. Not so much the *being into women* part. More the *I can't believe I spent the last twenty years thinking I was into men* part.

Lisa just didn't know what to call it. Men *were* attractive. But more to look at than actually date. Was there a word for that? Maybe Pat would know.

That was the other problem. She would have to deal with what she had just done to Pat. Pat who was quick-witted and grumpy and acerbic and drank her coffee black because who the fuck drinks black coffee and still makes it look so *hot*?

And for some unknown reason, looked out for her like a Pitbull. Her Pitbull. She hoped.

If there were any other queer women in this godforsaken town, she could *maybe* distract herself from the fact that she *still* hadn't gotten over the first woman she'd had a crush on. That's what Phaedra had been, hadn't she? A distraction. A very pleasant distraction.

She hadn't planned on being so bold with Pat. But God knows, everything she'd learned about flirting with men hadn't worked. Lisa threw her head back and groaned in frustration. She hoped she hadn't found Pat after all these years only to ruin everything with one poorly-timed kiss.

Oatcake pawed at her leg. Lisa looked at her phone. Getting dark at five, but Josh would be another couple of hours still. She stood and walked to the kitchen. She couldn't bear to eat, being a bundle of nervous energy right now. Oatcake had no such issue. She spooned the overpriced cat food into her bowl.

Lisa took her wine to the sofa and lay back. What if she could rewind the clock? What if she had never kissed Pat? She shifted against the cushions. That would never have happened. She'd been circling Pat like one of those penny-whirlpool donation boxes ever since she'd known Pat was here. It was inevitable.

Only because of Josh, she told herself. *You wouldn't have cheated if you'd been with Phaedra.* Did that count as cheating? When you'd planned to leave him anyway? Lisa nestled deeper into the sofa. *Of course it did, but it would be irrelevant in a few hours.*

Lisa finished her wine and refilled her glass. Phaedra would have been so bored here. It would never have worked. Unless Phaedra could single-handedly make this town cool.

If she'd managed to set up a piercing studio that was so cool that people would travel here just to be pierced by her? *She did like attention.* Phaedra would have loved having the entire town adore her.

Pierced By Her. Lisa giggled at the innuendo. It must be the wine. She never *did* get to see whether strap-ons were close to the real thing. Phaedra didn't have one. Or if she did, she never mentioned it. They had only dated for two months. Phaedra preferred being more tactile.

And the piercings. God, did she know how to use her tongue stud. That alone could have turned her into a household name. Lisa smiled, imagining every unsatisfied woman in this self-important backwater pressuring their men to get a tongue piercing.

Brad, who ran the town's local paper – a double sided 8 ½ x 11 composed mainly of dad jokes, puns and ads for the same four businesses every month, would write a headline. *Local Piercer Brings You Closer to God – Because You Get More HOLEY!* Wilma would consider it sacrilegious. Phaedra would ignore her and hang a sign that would read *Jesus Had Four Piercings* just to piss her off.

Brad would run a picture too. Phaedra's face with its crooked smile and smoky eye-shadow framed by a messy wolf shag. She'd lean arrogantly against the side of her shop on main street with a cigarette dangling from her fingers.

He would tell her she couldn't have it in the picture, but she'd refuse and eventually he would cave. Who the hell smoked actual cigarettes anymore? Phaedra did, that's who.

If it were legal, tobacco companies would line up to pay her to smoke outside of high schools. And she would. All the wannabes and posers with their cotton candy birthday muffin vapes would be whinging when the girls they liked flocked to copy Phaedra. Pat would mock them until they cried.

Lisa released a long, slow breath. She couldn't deal with Pat invading her fantasies right now. Pat was too real. Too close. Her thing with Phaedra had already ended. She wouldn't have to see her face and be reminded of what could have been. A fantasy with Phaedra could stay a fantasy without threatening to spill over into reality. Her heart would be safe.

Lisa took another, larger sip of wine. She sighed and settled back into the sofa, trying to concentrate on Phaedra's smirk. Phaedra wouldn't care enough to laugh at a bunch of high school boys. She would finish her cigarette, hop on her bike and drive over. Not just any bike - an Indian Scout. The only reason Lisa knew was because Phaedra loved that bike so much that she was on it the second the snow started to melt. Lisa didn't know anything about bikes, but she could listen to Phaedra talk about them for hours. Something about a woman's voice talking about engines made her heart race.

There would be a deep rumble just before the ignition shut off and Phaedra would ring the doorbell. She would lean against the brick wall. She liked the way the porch lamp highlighted her jawline. Lisa liked it too. Whatever mixture of products she used reminded Lisa of cherry cola.

Phaedra would smile. Arrogant. Cocky. Her incisors would be just a bit crooked. And she would never push it. She would just stand there, smiling until Lisa invited her in.

Lisa would offer her a glass of wine, but Phaedra would only give her a small, breathy laugh. It was a game they played. She knew Lisa had IPA in the fridge. Lisa always had IPA in the fridge just for her. Some local brewery. A different one every time. Exploring them had been their thing in the city. Lisa knew she missed it. She wanted to make the transition here as comfortable as possible.

She would take a sip, but she wasn't here for beer. She was here for Lisa. She would connect her phone to Lisa's speakers and show her the new house mixes she'd found while it was slow at the shop. It was the only place in town that played music like that. Everywhere else played country. Lisa suspected that a lot of the local clientele only hung out in her shop for the music.

Lisa would dance. Always tentatively at first. She could never immediately let go. Getting over the self-consciousness built from a lifetime of airbrushed magazine photos and Jane Fonda workout videos took time. Phaedra staring at her like she would eat her if she could helped. When Phaedra would join in, her movements were always slow and deliberate. Her hair bounced. Her ice blue eyes would rake over Lisa's body, as if stares could unfasten every button along the way.

They would move together. Closer and closer until one of them brushed against the other. Until a hand snaked around a waist. Until an arm draped across a neck. Pulled lips into a kiss. Tongue into a mouth. Deeper. Until you could feel the other's heartbeat. The vibration of the quietest whimper against your breath.

Phaedra would always break away first. She liked to lock eyes and revel in Lisa's stare. Lisa always felt like prey. Crude, but it always got her wet. She could see that gaze a thousand times and always need a fresh pair of underwear. Josh had never made her feel like that. Nor had any of the men she'd been with. How could she have denied who she was for this long? When women were right there?

Even the most experienced men always rushed things, but Phaedra knew foreplay. She knew that it was the salacious texts in the middle of the day. The single red rose left on the sheets they'd ruined the night before. The chaste kiss along the back of her neck while she did the dishes before she left. Foreplay was a whisper of a possibility tonight. A souvenir of the depraved things you did last week. The sideways glance at something innocuous, only to find out later how filthy her thoughts were.

Teeth sunk into her neck. Lisa exhaled. She loved it when Phaedra marked her. Even if she would have to cover up the next day. The reminder that her body had belonged to someone else.

Phaedra's fingers slipped under her shirt. The stiff blue cotton strained against the buttons, clinging desperately before spraying across the floor with a clatter. Oatcake batted at one of them. It skittered across the linoleum before she lost it under the stove.

Lisa braced herself against the wall, wrapping her elbows across Phaedra's neck, pulling her closer. She bit her collarbone and Lisa yelped before sinking into bliss.

Phaedra's finger hooked around the gore of Lisa's plain, nude-coloured bra. She didn't know how it was possible that Phaedra could sever the underwire but that was a puzzle for another moment. Her breasts relaxed, released from their constraints. She hung exposed and wanton.

The neighbours would see them, skin washed out in the blue-green fluorescent lights, like a cheap amateur porn set. They would see Phaedra's tongue wrapped around her nipple. They would see Lisa's head thrown back against the wall, auburn hair loose and splayed across the garden vegetable-themed wallpaper. They could see Phaedra's fingers fumbling with her belt buckle.

Lisa didn't care.

They could talk. Wilma could tell the entire church about the unrepentant display of lesbian sex she'd seen in the new police officer's house last night. *New* even though she'd been here sixteen years. Pastor James would craft a sermon about the evils of homosexuality. The church billboard would read *Marriage = one man + one woman* until some bored teenagers rearranged the letters to spell *Marriage = man + ramen.*

Lisa still would not care.

Phaedra hoisted her up, giggling and leaving her trousers in a pool on the floor. She deposited Lisa onto the counter, somehow without breaking the kiss. Lisa thanked her past self for cleaning the kitchen earlier, but those thoughts were short lived. Phaedra's hot breath teased her centre. Lisa squirmed, but Phaedra only bit her thigh. Lisa squealed, trying to angle her hips, but Phaedra wouldn't relent. Her efforts only gained her a slippery countertop.

Desperate for contact, Lisa grabbed Phaedra's hair, pulling her in. Phaedra gave in. Lisa almost came right then and there. Lisa tried to lean back and angle her hips better, but couldn't because of the cabinets in the way. Phaedra's solution was to simply sweep everything off of the counter. Ceramic shattered and kitchen tools clattered. Oatcake ran off to the bedroom.

"I'll pay for new ones" Phaedra's voice came out huskier than usual . She clambered up onto the counter, lowering Lisa across the stove. She didn't have time to protest - Phaedra's tongue was lapping at her hurriedly, like she was melting ice cream spilling over and coating her fingers.

Lisa grabbed the edge of the counter, thrusting into Phaedra's mouth. The buildup was unlike anything she'd felt before, like her whole body was ready to come apart. Every drag of her clit across Phaedra's tongue felt like it would send her, but she just kept easing off.

She whimpered. Phaedra smirked and snaked up her body for a kiss. "Such a tease." Phaedra made a show of licking her fingers. Lisa thought she might come from the sight alone. Phaedra teased her entrance, sliding delicately along her lips. "Fuck. Please?"

Phaedra obliged. One at first, drawing a lazy line across her front wall. Lisa's eyebrows knit together told her it wasn't enough. Two then. The salt and pepper shakers that remained on the stove rattled as she arched her back.

Phaedra plunged her tongue into Lisa's throat. Lisa moaned into her, brow furrowed when she unravelled around Phaedra's fingers. She didn't stop. Phaedra kept pace, guiding Lisa across that wave until it crashed ashore, leaving them spent and exhausted on the beach.

Which is when the door opened.

"What the…?"

The coffee table had been tipped over at some point, magazines, pens and a tissue box spread across the floor. The remnants of a wine glass and its contents shattered.

Josh swivelled his head, looking for an intruder, only to see a pair of trousers crumpled against the wall and the smell of sex and cherry cola hanging thickly in the air. He felt dizzy for some reason.

He followed the debris into the kitchen. Blue ceramic shards scattered across the linoleum, a few wooden spoons. A ladle.

The light from the hood fan illuminated Lisa's body. A pool of blood fed from a wound at her neck gathered on the glass stovetop. She still wore her blue RCMP blouse, but her breasts were exposed and covered in puncture marks. She was naked from the waist down.

Josh rushed toward her but Willow materialised from the shadows between them.

"Rowan?" Josh had difficulty seeing clearly. He rubbed at his eyes. "Lisa?" But why were there two of her?

"Josh, was it?" She put a hand against his chest.

Josh nodded, suddenly woozy. A thin haze surrounded everything. He shook his head, trying to clear his vision, but the fog remained.

"Why are you?" he tried to turn away, but Willow pulled his chin back to face her. He still averted his eyes. "Why are you naked?"

"Am I?" Willow tilted her head. The room spun along with it. Josh tried to remember what he was doing before, why he was here, but everything except Lisa was too blurry

"Y-Yeah. You're…" Willow slipped her arms around his neck and pulled him in for a kiss. Josh acquiesced. He couldn't remember why he shouldn't.

Willow drew a finger along his chest. She appreciated men with muscles and Josh had *some*. At least he wasn't doughy, like a lot of men his age. And, he had kept his boyish face. His stubble grated against the soft palms of her hands, a delicious contrast, she thought.

Her hands found his cock, hard already. "Boys are so quick," she murmured into his lips.

Josh's head swam. He couldn't remember. Something important. But it couldn't be *that* important if he couldn't remember. Could it?

Willow led Josh to the bedroom. He followed like a lost puppy. Her pheromones seemed to work remarkably easier on Josh than they had on Lisa. Maybe they worked better on men. Maybe men were simpler overall. She really wished she'd had more time to explore herself before she'd died.

She decided that she could happily spend hours pleasuring a woman, but when it came to her own, she couldn't imagine it without a man. Josh may not be the town hockey star all the girls drooled over, but he would do for now.

Willow guided him between her legs and was instantly underwhelmed. This was not how she remembered sex. Josh lay on the bed, lolling about in a stupor. Hard, but damn near comatose. She suspected he might even choke on his own tongue. Willow turned his head to the side. She supposed she could get off like this - if she did all the work, but if that was the case, she might as well buy a vibrator.

Pat had been very clear about biting men. But it was the blood that made you aggressive, wasn't it? A little venom would pick him right up, as long as he didn't bleed *too* much. Willow's fangs slid free.

Small town biology courses might not be up to the same standards as in the city, but Willow was pretty certain the jugular was a vein. Veins led to the heart, so if she bit him there, she wouldn't get too much blood in her mouth and the venom would spread quickly.

She missed and hit his carotid instead. Blood gushed into her mouth. Willow jolted back in surprise, but the taste overwhelmed her, flooding her senses. Tangerines and summer. So much more delicious than she could have imagined. She couldn't stop herself from biting again. And again.

And again.

And again.

And again.

twenty-two

Pat wiped the marble countertop and rinsed out the dishrag, only to find a crow perched on the window above the sink.

"What the fuck, Corinne? Now you're in my house?"

Corinne materialised, holding a small kennel. She promptly deposited it against the floor as if it were covered in filth. "You did invite me once. You're welcome."

Pat knelt on the floor and opened the kennel. Oatcake sniffed at her cautiously and then left to explore the house.

"You brought me Lisa's cat?"

"I'm still waiting for my *thank you*."

"Er, thanks, I suppose." Pat stood up. "Why did you think I needed a cat?"

"*You* don't need a cat. *Lisa* needs you to take her cat. And it's obvious you're in love with her, so I removed that problem and did what needed to be done."

"Alright, so, first, it's *not* obvious and second, what obstacle? Do you think you're helping get us together by making it look like I stole her cat?" Pat poured herself a smoothie. "Do you want some?"

"Yes, actually."

Pat handed her a glass.

Corinne took a sip. "Not that I care if you get together, but I needed to burn down her house and the cat was in the way."

"You what?" Pat nearly dropped her own glass.

Corinne looked at her like she was stupid. "I burned down her house. Just a little grease fire in the kitchen that became a *big* grease fire." Corinne spread her hands wide. "Because of that immature fool you created and haven't been looking after properly."

"But I haven't taught her anything."

Corinne rolled her eyes. "That's for damn sure."

"What happened?"

"Well, she had the balls to bite Lisa, unlike some people," Corinne side-eyed her. "But then she bit the boyfriend."

"What?!" Pat set her glass down before she *did* drop it.

"You *did* tell her she shouldn't bite men, right?"

"Of course I did!"

"Well, she didn't listen." Corinne tapped her foot as she thought. "I cleaned up this mess for you, but you're going to have to do something about the rest of it."

"Like what? I don't own her."

"I gave you the cuffs for a reason."

Pat's lips thinned into a white line. Willow hadn't returned last night. Now she needed to figure out where she was before she caused any more damage.

"Where's Lisa?"

"On her way here. You didn't think I'd burn down her house with her in it, do you? I'm a monster, not an arsonist," Corinne huffed.

Pat stared and then pinched the bridge of her nose. "Are you stupid?"

"Excuse me?" Corinne placed an elegant hand on her chest.

"Sorry," Pat breathed in frustration. "I know you haven't really interacted with people in a while, but just think. Please."

Corinne rolled her eyes.

"You waited for her to leave and then you burned down Lisa's house."

"Yes. To clean up *your* mess."

"And you brought her cat here. To me."

"We *have* covered this. I thought you were smarter."

"And Lisa is on her way here."

Corinne cocked her hip, waiting for Pat to get to the point.

"What do you think Lisa is going to think when she gets here and sees me with her cat?"

"She'll be overjoyed that you rescued her. You lot love cats, don't you?"

"You mean *lesbians?*"

"Yes, yes, whatever." Corinne waved her hand dismissively. Pat wasn't going to explain the euphemism.

"Does she know her house burned down?"

"No. Of course not."

"Then you don't think she's going to wonder why I have her cat?"

"I have the utmost confidence that you are capable of explaining that." Corinne placed a palm on her shoulder. "I believe in you."

"She's going to think *I* burned down her house." Pat waved frantically.

"Well, that's going to be awkward. I'm sure you'll come up with something. Best of luck." Corinne sped away in a flurry of black wings.

Pat shook the annoyance from her head and went off to find Oatcake. There was no time to make up anything remotely reasonable, so she hoped the truth, minus a few details, would suffice.

The crunch of gravel alerted Pat to Lisa's arrival. She threw on a coat and walked out to meet her. The truck door opened and Lisa fell into her arms.

Pat couldn't remember feeling this conflicted in a long time. The wound at her neck had mostly healed into a pair of bruises, but it was clear that Willow had been careless. She had *hurt* Lisa.

"You're growling. Are you okay?" Lisa looked up at her with tear-stained eyes and mascara running everywhere.

Pat hadn't realised she had been growling. She needed to deflect. "Never mind me. What about you? What happened?" Pat knew very well what had happened, but Lisa didn't know the half of it. She needed to ease her into it before she had a panic attack. "A friend said your house was on fire. They brought me Oatcake."

"What?!" Lisa's mouth fell open in shock.

"It's alright. You can stay here as long as you like. I'm just glad you're safe."

Lisa's face contorted, confusion and loss fighting for dominance. "I don't… I don't…"

Pat led her into the house. "Come inside. You're in shock."

Lisa struggled to understand what had happened. Did she dream all of that? Did she really see Josh's body reduced to bloody strips? Why was Phaedra there? Had she been drugged? Did Josh give them to her? Why would he do that? What else made sense?

Pat lowered Lisa to the sofa and wrapped a quilt around her. "Stay there. I'll go make some tea."

Lisa nodded, still trying to piece things together.

Pat returned holding out Lisa's old RCMP mug. Lisa reached out and took it.

"Ouch."

Pat quickly took the mug back. "Shit, sorry. It's hot." She set it on the coffee table in front of her and sat at the opposite end of the sofa.

"What happened?"

Pat took a deep breath. "I was told it was a grease fire."

Lisa frowned. "Did I start it?"

Pat shook her head. "I have no idea."

"And Josh?"

Pat shook her head.

"I think I was drugged, but I don't know where it would have come from." Lisa moved her fingers absently. "I remember Phaedra being there, but that's impossible, and…" Lisa blushed, suddenly remembering what she had pictured Phaedra doing.

"And what?" Pat held Lisa's tea out to her again.

Lisa took it. The mug had cooled down a bit this time. "We had… sex? I think? I can't remember."

Pat bit the inside of her cheek, taking deep breaths to avoid growling again, but Lisa noticed. Pat made a joke instead. "You never used to be this prudish about telling me details. What has this place done to you?"

Lisa saw through it. "Do you know what happened, Pat?" She looked directly at her.

Pat had a good idea of what happened, but there was no way she could tell Lisa. No way Lisa would ever believe it. "I wasn't there, Lisa. All I know for certain is what my friend told me."

"Which friend? I thought you hated everyone here."

Fuck. "Corinne."

"Fred's wife? I thought she never left her house."

Pat shrugged. "Fred passed. It's not public knowledge yet. Apparently, I'm in the will."

"What was she doing at my house?"

"Rescuing Oatcake." *From the fire she caused.* "You'll have to ask her about it."

Lisa set her tea aside and leaned into Pat. Pat shifted so she could lay her head on her lap.

"You smell like ice cream. Neapolitan." Lisa mumbled.

Fuck. Pat glanced over at the windows. Heavy curtains blocked the sunlight from coming in. The last thing she wanted was for Lisa to start hallucinating again.

But Lisa only moved closer, burrowing into her. Pat sighed and brushed the hair out of her face, exposing the wound Willow had left. A wave of anger bubbled up. Lisa hummed and closed her eyes.

Oatcake decided the two women looked like a comfortable spot to nap and promptly curled up on top of them both.

Pat stared at her. "What the fuck?"

Oatcake twitched her ears and turned her head, but she didn't move.

"I suppose I'm not going anywhere for a while then," Pat muttered, but only her and the cat heard.

She stroked her fingers through Lisa's hair and let her sleep. Maybe it would do her some good.

By mid-afternoon, the sun had moved to the south facing window that wasn't blocked by a heavy curtain.

That should take care of the pheromones, Pat thought, relieved.

Oatcake hopped down and sauntered off somewhere, but Lisa still slept. It was like she didn't want to leave. Pat couldn't count how many times she had dreamt of moments just like this, but right now, she only felt anxious.

What would happen when she realised Josh had been *bitten* to death? That the girl they had pulled from the wreckage had been dead for almost twenty years? That she had hallucinated *Phaedra*. That Pat had been the one responsible for turning her during a moment of teenage stupidity. Whatever tenuous connection they had would snap, irreparably damaged. Lisa would be furious. She would never see her again.

Pat had survived a lot, but she wasn't sure she could handle Lisa hating her.

Lisa stirred and yawned. She craned her neck to look up at Pat. A brief respite before the realisation that she no longer had a house and her boyfriend was dead slammed into her. Pat's heart broke watching the change come over her face. Lisa started hyperventilating. Pat shushed her and petted her hair until her breathing calmed

But only a single lonely tear welled up and fell. Lisa simply didn't have the energy to feel anything more.

Pat met her eyes. The emotional exhaustion obvious. "Police training?" she guessed.

"I don't know. It's like I'm *numb*." She turned to look away.

Pat stroked her hair. She didn't know what else to do.

"I feel guilty, you know?"

"About Josh?"

Lisa tried to nod, but the quilt restricted her movements. "I wasn't in love with him, but I didn't want him *dead*."

"Did you break up with him? You know, before…" Pat trailed off. She *liked* Josh. He was a fool, said inappropriate things. Was inadvertently homophobic. But Josh actually gave her hope that this town might not be this way forever.

Lisa tried to remember. "I invited him over to have the talk, but everything is fuzzy after that." Her face grew sour. "You don't think… you don't think he reacted badly? *He* didn't do that, did he?"

That certainly would have made things easier to explain, but Pat knew he wasn't responsible. Pat knew exactly who did it, even if she wasn't there herself. Only one person *could* have done it. Not person, *monster*.

And now she had to deal with it.

Pat inhaled sharply. "I didn't know Josh that well, but from what I *did* know, I can't believe he would do that."

Lisa shifted, turning so that she rested on her stomach between Pat's legs. Looking up at her with those tear-stained eyes, searching for answers. It almost destroyed Pat's resolve.

"But what if it *was* drugs? I'm a cop, remember? I see what meth does to people all the time."

"I thought you had a fentanyl problem here, not meth." Pat scrambled to find a different explanation for Lisa other than blaming Josh. It wasn't fair to him, even if he was dead and couldn't protest.

Lisa kept her eyes locked on Pat. Sunlight glittering, bringing out the golden streaks in the coffee brown. Pat tried to look away, but that would come off like she was trying to avoid it. Which she was.

"The fentanyl isn't pure. If it was, he would have just gone to sleep and never woken up. They cut it with who knows what?"

"I don't know, Lisa. Even if it *was* drugs. It's not who Josh *was*." *There*, she thought. *I can work with this line of reasoning*. "Josh wouldn't have been the one buying them. Josh would have been poisoned. How, I can't guess."

Pat tried to raise her hands to gesture, but Lisa had shifted and had pinned them down under the blankets.

She lay her head against Pat's chest. That seemed to resolve her questioning - at least for now. Lisa sighed, her fingers spread out next to her cheek. "Am I a bad person?" she mumbled against her work shirt.

Pat tucked her head into her neck, trying to look at her, but Lisa was looking away. "What? Why would you be a bad person?"

"Because I was trying to break up with him. And now he's dead." She pinched absentmindedly at a wrinkle on Pat's shirt. The soft flannel provided a small measure of comfort.

"No," Pat shook her head, rustling against the arm of the sofa. "You can't blame yourself for that." Pat bit her tongue. She had a habit of launching into tirades about women staying with men only because they feel responsible for them and how they need to look out for themselves. Her speech would have slotted nicely into place here, but now was not the time.

Isn't that what you're doing? Pat scowled at the voice in her head. *You're not responsible for what Willow did. You didn't kill Josh. You didn't bite Lisa.* That might be true, but Pat knew very well that Willow was her responsibility. Pat had *made* her.

But you told her she couldn't bite men and she did anyway. That's not your fault!

Lisa shifted and Pat looked down. Somehow, her face had gotten closer. Uncomfortably closer.

"Pat?"

"Yeah."

Lisa took a deep breath. She hoisted herself forward and kissed her.

twenty-three

It wasn't a deep kiss. Nothing earth-shattering or romantic. Just a kiss. On the lips.

"Thank you."

Pat wasn't sure how to respond to that, so she tried to pretend that it hadn't happened. Friends kiss each other on the lips all the time, don't they? Despite desperately wanting her to do it again, Pat's brain refused to accept it as real. Just gals being pals. "Er… For what?"

Lisa sniffed. "For everything. For dealing with my bullshit as a roommate. For helping me come out. For being here now, right when I needed you." Lisa's fist tightened around the fabric. "I know I'm not what you want." She swallowed and glanced away before locking eyes again. "But thank you anyway."

Pat scrunched her eyebrows together. "What are you talking about?"

"I know I'm a lot."

"No, you're not."

"And sorry for kissing you."

Pat looked stunned. "Why?" Her voice rose at the end.

"Because I'm not your type."

"Type?"

"Yeah. The type of girls you normally go for."

"Okay, so one, I don't have a *type* and two, why would you care about who I *go for*?" Pat wriggled her arm free of the blanket. "Have I *ever* brought anyone around? How would you even *know* what my type was if I had one?"

Lisa tucked her head back down into her chest. "Because you don't go for me."

"Lisa...I..."

Pat's mouth opened and closed several times. How was it possible that Lisa hadn't noticed her staring? Or avoiding staring? Or how she stayed up until all hours of the morning waiting for her to come back from a date? Or how Lisa could talk to her about anything, no matter how absurd, in the morning - before she'd had her coffee? *Obviously,* Lisa was her type. But Pat had refused to consider the possibility for so long that it had become fossilised. As if someone had spraypainted *NOT FOR YOU* in giant red letters over her.

"You're in shock." Pat decided. Lisa did not know what she was doing. She was reaching out for comfort in the only way she knew how.

Lisa looked back up at her, eyes wide in disbelief. "Shock?"

"Yeah, you're in shock. I don't want to take advantage of you like this."

Lisa's heart flipped. At least Pat had indirectly confirmed that she *did* want her. "How could you think you're taking advantage of me?"

Pat twisted her head and looked at her from the side. "Because you just had something unbelievably traumatic happen? Because you're here? Depending on me to put you up until we rebuild your house?" She looked away. "Because I'm a traumatised arsehole who can't say anything nice." she muttered. "You don't want me. You just think you owe me."

"Are you really that dense?"

Pat had not been prepared for that. "Er, no?" *I'm not, am I?* Pat thought. *She's awfully upset about me looking out for her.*

Lisa's lips turned into a thin white line. "Pat."

By the way she said it, Pat felt like she was in trouble somehow. "Yes?"

"Don't."

Fuck. Maybe she really was that dense. Pat tried to figure out what she wasn't supposed to do. She winced. "Don't what?"

Lisa exhaled. "Don't tell me that I'm just in shock. Don't tell me what I want and what I don't want. I've been throwing myself at you for *years*. How many times have you seen me naked?"

"Er," Pat stalled. "I always looked away. I thought those were accidents. Or that you were more comfortable in your body."

Lisa slapped her collarbone. "Are you serious?"

Pat tried to look away, but couldn't. Lisa eyes bored into her, pinning her in place. Her face got closer. Pat's lips parted.

Lisa took her bottom lip, but didn't break eye contact until she was sure Pat wouldn't pull away. For someone who looked so hard on the outside, her lips were so soft. How had she not noticed that before? God knows, she'd stared at them often enough.

Pat released the breath she was holding, letting herself melt underneath Lisa. The weight of her pressing Pat into the sofa. Pat had kissed plenty of women since she had turned. She had wanted to kiss plenty more. This was different. This was a kiss that had the pent-up longing of decades behind it.

Lisa's tongue slid between her teeth, tentative at first, and then bold. Pat whimpered. She couldn't remember doing that before. How was this all so new? She became aware that her free arm stood, resting straight up on its elbow, wrist, fallen askew. How did she not know what to do with her hands?

She let it fall, slow as a feather on Lisa's head, fingers pulling through her auburn waves, greying streaks at the temples. Lisa hummed into the kiss, smiling like a cat that had finally caught a mouse against her lips.

She *was* caught. How had that happened? *She* hunted other women. For food. Pat tried in vain to sort her feelings about it, but too many new ones kept coming.

She grasped at Lisa's hair, pulling her closer, a play at control. Lisa complied, but only to deepen the kiss. It didn't feel fair. *Pat* was the predator, not Lisa. Lisa was sweet and kind and giving and felt guilty about dumping a boyfriend with the personality of mayonnaise.

But Lisa was most definitely the one in control here. She propped herself up with one arm, listing to the side. Pat took a breath, immediately to have it stolen by the sight of Lisa hovering above her. Her hair curtained the two of them. Pat brushed it away as casually as she could. If this was going to happen, she wanted it to be real, not because of pheromones. She needed to be sure.

Sunlight dappled against her face. Pat squinted and Lisa giggled. Why had she waited for this for so long?

How could she have been so blind? That Lisa wanted *her*? How could she have let her own foolish opinions about what Lisa wanted stop her from *this?*

Pat arched her neck to catch Lisa, but Lisa pinned her down with a hand at her chest. She leaned into it, pressing Pat deeper into the sofa and plunging into her mouth. The hand fisted the work shirt and pulled. Pat got the message and wriggled awkwardly, trying to unbutton one-handed the offensive garment.

Lisa sat up to allow Pat to free herself. Pat crossed her arms over her head, Lisa's smile askance.

"How are you all abs and sports bra?"

Pat lifted her shoulders sheepishly. That wasn't a look that most people appreciated. Lisa ran a finger from the hollow of her neck, hooking it against the cotton bra.

"Please?" Lisa tilted her head.

"This hardly seems fair." Pat pursed her lips.

Lisa rolled her eyes and pulled her T-shirt over her head. God she was beautiful. Flowing hips, the swell of her breast only modestly hidden by a plain turquoise bra that had probably been purchased in the city five years prior. It wasn't lacey lingerie, clinging salaciously, but that's what made it hot. Lisa was *real* – not some figment of her imagination or a fantasy at two in the morning. She was here and she was *hers*.

Lisa unhooked the old bra, letting it fall away. Pat dared to skim her fingers up her abdomen. Lisa made no attempt to stop her. Pat splayed her fingers across her breasts. Lisa leaned into her and stretched her neck to nip at the fabric of Pat's sports bra.

"Now things aren't fair." She sat back up.

Lisa reached underneath her and unhooked the stretch cotton bra from the back. Pat pulled the straps through her sleeves.

"You're keeping your shirt on?"

Pat still worried about her pheromones. "If you keep complaining, I'll button it back up." She smirked.

Her breasts were nowhere near as generous as Lisa's. Most would consider her wiry, manly-looking, but her nipples stiffened nonetheless - a reminder of her femininity sitting atop the crest of her slight curves.

Lisa stared, mouth slightly open. "When did you get your nipples pierced?" The twin black metal rings usually made the few people who had seen them afraid of her. Pat loved watching their trepidation, but Lisa only looked hungry.

"Back when we were roommates." Pat cocked an eyebrow. Lisa realised that she'd never actually seen Pat topless. Lisa, on the other hand, had *accidentally* exposed herself more times than she could count. Pat had never said a word about it. Lisa was determined to rebalance those scales.

Pat could have been a lingerie model if Lisa had anything to say about it. She wanted her. All of her - piercings included. There was no caressing. No tentative exploration. Lisa's mouth, hot and greedy, took her without hesitation. Pat inhaled sharply, a small yelp coming from her throat. If Lisa heard it, she didn't show it. Her tongue swirled and snaked around Pat's nipple, tugging at the ring as if it were the cherry in a Manhattan.

Pat raked her fingers through the auburn mass of hair, now in an unkempt pile. Propriety had left the building. Every action sure and unquestioned. Her arms pinned Lisa against her chest.

Lisa sat up again, pulling Pat with her. Her short fingernails dug into Pat's muscles. *God they were delicious.* She knew Pat was strong, tightly corded. She *didn't* know just how much muscle she had.

It felt so much different than with men too. Not lumpy, or mean. Gentle. Soft. But still powerful. She imagined they could easily lift her up and throw her around if she wanted.

And Lisa wanted.

Pat kissed back.

Finally, Lisa thought.

Pat was a damn good kisser. Her tongue fought its way into her mouth. It pulled her tongue back into hers. *How many women has she kissed?* Lisa thought she might feel jealous at the idea, but for some reason, it just felt *hot.*

Lisa caught her eyebrows pinching together. Pat nipped against her bottom lip when she pulled away. Lisa's eyes darkened in the shadow cast by the sun, dipping beyond the window frame.

Fuck, Pat thought. She wasn't about to explain things right now, she just needed to stay in the sun. Yes, she was a monster. Yes, she fed on women. But she actually *liked* Lisa. More than *liked,* if she was being honest.

Pat wrapped her hands under Lisa's legs and hoisted her up with a squeal. It was more forward than she usually acted, but she would explain. Later. Much later. Maybe they could be like Fred and Corinne. It would be more than Pat could hope for.

Pat carried Lisa up the stairs, her legs wrapped around Pat's waist and giggling the entire way. Pat sighed in relief to see her bedroom bathed in the late afternoon sunlight.

Lisa fell backwards onto the mattress, the sturdy overbuilt frame refused to budge. Lisa would admire the furniture later. Her auburn hair fanned over the blue and white quilt. Lisa bit her bottom lip, eyes rapt at Pat's hungry gaze from above.

Pat *was* hungry, but she could control herself. She leaned over, half kneeling on the floor, trailing kisses across Lisa's stomach. Lisa couldn't help the grin, fingers lacing across Pat's short hair.

Pat unhooked the button of her jeans with her teeth. Lisa was about to ask where she'd learned to do that, but thought better of it. That was a question for another time. Right now, after this long, she was determined to enjoy the ride.

And she would. Pat peeled the denim from her hips like one of those magic tricks where someone snaps a white table cloth out from under a full spread. Lisa's teeth raked across her bottom lip. Pat pulled a leg over her shoulder, hot breath cascading across the inside of her thigh.

Lisa hummed her appreciation. Pat kissed along her skin, the swell inside her leg. Her cheek brushed against her dark hair and Lisa whimpered.

"Do you tease all your women like this?"

Pat smiled against her thigh, but didn't answer. She just needed to bask in her scent for a few moments longer. Lisa smelled delicious. Now she understood how frustrated Corinne got after spending so many years with Fred. Her teeth itched, but she was a big girl. She could keep them in check.

Or so she thought. Lisa knew what she wanted and refused to let Pat hesitate any longer. She pulled Pat into her in giddy frustration. Pat nearly lost it. Her canines slid free against the slick of her cunt. Salivary glands gushing painfully, she tried to relieve the tension in her neck by extending her tongue, but Lisa bursting across her tastebuds only made it worse.

Pat tried to inhale. *It might calm me* she thought. It did not. Each breath only brought more of Lisa into her senses. She had to make a decision – either bite now or get up and leave. Pat did not want to get up and leave.

Her mind raced to come up with a plan. Pat hoped her idea would work. Two fingers slid in effortlessly. Lisa gasped, masking the sound of Pat biting down hard on her own wrist. Her body would metabolise it quickly and she would have to mind her strength, but it was enough to make her fangs retract.

The rush of venom sped along her arm. It wouldn't take long before it hit her heart and then she hoped she could control herself. She hoped she hadn't averted one crisis by causing another.

She needed to come up with a better plan before the rush hit. Lisa settled into a steady rhythm around her fingers. Pat could move her teeth to a safer place, at least.

"Did you ever get to compare dicks to straps?" Pat pulled her head back. Her pupils had blown and a halo of light surrounded everything, but at least she was no longer in danger of biting Lisa.

Lisa propped herself up on her elbow and pulled Pat into a kiss.

Pat flooded herself. The venom had started working.

"No. Phaedra didn't use them."

Thank God. Pat thought to herself. She peeled herself away. Her fangs may have retracted, but now she was dangerously aroused. She would just have to hope that Lisa was capable of satisfying those urges. She whimpered when Pat pulled away.

Pat withdrew a pair of briefs and an assortment of straps and lubes from a beautifully joined walnut dresser.

"You've used toys, though, right?" Pat panted facing the dresser to hide how heavily she was breathing.

"Yeah." Lisa had snuck behind her. Arms wrapped around her waist. *Fuck, this is going too quickly,* Pat thought.

Pat moved to the side so Lisa could see. "Which one?"

Lisa fingered a plain, but solid-looking violet dil. She passed it to Pat with a smirk that she hoped covered her apprehension.

Pat caught it, but was too preoccupied trying to lower her heart rate. Her movements fitting the strap to her briefs felt violent and jerky. *Only a few more minutes until things even out,* she told herself.

Lisa slipped into her arms, her hips pressing the base of the strap against Pat. Her breath hitched and a flash of heat ran up her neck to her ears. She flexed her fingers to relieve some of the tension before wrapping her arms around Lisa.

Lisa snuck her hand across her abdomen, fingering the elastic of her briefs. For a moment, Pat thought she would slip her fingers under them, but instead, she teased the length of the strap. Pat released a short breath, the frisson teasing at relief. The more of the venom that could be diverted into arousal, the faster it would wear off.

"What does it feel like?" Lisa stroked the silicone, almost lovingly.

"I can feel when it presses into me. The base covers a lot of area."

Lisa drew the tip of her tongue across her top lip. She stroked down, firmer this time. Pat gasped.

"I like this," Lisa smiled wickedly.

Pat raised an eyebrow.

Lisa felt the need to explain. "I don't have to worry about hurting you."

That's the opposite problem that I have, Pat thought.

She craned her neck to catch Pat's lower lip. Lisa walked her backward until she fell on the bed. Pat caught herself growling in surprise. She took a breath, hiding her strained fingers against the mattress.

Lisa crawled onto the bed, stalking like a predator. *The fucking irony,* Pat thought.

"I need to get acquainted first,"

Lisa drew a tongue up the shaft of the strap. A liquid warmth pooled in her briefs. Adrenaline converted to arousal, as though she needed any more. Lisa clawed at her thighs, wrapping her lips around the head of the strap like a chocolate covered strawberry.

Pat stared wide eyed, fighting the urge to scramble backward. She hadn't ever been pursued like this. Pat was the pursuer. Pat was the top. Why was she acting like this?

And then calm. Her body had metabolised the last of the venom. Her veins cooled, the fight or flight response dying down. All that remained was a mass of auburn hair worshipping a silicone cock. One that was attached to her.

Pat threaded her hands through Lisa's hair. Lisa climbed into her lap and kissed her warmly. Pat leaned back into the headboard.

Lisa reached behind, biting her lower lip as she inserted the strap into herself. Pat stared, transfixed at her face morphing into bliss. Her soft moans brought forth another rush of heat.

Pat angled her hips, thrusting into her, hands bracing against her waist.

"How does this feel for you?" Lisa asked, breath hitching with that last thrust.

Pat ran a thumb over her lips. "Even if I couldn't feel a thing, just watching you is all I'd ever need."

Lisa tried to roll her eyes, but the strap hit just the right spot and interrupted her cynicism with a moment of pure bliss. "No wonder you got all the girls," she gasped.

Pat grinned, rocking her hips, dragging the strap against her front wall. Fingers skittered across her skin. Lisa threw her head back, blood singing like a siren under the freckled skin of her throat.

Pat slammed her eyes shut, but it was no use. She could still hear it. It called to her with every beat of her heart. Pat's knuckles itched. She wanted to touch it. Feel the muscle thrum against the pads of her fingers.

You can't, she scolded herself. *That kills people.*

Her scent kept calling. Her teeth arched against her tongue. She buried her head in her neck so Lisa wouldn't see, but it only made the feeling worse. As Lisa approached her climax, her blood rushed faster. Rosewater and pineapple. She needed to get away, *now*.

Pat pushed and Lisa fell backward onto the mattress, a look of shock and confusion on her face. The strap waggled ridiculously.

"Did I do something wrong?"

Pat kept her mouth shut out of fear of exposing her fangs. Instead, she grabbed Lisa's ankle and flipped her over. Lisa squealed. Pat breathed a sigh of relief. Thank God Lisa enjoyed a bit of rough play. Pat lifted her hips and slid the top of her strap across her thighs.

"Why are you teasing me now?" Lisa arched her back.

"You've never tried edging?" Pat's fangs caused a lisp. Thankfully Lisa didn't pick up on it.

"What?"

She inhaled sharply, clearing her senses and trying to will her fangs to retract again. "Oh, we have so much catching up to do."

Pat ran her fingers across her back. The curve of her hips absolutely sent her, but she refused to rush this.

Lisa pushed back against her. Once she had relaxed, Pat slid in easily.

"Oh." Lisa's tone was guttural. She clapped a hand over her mouth. She had never heard such a noise come out of her before.

"Did I hit the spot?" Pat said, a lilt of amusement in her tone.

"Fuck yes, do that again."

Pat pulled out slowly. Lisa squealed. "Fuck. That…that feels. Oh my god."

Pat thrust in again, keeping her movements steady, drawing it out.

"Fuuuck. Oh my god Pat, fuck." Lisa thrust back again. Her body relaxed into the movement. Soon she had a rhythm going. Lisa sang into the pillows until she tensed. "Okay. I think I'm done."

"Oh honey." Pat threaded her fingers through Lisa's hair. "You're not there yet."

"What?" Lisa yelped, but the slide of the silicone cock along her front wall sent her reeling. She howled like an alarm, getting louder as the pressure built.

And then she hit the wall. Lisa shuddered, her knees buckling. Pat rode her through the wave until she collapsed against the quilt.

Pat slid, panting beside her. Lisa could only acknowledge her presence with a wide-eyed stare. Pat wrapped her arms around her. Lisa locked her arms, clinging to her as if she'd drift away otherwise.

twenty-four

Pat waited until the last rays of sunlight shied away from the window before putting on her oversized T-shirt and pyjama bottoms. She didn't need her pheromones ruining this moment. Lisa shivered, missing her warmth. She pulled the quilt back and slid under the covers.

Pat sat on the edge of the bed, pulling Lisa's hair away from her face. "You said you were done earlier. Why?"

Lisa played with the edge of the blanket. "It's been so long, I thought I was."

"Did you never..."

"With Phaedra. That was a surprise too." Lisa turned away. "I remember, I cried so hard after."

Pat stroked her cheeks with the back of her knuckles, "Why?"

Lisa sighed. She had dissected that moment to death. "I think," she paused. "I think it was because I *knew* that Phaedra would always be a fling. And that she had somehow ruined me for men." She buried her head against the sheets. "I know, that sounds stupid - how could you experience the best sex of your life with the one woman you slept with and not know you're a... I don't know what I am." She toyed with the hem of Pat's t-shirt.

"Not even with a vibrator?"

Lisa shrugged. "I always stopped before it got too intense." Lisa sniffed. "I don't think I was ready to give up the idea that I was into men too. It feels like I would be letting everyone down - everyone who thought I would be married and have kids. I never wanted that, but giving myself that label made it feel so *final*."

Pat could have taken it personally, but she didn't. She *knew* why. It was why she had died, after all. Nobody raised as a girl *wants* to be that. You want to be normal. To fit in.

You can flirt with monsters. Dabble with them. Even have a relationship with one.

It's a very different thing to *be* a monster.

"Phaedra made you happy."

The tears fell freely now. "She did. But we both know she wasn't who I wanted."

Pat did *not* know and the confession landed like a bombshell. She didn't know what to do with the sudden swell of emotion. How could Lisa just *say* that? How could she so casually punch a hole in Pat's wall? Didn't she know how much damage she could do?

Pat lay down beside her, an arm draped across her waist, hiding her face in the crook of her neck. Her scent felt like home. Pat stared into a mass of bare skin and crumpled blankets, blinking tears for all the wasted time away, a sliver of moonlight peeked through the window. She feared her fangs might descend again, but they behaved. She dared to inhale deeper.

She could smell it underneath her skin. Rosewater and pineapple. Saliva started to run, so she pulled her head back before she went too far.

"What does this mean?" Lisa spoke into the growing darkness.

Pat couldn't help but feel they were speedrunning things, but Lisa was almost forty. Grown adults with fully developed frontal lobes don't have time for faffing about.

Did she like Lisa? Obviously. Love? They'd already lived together. Carried feelings for this long. A Pat from a previous life would have jumped at this second chance. There was just one small problem. A rather large small problem.

But Corinne and Fred had made it work. Why couldn't she?

"Why do you have a twin bed?" Lisa turned around to face her.

"What?"

"A twin bed. Why would you make yourself such a small bed if you can make whatever furniture you want?"

"Er." Pat stammered. "I don't need that much space, I suppose. Is it too crowded? Do you want me to move?"

Lisa smiled and shook her head. "Don't you dare." She pulled Pat tighter. "It's the perfect size."

Pat laughed. "Alright then. You let me know if you want something bigger."

Of course she wanted something bigger, didn't she? Lisa thought about it. Previous lovers had done their thing and then she always felt the need to get as far away from them as possible. Exile them on the other side of a king-sized mattress.

Now she felt that the bed was too big. That Pat couldn't be close enough. That she would miss her if she weren't wrapped tightly around her.

Lisa traced Pat's throat. The skin was so soft there. All of Pat was soft, and yet, her muscles flowed so powerfully underneath it all. Her fingers found the collarbone. The slight swell of her breast. An areola so soft, it was practically pornographic. Then the nipple ring.

"When *did* you get these?" Lisa gently tweaked her nipple. Pat squirmed.

"Phaedra did them."

"What? Really? When?"

"I went to see her the day after you told me about her."

Lisa turned and frowned.

"I needed an excuse to see her."

"You were checking up on me?"

Pat laughed. "I checked up on all your dates, remember? Except Phaedra didn't have a dating profile, so I had to see her in person."

Lisa nuzzled in closer. "Why do you smell like ice cream?"

Pat supposed she wouldn't be able to help it now that it was dark. She closed her eyes and let Lisa sleep nestled into the hollow of her throat. She could tackle this problem tomorrow.

Lisa awoke to the sunlight beaming rudely against her face. Pat was absent. Josh was dead. Her house was gone. And only one of those concerned her at the moment.

She *should* feel upset at Josh's death, but all she could feel was *relief*. Her own cowardice had dragged a one-sided relationship with him for years past its expiry date and she hadn't even had to face him to end it. Josh deserved more.

The house, she could take or leave. Insurance would cover it and aside from a few old RCMP training mementos, she could replace everything else. And she'd gladly trade all of it for Pat. What she wanted was Pat. To live here with Pat. Which was absurd. Because yes, there was clearly mutual attraction and yes, she had just had some of the best sex of her life, but those were just hormones talking. She *should* be feeling sad and ashamed, but all she felt was relief and elation.

Oatcake nosed her way through the door, slinking inside. She hopped up onto the bed and bunted her face against Lisa's. Lisa moved her and held Oatcake close, kissing the top of her head. "Am I a bad person?" she whispered. Oatcake only purred.

Pat overheard, but she didn't say anything. She had a pretty good idea of what Lisa must be thinking. She knocked against the doorframe.

"I burned you some pancakes."

Lisa rolled over. Pat leaned against the wall, her adorable dimple and loose-fitting pyjama bottoms making her look far younger than Lisa knew she had to be.

"How do you look so good?"

Pat ran her hands over her buzzcut. "I don't have any hair to mess up."

Lisa bit her lip and crawled out of bed. She fell into Pat's arms, skin still radiating warmth from the bedsheets. Pat kissed the top of her mussed auburn hair. Why had she waited so long? *You know why. You still need to deal with that.*

Pat held out some folded flannel. "Jim-jams?"

Lisa smirked at Pat's ridiculous vocabulary and took them reluctantly.

"Alright, let's go eat."

Pat held a piece of pancake out for Oatcake, who sniffed warily at it. She decided it qualified as food.

"You can't feed cats pancakes!"

Pat looked surprised. "Really? I've never actually had a cat. I don't have cat-food either. I'll go pick some up later today. Sorry."

Lisa smirked, enjoying Pat's flustering.

"So," She picked at her pancake. It was terrible, but her heart still glowed that Pat had made an attempt. "I asked you last night, but you didn't answer."

Pat put down her fork. Lisa looked at her plate.

"What does this mean?" She locked eyes with Pat. "For us."

Oatcake pawed at Pat for some more pancake. Pat obliged. Lisa let it go.

Pat knew this had been coming. She'd practiced what she would say all morning. And now that she was in it, it still felt awkward. "Do you want something more?" It felt like a deflection. "Given that we're in Northton, I mean. I don't want to cause you problems."

Lisa very much wanted something more. She gave the barest hint of a nod. Pat sighed and Lisa's heart sunk.

"There's a lot about me that you don't know."

"You don't want me, I get it." A hot tear fell across Lisa's face. She thought she could be an adult about this, but apparently not.

"No!" Pat reached across the table and tried to take Lisa's hand. Lisa had not been expecting it and she moved to wipe her face. Pat's hand landed in a mess of syrup instead.

"Ah fuck." Pat licked the syrup off her fingers. Lisa laughed, but the tears still stung.

"It's not that," Pat said between licks. "There's just so much I need to explain."

"Is it about the toothbrushes?" Lisa looked toward the closet.

"What?"

"The toothbrushes with all the women's names on them."

"I told you, those are mostly pretty old."

"*Most* of them?"

"Andi and Phaedra were here last year."

"And the rest?"

Pat shrugged. "It's not what you're thinking." *It's much worse,* she thought. How do you explain that it's not a *sex* thing, it's a *feeding on willing participants* thing? Most vampires were straight and didn't participate in anything but voyeurism beyond that.

Lisa stared, searching for the barest hint that she might get what she wanted. "So that other house? The one you throw *parties* in?"

Pat thought of the space filled with chains, floggers and furniture unfit for your average living room. The only people who got off in there were the human donors, though the vampires with bisexual tendencies would sometimes put on a show.

Pat picked up her fork and stabbed at a piece of blackened pancake, wracking her brain for how she could possibly explain this.

Which is when a crow flew through the kitchen window and landed on the table.

"Are you fucking kidding me? What the hell is wrong with you?" Pat slammed her fork down against her plate.

Lisa jerked back. "Do crows always land on your table?"

It dawned on her a little too late that she had just been caught scolding a crow in front of Lisa. Pat gestured toward her. "You can't do this now." She hissed.

"Are you… talking to the crow?"

The crow snapped its head toward Lisa and then back again to Pat. It pecked at a piece of pancake and then promptly dropped it. The crow fixed its beady eyes on Pat.

Pat sighed. She raised her eyes to Lisa, who marvelled at this bizarre scene in front of her. She scrambled to think of something, *anything* that would make what was about to happen easier for Lisa to accept, but came up blank. It was going to be the truth. All of it.

Pat clasped her hands together and took a deep breath. "Things are about to get really fucking strange, but I *promise* you that this doesn't change anything."

The crow tilted its head.

"Alright, this changes *everything*, but not the way I feel about you."

"You feel about me?" Lisa's eyes rejoiced, but it was short-lived.

A dozen other crows flew through the window, morphing into the shape of a tall, elegant woman.

"Finally," she spat.

Lisa shrieked and ran into the kitchen.

"I did say things were about to get strange." Pat glared at the woman. "This is Corinne."

Lisa backed against the counter, keeping the island between her and Corinne.

"Oh relax." Corinne waved her hand. "I'm not going to bite you." She tilted her head toward Pat. "*She* might though. She's wanted to for years."

Pat turned red.

Lisa didn't run any father, which Pat took as a good sign.

"You know you could have done that outside and knocked on the door like a normal person."

"Yes, well, you were having *issues*."

"I was getting to it."

"Not quickly enough. I know you lot like to go at it for hours, once you finally manage to confess your feelings."

"I told you I was getting to it." Pat grit her teeth.

"How long did it take? Decades? It's beyond *Victorian* levels of pining." Corinne scoffed and rolled her eyes toward the kitchen, as though Lisa was in on her mockery of Pat. "We don't have another four hundred pages for you to write sonnets about her ankles."

"You've been pining for me for decades?" Lisa's heart flipped even as she cowered next to the Lazy Susan.

"You have no idea." Corinne's voice filled with disdain. "Watching her flounder around has been like having sex with an imbecile who can't find the clit. You want so badly to yell at him, but you know it would only hurt his feelings and he still wouldn't be able to find it."

"You do nothing *but* yell at me."

Corinne turned back to Pat. "Perhaps not loudly enough. But it seems you know where the clit is, so yay you."

"Were you watching? Is that why you're here?" Pat glowered.

"No. Your daughter is going on a rampage."

"You have a daughter?" Lisa nearly knocked the box of pancake mix off the counter.

"Ah, yes. You were *getting to it.*" Corinne glowered back before turning to Lisa. "She *bit* the first girl who kissed her and now we have *this.*" Corinne gestured broadly.

Lisa looked confused.

Corinne turned back to Pat. "You haven't told her *that* either?"

Pat dropped her head into her chest. "Getting to it," she muttered.

Corinne smiled sweetly at Lisa.

And then her fangs descended.

Lisa shrieked and tried to scamper further away. Corinne retracted her fangs. "I already told you I wouldn't bite you." She waved dismissively and turned back to Pat. "Find me at the cemetery when you finally manage to tell her everything. Just don't take another twenty years or there won't be a town left. Also, your pancakes are an abomination." Corinne exploded into a flurry of crows and flew off.

twenty-five

Pat set a mug at the edge of the coffee table and left to sit in the loveseat at the other end of the room. Lisa curled tightly against the corner of the sofa. She reached for the mug and held it close against her chest. Pat sipped her coffee, black as always.

"So, you're…?" Lisa let the sentence hang.

Pat nodded and took another sip.

"Have you ever bitten me?"

Pat breathed a laugh. "No."

"Why not?"

Pat chewed her lip for a moment and stared off into the late morning light illuminating the dust. It drifted slowly, but inevitably. The truth, like gravity, would always win eventually. She took a deep breath. "Forget what you know. I don't need to bite people to live. I don't sparkle in the sun. Or burn."

"But you *can* bite people."

Pat nodded slowly.

"Can I see?"

Pat stared at her for a moment before deciding that the damage had already been done. She opened her mouth and let her fangs slide forward.

"Does it hurt?"

Pat shook her head.

"Can I touch them?"

Pat set down her coffee and lumbered over to Lisa, shoulders stooped. Her demeanour had changed so drastically from the Pat she knew. Gone was the in-your-face confidence. She looked genuinely afraid. Pat knelt beside the sofa, fangs exposed, awaiting the monster's due.

"Come here," she whispered. Pat expected Lisa to run a finger along her fangs, but instead, she pulled her head into her lap.

Tears welled up and fell. Lisa ran her fingers across her short brown buzz cut. "Tell me about your… daughter," Lisa asked quietly. "If you want to."

"Corinne will get angry if we take too long," Pat murmured into the flannel pyjama covering Lisa's legs.

"Screw Corinne."

Pat laughed. "She's not actually my *daughter*. She's just called that because I turned her. Just like I call Corinne *mother*." Lisa waited. Pat took a breath.

"It's a curse. We're monsters. We don't *need* to drink, but we want to. I don't know if that makes it better or worse." Pat swallowed thickly. "Venom makes people not mind it so much." That seemed much more palatable than saying *makes you horny as fuck.* Pat couldn't remember the last time she had self-censored, but her defences were in such shambles, she felt utterly exposed. Like she was naked in the middle of Kings Cross with only her hands to cover herself.

The prickliness of Pat's hair tickled at Lisa's fingers.

Pat continued. "Like everything, there are limits. Venom carries a small part of yourself. You'll recover it if you drink, but turning someone requires a lot more

– too much to recover. And they have to die for it to work. Doing it more than once is impossible."

Pat played at the fabric of Lisa's pyjama. "That's not completely true. I suppose you could turn a second person, if you're willing to die for it. Which is a good thing because otherwise, there would be a lineup of girls at my door asking to become vampires. Most of them have no idea what that would mean."

Lisa snorted. "Has that ever happened?"

Pat nodded against her lap. "Phaedra asked me once."

"Really? She knows?" Another thing Lisa felt jealous about.

"Yeah. She found out years ago. I told you her and her wife stay here sometimes. It's nice having people around who understand."

Lisa wanted to ask about what they did here, but decided she wasn't ready to know quite yet.

"That doesn't sound like much of a curse."

"That's not it." Pat turned to look up at Lisa. "The curse is that you can't bite men. At least that's what Corinne thinks. Male blood sends you into a rage. You'll kill them."

Lisa blanched. "Is that…?"

Pat sighed, her heart stopping. She knew this would have to be said sooner or later. "I wasn't there, but Corinne said it was. She was the one who lit your house on fire to cover it up."

Lisa stopped stroking Pat's hair. "She what?"

Pat lifted her head. "Corinne is…" she gestured impotently.

Lisa huddled into the corner of the sofa, holding her knees tightly to her chest. Pat backed away. "I get it.

This is a lot. None of it is fair to you." Pat scanned the room, looking for something to focus on that wasn't Lisa's piercing gaze. "I'll find somewhere else. You can stay here as long as you need."

Pat scrambled to her feet and ran upstairs before Lisa could say anything else.

Lisa wanted to feel angry. She *should* feel angry. She should want to throw things and scream obscenities after what Pat had done to her.

Except she hadn't. None of this was Pat's fault. And even though a part of her wanted to lash out at someone, that *someone* wasn't Pat. Pat had done nothing except constantly try to protect her, even from herself. Even now, as she ran away. Try as she might to steel her resolve, Lisa's heart still broke. She couldn't lose Pat, no matter what she was.

Not after she'd been in love with her for twenty years.

Oatcake hopped up on the couch and batted at Lisa's legs until she released her grip on them and allowed her to curl up on her lap.

"You're not a vampire too, are you?" Lisa muttered. Oatcake only purred louder.

Pat returned a few moments later, but didn't acknowledge Lisa. She kept her head down and shuffled quickly toward the door. Lisa had never seen her like this. She looked like she was on the verge of erupting into tears.

"Stop." It was barely a whisper, but Pat turned around. A hoodie pulled up over her head, slouched forward and off balance with a stuffed duffel bag in her hand.

Pat's hazel eyes shone, magnified by the unfallen tears – almost pleading, but not apologetic. "It's okay. No-one wants a monster around."

"I do."

"You don't know what you're saying." Pat stood motionless for a few moments.

"Stop telling me what I want and what I don't want. You know I've been throwing myself at you since I met you and you refused to see it because you thought you knew me better," Lisa shouted.

Pat was stunned. Lisa had never yelled at her before, but she wasn't wrong. Pat *hadn't* given her a chance. She'd made a lot of assumptions – incredibly valid assumptions, but assumptions nonetheless. Pat set the duffel bag down and jammed her hands in the pockets of her hoodie.

Lisa tilted her head toward the end of the sofa. "Sorry, Oatcake took your spot. You'll have to sit over there." Oatcake purred smugly.

Pat breathed a laugh and folded her legs under herself in the corner. She locked her eyes on the cat, not knowing where else to look. "What do you want to know?"

"You said you're cursed. Is there a way to break it?"

"No," Pat turned away. "I'm already dead. Breaking it would kill me again. Though," she scoffed, "I think the *real* curse is that we're stupid. Corinne turned me on accident. I turned Willow because I was a lonely idiot."

Lisa buried her fingers into Oatcake's fur. "How did she turn you on accident?"

"It's a long story."

Lisa tilted her head with a scowl that indicated in no uncertain terms that she was unwilling to deal with Pat's evasive bullshit anymore.

"Okay." Pat held up her hands and took a deep breath. "I didn't have a happy life before." Pat darted her eyes from place to place, but Lisa refused to stop looking at her. A full minute passed before Pat continued. "I grew up really religious - as in, the type of church that would shun you. Floor length dresses, girls pick up after their brothers. That sort of thing. I got caught with another girl. They shaved my head." Pat ran her fingers across her buzzcut. "I liked it. They said I was *unrepentant* and they told me to leave. Got a job doing construction to get by. Just manual labour, that sort of thing. I pretended to be a boy. When I did, I started packing."

"With those...?"

Pat nodded. "One of my mates figured it out. Then he wouldn't leave me the fuck alone." Lisa winced. Pat massaged her forehead. "We were out drinking after a shift and he got more and more insistent that I give him a shag to keep my secret. I refused, so he outed me. The rest of the crew beat the bejesus out of me until Corinne chased them off."

"She rescued you?"

Pat scoffed. "On accident, remember? She also thought I was a man. Thought she could inject a little venom, get me nice and hard and then fuck me. When my pack didn't get hard, she kept biting me until she pulled down my trousers and discovered it was silicone. By then, I had died and she'd injected enough venom to turn me."

"Why would she...?" Lisa frowned.

"Because she wanted to fuck a man."

"Couldn't she just do that without biting him?"

Pat bobbed her head back and forth. "Yes, but it's not that simple. It's really hard to fuck someone without biting them. You're close. Heartrates speed up. It's like putting drugs right under an addict's nose."

"But we…"

Pat nodded.

"And you didn't?"

Pat nodded again.

"But you wanted to?"

Pat locked eyes with her and nodded slowly.

"Oh."

Lisa stared at Oatcake. Pat stared at Oatcake. Oatcake arched her neck so Lisa could scritch under her chin.

"What does it feel like?"

Pat refused to pull her eyes away from Oatcake. "You've already felt it."

"I thought you said you didn't bite me."

"*I* didn't. But Phaedra was never at your house."

Lisa's eyes widened.

"You probably don't remember much because of the pheromones we secrete. They're a sort of hallucinogen."

"You make us hallucinate? Am I hallucinating now?"

Pat shook her head. "I'm guessing it was dark and *Phaedra* wasn't wearing much."

Lisa searched her memory. *Phaedra* hadn't been wearing much. It should have been odd at night in early spring, but she had ignored it. Why the hell had she ignored it?

Lisa stopped petting Oatcake and took a deep breath. "So, what happens now?"

"What do you mean?"

"I mean, I know you're *you*. And last night, I asked you what does this *mean*?"

Pat found it suddenly difficult to breathe. "You want...?"

Lisa opened and closed her mouth several times trying to come up with words that would be adequate to express the situation.

"I..." she started. "I don't know what label to put on it. I do know that I spent the last sixteen years in Northton, killing time. I wasted years with the nicest man that I had no real attraction to. And I feel horrible – not that I wasted my life, but that I wasted what little was left of *his* life. I think," she lifted her hands and let them fall on her lap. Oatcake looked at her and then curled up tighter. "I think that I might *never* have been attracted to men."

"Didn't you try to get me to like Hugh Jackman at one point?"

"Yeah. I did. And looking back on it, I can't believe I did that. He *was* attractive. But I don't even know if *I* was attracted to him. I just knew that's what attractive men *looked* like. Do you know what I mean?"

"Er." Pat looked at Oatcake. Oatcake was no help. "Not really? I was kicked out because I liked girls. I always knew. But if it makes sense to you." Pat shrugged.

Lisa leaned forward to put a hand on Pat's leg. Oatcake mewled in protest, but didn't move. "And that's what I love about you. You have this amazing self-confidence in who you are."

Pat frowned. "It got me killed, remember?"

"Well, that won't happen a second time, will it?"

Pat gave an awkward grin. "It feels really strange that you know all of this now."

Lisa slapped her leg playfully. "Deal with it. I've been waiting for you for this long and I'm not letting you go again."

"Even if I'm a monster?"

"Even if you're a monster."

"You know that I'm not going to age the same as you, right? You're prepared for people to start wondering why you're kissing your daughter like that?"

Lisa laughed. "You're the one who's going to have to kiss an old woman."

Pat grinned, bashful, but also salacious. Lisa's heart did a backflip.

"So, can you?"

"Can I what?"

Lisa's eyes fell over Pat's lip. "Bite me."

"Now?" Pat drew her head back in shock.

"I want to know what it feels like. While I'm not hallucinating or whatever happened to me."

"But Corinne..."

"I believe I said *screw Corinne,*" Lisa interrupted. "Just a little bit. Please?"

Pat unfolded herself from the couch and knelt behind Lisa, slipping her arms across her neck. Lisa tilted her head to the side and shuddered.

"Are you sure you want me to do this? You seem nervous."

Lisa reached behind her and wrapped her fingers around the back of Pat's head. "Shut the hell up and bite me."

twenty-six

Even if she hadn't planned on biting her, Lisa's forwardness overcame the modicum of self-control that Pat had left. Fangs sprung free, finding the carotid of their own accord. Pineapple and rosewater burst across her tongue. She had been dying to taste Lisa for twenty years and she was determined not to waste a drop.

Lisa's pupils blew instantly. The venom flooded her system, first her arm - sparkles, like someone had injected her with Pop Rocks. The delightful sensation of lemon sugar flooding every cell from her shoulder to her fingertips.

Lisa pulled her hand away, staring in amazement. How could her fingers feel *good*? And then it hit her heart.

Like a drugged glitter bomb, her pulse raced, a deluge of energy. *Want*. She could feel her blood vessels dilate. Feel herself open. Feel a void expand that only Pat could fill. She could swear that she could hear her hormones rush to her core.

Lisa had expected it to feel similar to the last time. Hunger, of course, but one she would satiate by *allowing* Pat to take her. Perhaps guided by gentle persuasion, flirtatious banter and maybe a few direct instructions.

In the sunlight, without the pheromones in the way, Pat knew better.

Lisa turned to face Pat, chest heaving. Oatcake scurried away after being so rudely interrupted. Lisa launched herself forward, crashing against Pat's lips. Her mouth had barely parted before Lisa's tongue barged in like a battering ram.

Pat had never choked on a tongue before and she had to admit that the sensation was not entirely unpleasant. She didn't have long to ponder, since Lisa had managed to crawl over the arm of the sofa and wrap her legs around Pat's waist, grinding herself against her middle.

Pat knew better than to attempt to reason with her. In this state, only one thing would work to relieve the pressure. Or, more accurately, given that Pat had probably been a bit too enthusiastic with the biting, one thing multiple times. Corinne was going to kill them.

Pat braced Lisa against the wall, peeling her legs from around her waist. Lisa did not appreciate the interruption and only relented once Pat's fingers found their proper place. Pat buried two of them without resistance inside of her, thumb swirling a swollen clit.

Lisa bit as she approached her release, far harder than she would have had she been in her right mind. Pat allowed it. She only let go to scream while Pat rode her through her first.

Lisa pushed Pat to her knees, wrapping a thigh around her head. Pat lapped gratefully, her fangs springing forth once again in the midst of her scent. *Patience,* she told herself. *You still have shit to deal with.*

But it was so hard to concentrate with everything she wanted immediately on the tip of her tongue.

Pat cradled Lisa's clit in the flat of her tongue, humming her praise. Lisa sang in chorus. Fingers found the spot inside, gently stroking, but Lisa needed more. She clawed at the back of Pat's head until she curled her fingers violently against her wall, releasing a flood. Lisa howled, clenching tightly. Pat's wrist cramped. Lisa peered down at her, like a queen. Like Pat would be her loyal servant forever. Pat stared up in adoration.

"Upstairs. Now." Lisa ordered. Pat obliged. Lisa took the steps two at a time. By the time Pat had caught up to her, Lisa was already holding her choice of strap and lube. Pat did not have time to give a cocky smirk - Lisa simply thrust the objects toward her.

Lisa threw Pat's oversized pyjama shirt over her head. Pat struggled to fit her briefs on with Lisa's mouth glued to her nipple. Lisa cupped her hand under Pat's strap, finger stroking the length of her slit. Pat whimpered.

Lisa drizzled lube across the strap. Half of it splattered wetly on the floor, but neither took any notice. Lisa ran her hand along the shaft and let go of her nipple, burying her face into Pat's neck. "Do what you did to me last time."

Pat arched an eyebrow.

Lisa nipped her throat. "But rougher. I want to feel it tomorrow morning."

A rush of desire saturated her briefs. Pat spun Lisa around and bent her over the bed. She dragged the length of the shaft along Lisa's swollen lips before notching the tip at her entrance. Pat's breath hitched.

She eased herself into Lisa, but Lisa was having none of it. She reached behind her, digging her nails into Pat's thighs. "I said *rougher.*"

Pat obliged. She buried the strap to the hilt, forcing the air from Lisa's lungs along with a guttural sound she was certain she'd never heard before. Lisa grasped at the sheet.

"Fuuuuck. Yes. Right there." Lisa attempted to muffled her cries in the mattress. Her next orgasm came out of nowhere. A single long note, punctuated only by the staccato rhythm of Pat riding her through it, only building into the next one. Pat released her grip on Lisa's hip, slipping her fingers across Lisa's abdomen, pressing her spot into her silicone cock. Lisa gasped once before shrieking, clenching so tightly that Pat was forced to stop.

Lisa collapsed onto the bed, allowing Pat to extract herself.

"Was that…okay?"

Lisa raised her eyebrows, but couldn't answer until she caught her breath.

"Are you kidding?" she panted.

By Pat's face, Lisa could tell Pat didn't know. Lisa sat up, lacing her fingers through Pat's. "Women would pay actual money to experience that."

Pat turned away, a sheepish smile on her face.

Lisa squeezed her hand. "How do you not know this? Don't you have a basket full of women's toothbrushes?"

Lisa had put two and two together and there wasn't much denying it now.

"Well, yeah, but it's dark when they come over. Sure, we make sure they're taken care of, but it's not the same."

"*Taken care of*?" Lisa laughed. "That was amazing."

Pat blushed and turned away again.

"What about Phaedra and her wife?"

"Andi?"

"Yeah. Do they have a *good time?*"

Pat frowned. "I'm not sure what you want me to say."

Lisa took a deep breath. "Have you ever bitten either of them?"

"Me? No. I told you they come here to relax."

"How did they find out?"

"Another woman was staying over while they were here. I had blood on my shirt and she was still under the influence. Phaedra thought I was abusing her. I panicked and had to explain everything."

"You thought telling her you were a vampire would be less shocking than abuse?" Lisa laughed.

Pat threw up her hands. "I told you, I panicked!"

Lisa shook her head in mock disbelief. "So, what, you just have girl parties out here in the woods?"

Pat shrugged. "I suppose you could call it that? A few vampires I know and some willing participants who want to experience the high. There's a jacuzzi and some other equipment. I won't have anyone over if that makes you uncomfortable."

"Wait, *other* equipment?"

Pat rubbed her face. "Are you sure you want to do this now?"

"Definitely."

Pat rolled her eyes. "Fine. Let me put some clothes on first."

Moments later Pat found herself giving Lisa a tour of the pool house and the various other equipment.

"St. Andrews cross, rack, pommel horse. Floggers and crops are in that cupboard over there. Ropes and cuffs are in that one over there." Pat pointed at each nonchalantly as though everyone had a private kink space on their property.

Lisa looked at her in astonishment. "Jesus, Pat."

"What?"

"How often does this get used?"

"There's a group of, er… like-minded individuals in the city that rents the space once a month. It's invite-only."

"And you?"

"I throw a private party once a year. The women who want to experience being bitten have other kinks. The equipment is mostly for them. It's hard for vampires to get into it when pain doesn't really mean anything."

Lisa raised an eyebrow. "I thought you'd…"

Pat shook her head.

"Huh." Lisa bit her lip. She was learning all sorts of things today. She wasn't sure how she felt about it, but if you're in love with a vampire, she supposed sex and blood would have to be part of the package. Unless she was going to be Pat's sole source. She didn't know how much blood Pat needed.

Pat locked the door to the unassuming A-frame. A crow yelled at her from the roof. Pat rolled her eyes. "Yes, we're hurrying. Fuck off." She gave the crow the middle finger. The crow flew away.

"What's going to happen?"

"I'm not sure. I assume Corinne is expecting me to help stop Willow."

"Wait, *the* Willow?"

Pat sighed and nodded. "She's the one I bit. She killed Josh. And who knows who else." She neglected to mention that Lisa had already met her, that Willow was the girl they'd pulled from the truck.

"And Tyler?"

"That was probably Corinne."

Lisa jerked away.

"I don't know, you'll have to ask her. Corinne doesn't usually kill someone without a reason."

"I thought you said she killed you."

"Yeah, 'cause she thought I was a man and she thought she could fuck me. You know how the venom feels."

"And she wanted to…" Lisa made a face. "With *Tyler?*"

"You're more of an expert on men than me."

"Maybe I'm less of an expert than I thought." Lisa looked away in disgust.

"Listen." Pat took Lisa's hands and stared pointedly into her coffee brown eyes. "I don't know how this is going to end, but I don't want you getting hurt. You should stay here."

"Absolutely not. I might not have loved Josh, but I owe him for what happened. And," Lisa placed her palm on Pat's chest. "I don't want you getting hurt either."

Pat blew out her cheeks. "Give me a second." Pat ran back into the pool house. She emerged a few moments later with a pair of handcuffs.

"I thought you said that sort of thing didn't interest you anymore."

"Cheeky." Pat held out the cuffs. "They're silver. They'll prevent her from being able to escape. You have police training. If she gets too close to you, use these."

"No crosses?"

"No. I've been in several churches. The only thing repellent about them is the smell of cheap furniture wax and old people."

"What about garlic? Or wooden stakes?"

"I could get you to stab me with a garlic infused hemlock stake, but we don't have time and not really my kink either. Corinne is already impatient." Pat held out her hand. Lisa took it.

It felt like coming home to a place long forgotten. Like somewhere she never should have left. Yes, details would need to be hashed out. Expectations would need to be tempered. Mundane tasks like food that wasn't blood or burnt pancakes.

But none of that mattered right now. *Now* was that perfect moment of twilight, just before night bled into day. That moment where the sun began to peek above the horizon, just before everything changed. Even though it was inevitable, she could still look back on what was.

Embrace it.

And then let it go.

twenty-seven

Southern Alberta receives some of the most unobstructed sunlight per year in the world – well over two thousand hours. Two vampires and a woman met by Bill's toolshed next to the town graveyard, sun splashing over their faces. That was on purpose.

Corinne stood in heels, piercing the damp, half thawed earth. A cigarette dangled from her slender fingertips.

"Smoking will kill you," Pat said loudly as she and Lisa approached.

"Fucking women will kill you." Corinne flicked ash in Pat's direction. "I'm pretty sure you lot have a higher death rate than smoking."

"Did you look that up?"

"On what? The *internet*." Corinne rolled her eyes. "With the blithering of soccer moms whinging about fen-phen and yoga so they can keep up with their spawn and the libidos of their bloated dough ball husbands."

"Are those Louboutin's?" Lisa pointed toward Corinne's heels.

Corinne pointed her cigarette toward Lisa. "I like her. It's about time you did something right. Just don't fuck it up."

"You're in a mood today. I thought you enjoyed biting those dough balls."

"*Biting* them, yes. Giving a shit if they fuck someone else?" Corinne waved her hand dismissively. "They aren't the prize these internet women seem to think they are." She tapped the ash from her cigarette and took a deep drag. "Anyway. We're not here to discuss marital fidelity."

Pat looked sceptical. "We're here because you care about people dying?"

"Not particularly. But there *have* been an awful lot of them lately."

"Weren't you responsible for at least one?"

Corinne huffed. Curls of smoke circled her head like an arrogant dragon. "That boy deserved to be bitten a long time ago. You had the right idea when you hit him with your truck."

"You know that Fred was the one who got me out of that?"

"What did you want me to do? They thought I killed that man with the woodchipper."

"You did."

"No, I killed him *before* he fell into the woodchipper." Corinne shook her head and took another puff.

"Whatever. Where is she?"

Corinne pointed toward a filthy stone mausoleum standing ostentatiously in a sea of flat grave markers. "You'll need to do this in the sun."

"I know."

"I know you know. *She* doesn't." Corinne tilted her head toward Lisa. Lisa looked confused. "I need you to make sure no-one gets close to the graveyard. Or we're going to make national news and the *internet* is going to take a break from talking about whiskey suppositories."

"You mean *butt chugging?*" Pat narrowed her eyes.

Corinne flapped her hands. "Yes, yes. It's all the rage now."

"What websites are you *on?*"

"Never mind that."

Lisa looked toward Pat. Pat nodded. Lisa turned to leave.

"Not so fast." Corrinne threw her cigarette butt on the ground and exhaled a thin stream of smoke. "I need to talk with her. Alone."

"Why?" Pat stood between Corinne and Lisa. Lisa peeked from behind Pat.

"Did you fall from the Christmas Tree? You should know better than to ask stupid questions. I've seen ahead. If you know, it won't go the way it needs to."

Pat pinched the bridge of her nose. Lisa laced her fingers through Pat's other hand. Pat relented. "It's okay." Pat squeezed. "She doesn't even *like* women. She won't bite you, she's just a bitch."

"A bitch who's helping you clean up your mess. You could say *thank you.*"

"Thanks, mom." Pat mocked.

Corinne waggled her fingers and shooed Pat away. Pat trundled off toward the mausoleum. Out of the corner of her eye, she saw Lisa walk back toward her truck. Corinne lit another cigarette.

The shadow of the mausoleum retreated, leaving what was left of the naked snow to fight in vain against the sun. Inside, two blue eyes glowed. Pat leaned against the smooth brick entrance, jutting her chin at the mess of mangled meat and blood cooling against the concrete floor.

"This your handiwork?"

"No, I found him like this. CPR didn't work."

"He have a good time, at least?"

Willow stepped over the corpse. "Bill was eighty, Pat. I don't think there are enough drugs in the world to have made him hard."

"Then why?"

"It brought you here."

Pat rubbed her jaw. "You know where I live. You could have come by at any time."

"Fine." Willow pursed her lips. "I tried. Do you know how humiliating it is trying to have sex with an eighty-year-old? Because that's my option? Slinking around in the dark, trying to find someone? Anyone?"

"What about…?"

"Women?" Willow interrupted. "I'm bi-curious at best, Pat. I'm sorry, but I tried it. Not for me. Even you." Willow bobbed her head back and forth. "I mean, if you had a dick and you bit me? But with a clear head? I just can't see it working out."

"Tell yourself what you want, but I didn't bite you in the wood shop."

"I wasn't *me* in the wood shop." Willow's nostrils flared. "Besides, you told me you were used to it."

Pat nodded slowly, staring at the pool of blood trickling toward her boots. "I'm sorry. I really am."

A fist cracked against her jaw, knocking her head back against the brick.

"Sorry?" Willow shrieked. "You have no idea."

"I have no idea, huh?" Pat cracked her neck. "Remember when I moved to this absurd shitsmudge of a town? I must have forgotten about all those women throwing themselves at me." Pat scoffed. "You saw what I went through. What you put Kyle through. I could have murdered every one of you quisling cockstains at any time."

"I wasn't part of that."

Pat tapped the toe of her boot against the ground. "No. I thought you were different."

"That's what I get for being nice to the town dyke."

Pat glowered. "That's what you thought you were doing?"

Willow met her stare. Neither blinked.

"*You* chose to hang out with *us*. Because your shit friends in this shit town ditched you when you dumped your shit fiancé."

"I was there for Kyle, not you."

"You kissed *me*, not Kyle."

"And *you* thought it meant *true love*," she mocked.

"And you did it again in the wood shop. Not as straight as you thought you were."

"Stockholm syndrome," Willow spat. "You wouldn't have taken me in if I was just a random woman in that truck. Or maybe you would have. You *do* like to play fast and loose with consent."

Pat stood up straighter. "I'm *always* invited. Somehow, I don't think Bill invited *you* in."

Willow grinned. "No, but Lisa did."

A pang of jealousy shot through her. Pat had inferred that's what had happened, but hearing it out loud made her enraged. Willow caught the twinge of pain across her face.

"She was delicious, by the way. Tropical fruit, a bit floral." Willow licked her lips. "And her pussy!"

Pat winced. "Not gay, eh."

"Oh, I didn't *really* care about that." Willow took a step toward her. "I know I can't hurt you. At least not in any way that counts." Willow grit her teeth and jammed her fingers into Pat's liver. Pat growled and grabbed her throat, but Willow's smirk didn't leave her face. Pat clenched her abdominals. There was a sickening crack of fingerbones snapping and a squelch when Willow withdrew her mangled hand.

Willow reset her fingers. "See what I mean?"

"So, what? You're just going to be a bitch to me forever? Get in line." Pat hoisted Willow off the ground, her feet dancing in the air like a hanged man. "Gotta admit, I was hoping for more creativity, but I can respect a classic - provided you can pull it off. Most covers are worse."

Willow wriggled against Pat's grip but still managed to croak out. "Twilight fanfics were better than the original."

"Only when she ends up with Alice."

Willow curled her lip.

"Into the Jacob-Edward ships, eh? How common. Sorry you went through all this only to find out you really are the same as the rest of them."

Willow dissolved into the shadow of the mausoleum, but only far enough to escape Pat's grip.

"What a surprise. A man-hating lesbian." Willow massaged her throat. "What a boring stereotype."

"I didn't try to fuck an eighty-year-old. I suppose that shows more commitment to getting male attention than your average basic white girl, so you win. Where should I mail your prize?"

Willow screamed and launched herself toward Pat, arm poised to strike, but Pat caught her wrist and held it effortlessly.

"I'm sorry you're not that special, even as a vampire. There are only three of us here, and the other one hates me too. Common as fucking dirt."

Pat smirked. Willow spat.

"What about you? Do you hate yourself too? It must hurt the ego knowing that women only fuck you because you drug them."

"Tell yourself what you like," Pat scoffed. "Apparently even straight girls chase me."

Willow sulked. A lifetime of abuse had sharpened Pat's wit to a razor's edge. She couldn't compete. "Must be nice to bite the people you actually want to fuck."

"It is."

"Have some empathy." Willow clenched her fists. "Think of what it would feel like if you could only bite men."

"Oh, now you want empathy. After you hateful bastards beat me within an inch of my life? After I was turned on accident because Corinne can't tell the difference between men and women? After you snivelling bloodbags exhausted yourselves trying to make the new kid miserable? How's this for empathy? I *can* bite men."

For a few moments, the only sound was Willow's ragged breathing.

"What?"

"Male blood doesn't affect me. They just taste like a skid mark," Pat sneered.

Willow flailed uselessly, but Pat's arms were longer.

"Do you know *why* Corinne hates me? Because I refused to turn Fred. But even *she* knew it was a terrible idea."

Willow growled and slipped into the shadow again.

Pat grinned. "There are no shadows outside of these walls."

Willow seethed in the corner. "Let's get one thing straight."

"I don't do straight."

Willow rolled her eyes. "*You* did this to me. *You're* the one who brought me back just to live a sexless existence skulking in corners, preying on frustrated women."

"I already told you that you don't have to."

"Oh, how kind." Willow mocked. She leaned against the wall. "I get to live like a nun, forever hungry with no abilities and the constant urge to bite people. Fuck you."

"I already apologised." Pat moved over to Willow and leaned against the wall with her. "And yeah, you're right to be angry. But you can't take it out on random people."

Willow turned to look at Pat, a glint in her blue eyes. "Oh, I can. See?" She pointed at the mass of flesh that had been Bill. "Remember? Monsters." Willow gestured back and forth between the two of them.

"You'd better plan on moving to a city then. You're going to run out of men at the rate you're going."

"Oh, I'm not going anywhere." Willow laughed and made toward the door. "You brought me back to live in this hell. I'm going to make sure you regret it forever."

twenty-eight

Lisa pulled a ribbon of yellow police line tape across the gate to the cemetery. The department had ordered an entire case of it ten years ago and Jacob couldn't remember the last time they'd gotten to use it. He acted like a kid getting a new puppy when Lisa burst into the precinct and ordered him to get it. Sherri didn't even ask what had happened. She just shook her head and kept typing.

As soon as Lisa finished unrolling one spool, Jacob handed her another.

"I think we have enough, Jacob."

"Yeah, but someone could come from over there." Jacob pointed to the Miller's farm on the east end of the cemetery.

"No-one is coming from over there." Lisa tried to control her tone, but Jacob practically vibrated with enthusiasm.

"But what's stopping them?"

"An entire quarter section of dead flax?" Lisa looked at him like he was simple. "You'd have to walk all morning to cross it. And the road's already blocked off." Lisa waved her hand toward the squad trucks with their flashing blue and red lights.

"Still." Jacob bounced on his toes.

Lisa sighed. "Fine. Take some stakes and string up some more tape." Jacob ran off, almost at a gallop. "But you're taking it all down when we're done here," Lisa yelled. Jacob didn't hear her.

Lisa blew an errant lock away from her face. Corinne had told her to block off the road. And then to stay by the gates. As if she had any authority to tell an RCMP officer what to do. And Lisa had done it anyway. Maybe it was compulsion, but Pat hadn't mentioned anything about that. She would have to ask her later, when she gave Pat the message Corinne had relayed.

Lisa craned her neck to see if she could spot Pat in the field. All she saw were the patches of snow on the flat grave markers melting in the sun. Soggy brown grass covered everything else.

She felt the urge to go look for her, but Corinne had been very clear.

"Deviating, even a little, will bring catastrophe." Corinne had said.

"What sort of catastrophe."

Corinne listed off consequences with the nonchalance of a grocery list. "You'll die. Pat will die. So will most of the people in this festering herpes sore of a town."

Lisa felt her ears heat. "You hate this town."

"Very much so, yes."

"Then why do you…"

"I'm telling you this for *your* sake, not mine." Corinne swatted the question away before Lisa could complete it. "On your own head, be it."

"Psalm 7:16." Lisa spouted. She surprised herself at the automatic response. It had been years.

Corinne raised an eyebrow.

"Religious family." Lisa looked at the mud sheepishly.

"Do they know you're…" Corinne gestured up and down Lisa's body."

"Gay?"

"Whatever you're calling yourselves now. I don't keep up."

Lisa shook her head.

"Hmm. Where do they live?"

"Regina."

Corinne straightened her posture. "I'll take care of it."

"Take care of what? You're not going to kill them, are you?" Lisa scanned the horizon for Pat.

"Why? Should I?"

"No! What are you, a vampire mafia? I can just put out hits on people?"

"A brilliant idea that I should have had years ago. Completely unfeasible *now*, of course, with all of your cameras and other baubles. But I knew I liked you for a reason." Corinne smiled sweetly. "Much better than that other one. I'm so happy she's finally come to her senses."

"What? Who?"

"Pat, of course."

"I thought you hated Pat."

"Whyever would you think that?" Corinne curled her lip.

Lisa poked her tongue against her cheek. "She told me you hated her. And you treat her like she's an idiot."

"A mother can be disappointed in her daughter, you know. It doesn't mean I *hate* her. *You* of all people should know *that.*" Corinne crossed her arms pointedly. "I'm sure *your* parents wouldn't approve of *you,*" she muttered.

Lisa crossed her arms back. "Pat told me about how *disappointed* you were that she wasn't a man."

Corinne brows pulled in. She hadn't had to deal with people in a very long time. It felt invasive that Lisa knew this about her. "Yes, I *did* try to eat her. But she's still my daughter. I don't *want* to see her miserable." Corinne placed a finger on her lips. "Most of the time. Sometimes it's entertaining."

Lisa covered her mouth to hide her lip curling in disgust.

"Oh stop. You only think she's so wonderful because you're smitten. I can't fathom why."

"I don't," Lisa blew out her cheeks. "I don't understand your weird family dynamics. You say you don't hate her, but you act like she's the worst person alive."

Corinne sighed and looked at the ground for a moment before meeting Lisa's stare. "Patrice is the strongest woman you or I will ever meet. She refused those filthy men in the bar and they nearly beat her to death. She stood up to these backwater bastards and they shot her. She even stood up to me." Corinne lowered her eyes. "She never fails to jump at the sun with a hoe, but she was right every single time."

"Then why do you treat her like that?"

"Because I can't forgive her for it."

Lisa watched Corinne stare at her extinguished cigarette for several moments before she was ready to meet her eyes.

"When all of this is over, tell her something for me, will you?"

"You can't tell her yourself?"

Corinne scoffed and waved her hand. "I'm leaving this humourless joke they've convinced themselves is a town."

Lisa rolled her eyes. "Fine. What do you want me to tell her?"

"Tell her that I'm proud of her and to get to the crematorium." Corinne turned away to face the toolshed.

Lisa waited for her to say something further, but Corinne just waved her hand dismissively and refused to turn around.

"You just do what I told you. Quickly, now!"

The early March sun had begun its descent, but the clear Alberta skies and the lack of trees meant that shadows would not appear for another hour still.

The sunlight warmed the air a lot more than the patches of snow would indicate. Lisa sat in the squad truck with the door and her vest open.

Corinne had been scarce on the details - only insisting that she stick to her instructions. Lisa caught a figure approaching from the corner of her eye. Her heart leapt at the thought of Pat returning to her, but she didn't walk like Pat. The figure had cropped, dark hair. Messy, like she'd cut it herself.

Lisa got out of the truck and waited. Something about the woman walking toward her made her nervous. She shook her arms, trying to relieve the tension that shouldn't be there. Lisa didn't see any weapons or indication that the woman meant her harm.

But why was she there? The cemetery had been empty when they had arrived. Had she shown up in the ten minutes it took Lisa to gather Jacob and his box of police tape? Maybe Jacob was right and she'd been just on the other side of the Miller's flax field. Lisa craned her neck to the east to see if Jacob was anywhere nearby, but all she saw was yellow plastic ribbon flapping lazily in the gentle breeze.

Lisa activated her radio. "Officer McLeod, come in." A few moments of quiet static passed. "Officer McLeod." Still nothing. "Jacob, answer your damn radio."

"This is dispatch. He left it on his desk again."

"Goddammit Jacob," Lisa swore.

"When you find him, tell him he owes us all coffee. Again."

Lisa shook her head. "Thanks, Sherri."

The channel went silent. Lisa turned her attention back to the woman who had now crossed most of the cemetery. Blood covered her face and most of her shirt. Lisa sprang into action. She grabbed the first aid bag from the SUV and ran.

At twenty feet away, it hit her. It was the girl Pat had pulled from the wreckage, but her hair was different. Pat had said she'd left! What was she doing here? Lisa realised that she had never been told her name.

"Officer Tanner, RCMP," Lisa shouted. "I can provide first aid. Can you show me where your injury is?"

The woman stopped and tilted her head. "It's not my blood."

"Can you take me to the person who is injured?"

The woman stared at Lisa a bit too long, seemingly confused by the request.

"You might be in shock." Lisa pulled a foil blanket from the bag and draped it across the woman's shoulders. "Do you remember me? I was there when Pat pulled you from the truck." Lisa looked into the woman's eyes, checking for uneven dilation.

The woman nodded. "I remember."

Lisa pulled on a pair of gloves. "Can I check you for injury? There's a lot of blood around your face."

The girl nodded.

Lisa examined the woman's head and face, but found nothing that could have possibly produced this much blood.

"I told you, it's not mine."

Lisa handed her some paper towels. "What happened?"

The woman wiped her face. "I'll show you." She pointed toward the Miller's property.

She walked off, foil blanket snapping in the breeze like a cape. Lisa followed. Yellow police tape demarcated the edge of the cemetery, right up to a small hillock with a small copse of trembling aspen, buds still unwilling to accept that spring lurked just around the corner.

The woman turned to skirt the hillock.

"The last time we met, you couldn't remember your name. Do you remember mine?"

"Lisa." The woman didn't turn around.

I need to keep her talking so I don't lose her to shock, Lisa thought. "Pat said you'd recovered your memory before you left. Can I have your name?"

The woman turned and flashed her a smile. They seemed familiar, but she couldn't place it. Lisa dismissed it. She must just be remembering her from when they pulled her from the wreckage.

"Rowan."

"Nice to meet you, Rowan. Now where's this injury?"

"Just behind the hill." The woman pointed. Lisa jogged ahead to inspect.

The sun splashed aspen shadows toward the flax field. A body lay crumpled against the soggy vegetation.

Lisa dropped her bag. There would be nothing in it sufficient to deal with the extent of the person's injuries. Their body was simply too far gone.

Body was a generous term. The corpse gave the impression of a sack of ground beef, loosely held together by blood-soaked clothing.

Just like Josh.

Just like the man in the truck.

Lisa turned to the woman. Her iridescent blue eyes seemed to glow from her backlit silhouette.

"Phaedra," Lisa mouthed.

"Rowan," the girl corrected.

"Phaedra has brown eyes."

Rowan squinted. "I'm not following. Are you sure you're not the one who needs this?" She held out the foil blanket.

"Phaedra has brown eyes," she repeated. Lisa brought her hand to her mouth. "It was you that night. You killed Josh."

Rowan snorted and crossed her arms. "One, I did you a favour, and two, he sucked in bed. No wonder you were obsessed with Pat."

Lisa unbuckled the snap on her holster.

Rowan rolled her eyes. "Please. I'm sure you know by now that won't do anything."

"You're not *Rowan* either, are you? You're Pat's daughter." Lisa's head swam. Pat had known who she was when she'd pulled her from the truck. But then again, how could she have told Lisa? Lisa hadn't even known she was a vampire back then.

"Yes. Willow." She delighted in the realisation that spread over Lisa's face. "That's right. I'm *that* Willow. We have a few more moments until Pat figures out where I went. I'm curious what you've heard."

Lisa's hand didn't leave her pistol. "That the town bullied you after they found out you were gay. Then you killed yourself."

"I didn't kill myself. And I'm not gay. How the fuck does this town keep getting that wrong?" Willow threw up her hands in exasperation.

Lisa kept her eyes locked on Willow, bracing herself for any sudden moves.

"I overdosed. By accident," she emphasised. "And I kissed Pat *once*. That doesn't make me *gay*. She was the one stupid enough to turn me *after* I had died. Now I get to live like *this* forever."

Lisa huffed. "She said if people found out, she'd have a lineup of women begging to be turned at her doorstep."

"Yeah, well." Willow sucked her teeth. "Pat seems to think that this is all sunshine and roses. But most women like men, Lisa."

Lisa wasn't sure how to respond, but it didn't matter.

"No, you wouldn't understand." Willow continued. "Because you're a fucking dyke, just like her." She flew at Lisa

Lisa's fingers tensed around the pistol and fired. If she hit, it didn't matter. Willow's grip on her throat was too strong.

twenty-nine

At 6 o'clock, the only shadows in the cemetery were cast by the mausoleum and the tool shed. A slight dimming of the light simply wasn't sufficient. Pat had run from one end of the cemetery to the other trying to track down Willow, but all she had found were row upon row of flat grave markers.

A shot rang out in the northeast corner. Pat swore and sped off as quickly as she could. At full effort, it still took her three minutes to run the length of the field.

A stand of bare aspen trees and their lonely shadows provided the only hint of cover. A solitary crow perched in their branches. They must be there. Pat willed herself to move faster.

"There you are." Willow grinned, holding Lisa so that her toes barely touched the ground. Pat froze. Lisa's face had not yet turned grey. She must be trying to drag this out for as long as possible.

"Let her go." Pat jammed her hands into her pockets, walking calmly the remainder of the distance. "She's got nothing to do with this."

"This?" Willow spat. "What exactly is *this*?"

"Whatever issue you have with me. Take it out on me."

The light shifted from orange to red. Willow's murderous grin adopted the angry hue.

"Shadows won't save you," Pat warned. "You've had days of practice. I've had years."

"Save me?" Willow hoisted Lisa further. Lisa's hands wrapped around Willow's wrists. "You can't kill me anymore than I can kill you."

"How sure are you about that?"

Willow squeezed harder. Lisa sputtered. The red horizon slowly faded.

Pat flicked her eyes to Lisa's. "If you kill her, I'll spend every waking moment making your life a living hell."

"It already is," Willow hissed.

Pat crossed her legs and sat, ignoring the wet and cold grass. "You have an eternity. Why chase me around this dump? You'll get bored of it after a day or two. Go to the city, eat as many men as you want."

Willow started getting agitated. She wanted Pat on her knees, begging her to spare Lisa, but she acted like they were having a fucking picnic. What use was Lisa if Pat didn't care? She must be more heartless than she thought. More of a monster.

Her chest heaved with anger, fingers tensing around Lisa's throat. Lisa whimpered. If she survived, she'd need several visits to a physiotherapist after dangling by her neck for this long.

"Fine," she seethed. "I'll make you a deal."

"You may have dated a used car salesman, but that's not how this works."

Willow clenched her jaw. "I'll let Lisa live."

Pat raised her eyebrow. "Why haven't you killed her already? You weren't so kind to her partner over there." Pat jutted her chin toward the mangled body.

Willow growled.

"Or did you try to fuck him too? It's hard to tell with the mess you made. A bit of a cockup, to be honest."

"Fuck you."

Pat shook her head. "No, that was earlier. Back when you weren't insisting that you weren't gay."

Willow screamed in frustration, but she couldn't reach Pat – not without dropping Lisa. "This is why everyone hates you!"

"Huh." Pat pawed at the back of her neck. "I always thought it was the hair."

"No! It's because you're an asshole and you always have a stupid retort. *You* did this to me! *I'm* not the one being unreasonable here!"

"But you are holding someone by the neck."

"Pretend all you want, but *you're* the monster. Not me."

"Just like how you're not gay."

Willow grit her teeth.

"I know, I know." Pat held up her hands. "You tried to fuck an eighty-year-old to prove the point."

Willow trembled with rage, but Pat kept going.

"I know Jacob over there was related to Cory Winter, so his parts might not be what you expected, but I hope he was better than Bill."

"You," Willow hissed, "will go with me to the city."

"Why?"

"Because I'm going to pick one out and *you're* going to turn him."

Pat shook her head. "I can't do that."

The last of the sun's rays disappeared behind the horizon, camouflaging the change on Willow's face.

"I don't care if you don't like the taste. You *owe* me."

Pat sighed. "Venom carries a part of you. That, plus your death is enough to turn you. Turning another person requires a bigger sacrifice and losing that much venom would kill me. I couldn't even if I wanted to."

"Fine, then we'll kill two people."

"And you call me the monster?" Pat rested her head in her hands. "You don't get to choose which two people. Even if you could, I wouldn't."

"Why not?" Willow whinged. "I can't live like this. You owe me this much, Pat."

Pat picked at the dead grass. "I can bite men, fine. Their blood doesn't affect me as much. What happens after I turn one, though?" Pat threw a stalk absentmindedly and picked another. "Corinne hated me for not trying, but she knew what would happen. She knew that if I turned Fred, his own blood would drive him mad." She locked eyes with Willow. "Remember what happened when you, me and Kyle went to my place and you kissed me?"

"What does that have to do with anything?"

"Caleb and Tyler showed up. With a gun. Men can barely control themselves now. And you want me to make them worse?" Pat could see a flash of understanding cross Willow's face, but only for a moment.

"A male vampire will be like a stray with rabies."

"You just hate men."

"I mean," Pat shrugged and threw another blade of grass at the ground. "It was men who couldn't get over me not wanting to fuck them. Men who beat me. Men who shot me when I let you kiss me. If anyone has a reason, it's me."

"Not all men are bad. You seemed fine with Fred. And Josh." Willow lowered Lisa a fraction of an inch, her arm getting tired.

"You're the one who said I hated men. I just said I had a reason." Pat uncrossed her legs and stood, slipping her hands into the pockets of her Carhartt's again. "Yet, you've killed more of them in the last two days than I have in the last fifteen years."

The last of the sun's light melted away and Willow roared in frustration.

Pat pointed her head toward an aspen. "Put her down. You're both getting tired."

Willow grunted and slammed Lisa against the tree. Lisa gasped, but was too spent to fight back. Willow pinned her, using the tree as a crutch to keep standing.

"Look. I know how frustrating it is to want something and not be able to have it. I'll talk to Corinne and see if she'll teach you how to control yourself. I can do that much for you at least."

Willow grunted. The anger had exhausted her. "How did you find out?"

"Find out what?"

"That you could bite men."

Pat curled her lip darkly. "Corinne was there when I returned for the wankers that beat me senseless. She hadn't told me anything. Probably thought it would be amusing to watch me bite them to death. She's like that."

Pat flicked her eyes to Lisa to make sure she was still okay. "But it didn't go like she thought it would. I didn't kill them in a frenzy. I crippled them in a warehouse so they couldn't get away. I made sure they died properly. Made sure they knew that the woman who wouldn't serve her purpose hadn't learned her lesson. That no man would be able to teach it to me either. 'Cause I'm a monster, remember?

Willow didn't know that she could be afraid if she couldn't feel pain. But Pat's words, lacking all remorse, caused a shudder. They came from a dark place, deep within, built brick by brick from a lifetime of rejection and abuse.

But it wasn't enough. She had her own problems. Willow relaxed her fingers around Lisa's neck. She could accept that Pat had suffered. That Pat had been dealt an awful hand in her first life. She could wrap her mind around how Pat might want to make up for it in this one.

Because she wanted the same thing. She wanted to break free of her parents' control. She wanted to live beyond the confines of this town's expectations. She wanted to explore herself, her own desires. The difference was that Pat now had the opportunity and she did not. All she had was enough immortality to watch impotently as everyone else got to experience what she wanted.

Willow grit her teeth before she found the words. "I get that your life sucked."

Pat stared, unblinking at the shadow crossing Willow's face. She'd heard enough conversations that started with *I get* to know what came next.

"I get that you've been hurt."

"Killed," Pat corrected.

"And bullied. But you've had the last eighteen years to live how you wanted." Her eyes darkened. "It's my turn now."

Pat inhaled slowly. "You want me to kill myself so you can fuck a man?"

"You already got what you wanted!" Willow's fingers flexed.

"I'm not sure how I can be any more clear about what will happen. Even if, by some miracle it works, you'll be stuck with that one man forever. It will be Caleb all over again, but a million times worse. You won't control him, he'll control you." Pat made sure Willow was looking at her. "And I'll be dead, so I won't be able to help you this time."

Willow took several breaths. Tears gathered and settled on her face, glistening in the starlight as they fell.

"At least wait until you find one you want to be with forever."

"You get to fuck whoever you want," Willow grumbled. But she knew Pat was right. The only thing worse than her present circumstances was being a prisoner again. "But you *owe* me. When I find one, you're doing it."

"If. And I'm not making any promises. It wasn't just me who refused Corinne. Fred also refused."

Willow stared at her knees and shifted, like she was about to flee from embarrassment. She shifted again. Pat's eyebrows pinched together, trying to figure out what she was doing.

Willow looked over at Lisa, her fingers still loosely wrapped around her throat. Only now, her wrist bore a silver handcuff, the other end wrapped around Lisa's arm.

Willow screamed and tore her throat.

thirty

Lisa sputtered, blood cascading down her shirt. Her head lolled backward at a sickening angle against the tree. Willow tried to run, only to be jerked back to the ground by the weight of Lisa's body.

Pat slammed her fist into Willow's jaw, knocking her head back against the aspen so hard it shook. The lone crow cawed in annoyance and flapped away to another branch.

Lisa's injury was fatal. Anyone with eyes could see. They could be sitting in an operating room, prepped and ready with a team of medical professionals and every single one would be hanging their heads instead of springing into action. Her coffee-coloured eyes stared, grasping toward Pat, but she had lost too much blood to move.

Willow's head ricocheted forward from the trunk, vision doubled and blood running down her neck. She yanked impotently at the cuff. Lisa's arm dragged against the dirt, lifeless. Willow wasn't strong enough to break the chain that connected them, nor could she carry Lisa. She was trapped, but she still had the upper hand.

"Break it," she hissed through pointed teeth, Lisa's blood still coating them garishly.

Both of them knew the choice. Free Willow and save Lisa at the cost of her own life, or live, take revenge and let Lisa die. Live with the memory forever. She had less than seconds to make it and both of them knew what she would choose. The crow cawed obscenities.

Pat slammed her hand against the tiny silver chain, smashing it against the tree. Willow scrambled to her feet and bolted, a single cuff still attached firmly to her wrist. She would have to find something else to remove it, but at least she had a head start. Bill's shed would have the tools she needed.

Willow ran toward the west end of the cemetery. It would be a five-minute jog on a good day, but it was dark and Willow's head still spun. The frailty of the human condition weighed heavily on her. Once she got this damn cuff off and was able to heal again, she would make them all pay. This time, Pat wouldn't be around to stop her.

Pat leaped forward and sunk her teeth into what remained of Lisa's neck. Pineapple and rosewater. The last taste of the only woman she had ever loved.

Pat did not know what to expect. It had been so long since a vampire had attempted to convert a second person that such knowledge was lost. If Corinne knew, she had never mentioned it.

Venom flowed, along with the last of herself. Even as she drank, her teeth retracted. The borrowed years piled on. Every torn muscle. Every breath of overexertion. Every cracked rib and broken bone that should have happened over the decades manifested themselves. Her lungs burned. She gasped, rolling backward against the sodden grass.

Pat had forgotten pain - not the pain of heartbreak, or the death of a loved one. Those would never disappear. Actual, physical pain. She had forgotten how it took away your ability to breathe. How it lingered stubbornly weeks after the injury had faded. How it could blind you, even though the blow had landed nowhere near your eyes.

The world faded into a swirl of dark greys and stars smeared across the sky. Alarmed voices turned into a muffled wash. And then a trickle until all that remained was the liquid *whoosh* of blood passing through her veins from an ever-slowing heartbeat.

Another flash of pain told her that Lisa's teeth had found her neck. Lisa would live. Lisa would take her vengeance, but Pat would not be there to see it. She would make a better vampire than Pat had ever been. A smarter one, at least.

She would need to flee this town. It's what she wanted anyway. Her and Willow could fight for eternity. Or fuck. She didn't know. Or care. As long as Lisa was happy.

Willow.

She would never get what she wanted now. Pat was gone and with her, her only chance at turning a man. A pity, Pat thought. She could have learned to control herself. Corinne could have taught her. But she had refused. Willow wanted everything immediately and now she had ruined her only chance. Foolish. But then again, so was Pat at that age.

Corinne had been wrong. Pat was not the one who would break her curse. If it even existed. Her ability to see ahead hadn't helped them either. Pat didn't know how far her vision extended. Corinne had always been cagey about her abilities, only showing them off when she thought it would impress you. Or annoy you.

She hoped Corinne would be nicer to Lisa. She would need some help and she doubted Willow would give it. Willow didn't know anything anyway. She had done nothing but cause problems. *That's what you get for biting a straight girl.* Not straight. Not that it mattered now. Willow would probably run off somewhere else. She hoped she would. Even though Pat hated this town and everyone in it, the thought of Willow slaughtering them all didn't appeal to her.

Pat had had the opportunity. She had more reason to hate them than Willow. She had killed in revenge once already. She knew she was capable. But something had held her back. Even though they provoked her every day. Why, she didn't know. Perhaps she wasn't the monster she thought she was.

Another flash of pain. This time on the other side. Strange that Lisa would bite her twice. Or perhaps not. Lisa had only just found out Pat was a vampire. Pat and Corinne hadn't had time to explain much. She had no idea how things worked. And Pat couldn't stop her.

Unless they weren't Lisa's teeth. Willow maybe? Perhaps she was still so angry that if she couldn't get what she wanted from Pat, she would deal the finishing blow. That made sense. Pat knew she deserved it.

The dull sound of passing blood in her ears slowed. Pat recognised the feeling of warm glitter trickling through her arteries. First her arm. Then her chest. Her legs. The other arm. Finally, her head. The heartbeats slowed and stopped entirely. *Strange how dying feels like venom,* she thought.

Rather than a bright light, Pat found the opposite. The dark grey of her vision faded into Vantablack, first at the edges until the patch of lighter coloured darkness shrunk into a pinpoint. Like an old T.V. that glowed for several minutes after you clicked it off. The ghostly radiation of a connection to someone unfathomably far away suddenly severed, but you still felt the residual warmth of their fingertips where they had pressed against your palm.

Pat breathed her last.

If you ask someone who has been declared dead, they will tell of a light, or memories of loved ones. That is not death. That is dying. Death is the absence of everything. It is the complete and utter erasure of all that you are and all that you ever will be. Coming back to your body is not possible, because who you are ceases to exist even before your body is reclaimed by the earth.

The exception is being turned. With venom, enough of the other person is within you that they can make that Faustian bargain on your behalf. They protect you from deletion by offering themselves in your stead. Which is why it can only be done once.

The exception again, was Pat – hidden away in a mother's embrace, shielded from Death's relentless and unforgiving stare.

Against the black, someone had thrown a bucket of red paint and now it coated the figures hiding in her vision. She could see them. Not clearly, but their liquid forms dripping as they moved. She saw their blood.

Pat lurched upward, teeth springing forth, latching onto one of them, drinking until the figure disappeared. Pat recognised the taste, but that had been years ago. It couldn't be her.

Her vision still tinged red, but now it was from wrath. She caught Willow's crimson-outlined silhouette fleeing. A silver bracelet around her wrist glinted in time with her arms in the starlight.

Pat sped through the shadows. There was no epic battle. No long-awaited nemesis. No thrill in the exertion of muscles or glee at the chance to prove her worth. This was a regretted execution. Willow was not a match for Pat, even without the silver handcuff.

Pat stumbled as she walked back to the copse of aspens, only now questioning why she still breathed. Lisa hunched over the ground. Pat tried but couldn't see what she was doing. Her eyes still wouldn't focus properly. Lisa turned, wide eyed to see Pat, covered in blood and holding Willow's head.

Lisa launched herself into Pat's arms, knocking her back several steps. Lisa appeared to have gained a significant amount of strength and Pat had been unprepared.

Lisa pulled Pat's head back to look at her. "I thought I'd lost you!"

"I thought *I'd* lost *you*!" Pat echoed back.

Lisa ran her hand over Pat's buzzcut. "Your hair is white!"

Pat rolled her eyes upward to see, but couldn't. "I'll take your word for it."

Lisa laughed.

"Does it look good at least?"

"It makes you look even more badass."

"I was going for *leave me alone*, but I'll take it."

Lisa planted her lips firmly against Pat's. Pat broke away first. She needed to know.

"What happened? What did you do? Why am I still here?"

Lisa shook her head. "I remember waking up angry. I bit you. I thought I could save you if I did, but nothing happened."

Lisa turned toward the spot where she had been crouching. Pat recognised Corinne in the rapidly decaying corpse. She started toward her, but Lisa held her back. "She's gone."

Pat glanced quickly back at Lisa. Lisa's tears glinted as they fell. "She pushed me away. She said I couldn't do anything more." Lisa pointed toward the body. Pat noticed the other end of the silver cuff. "And then she bit you and this happened."

Pat held up her arm with the cuff. "This is why. Do you have the key?"

Lisa fished around in her pocket and held it out. Pat unlocked the cuff and it fell uselessly on the ground. "You can't do most vampire things wearing silver. It's about the only things the books got right."

Lisa sniffed in confusion. Pat rubbed at her chest, staring blankly at Corinne's remains. "She was there when her mother got caught." Pat's shoulders slumped forward. Lisa placed a hand on her back.

"She told me that she was extremely cautious for years afterwards, and still, she almost got caught. She insisted that Carmilla was about her, so she fed a bunch of bullshit to Stoker. It worked, more or less." Pat breathed a laugh. "She's been staked a few times now. Turns out it was *me* that killed her."

Lisa slipped her arm around Pat's waist. "She told me she was proud of you."

Pat fell forward on her knees, her face contorted in an ugly grimace. Pat couldn't remember the last time she had truly cried. She had remained defiant when her parents had asked her to leave. Enraged at her coworkers when they had beaten her. Sorrow at the time wasted without Lisa. Confrontational in the face of constant harassment from the town. But tears hadn't streamed unrestrained until now.

Corinne may have been a bitch – an ugly word, but Corinne wore it proudly. She showed no empathy and resented her for doing the right thing. But she was a bitch who sacrificed herself for Pat.

"Do you want to talk about it?" Lisa skimmed her fingers across Pat's shoulders.

Pat stared at Corinne's corpse for a few more moments before she answered. "I don't know." She reached across her chest and laced her fingers through Lisa's. "I didn't know she loved me that much, but when I think back on everything she did for me? It was more than my own mother." Pat waffled her head "That was a low bar, though. I always thought she did it out of guilt or obligation. She certainly never said anything nice to me."

Lisa slid her arms across Pat's neck and hugged her. "You're terrible at reading people."

"What?" Pat turned her head.

Lisa planted a kiss on her forehead. "I've been throwing myself at you for years and you didn't notice."

"Oh."

Lisa rolled her eyes. *"Oh."*

"I thought it would never work, so I didn't consider the possibility."

"You had your head up your ass, you mean."

Pat groaned. "I'm sorry."

"You're such a golden retriever."

"A what?"

Lisa squeezed. "Never mind. Now you're *my* golden retriever."

"I'll be whatever you want."

"That's such a golden retriever thing to say." Lisa slapped her playfully.

"I don't..."

"You don't go on the internet at all, do you?"

"Why would I?"

Lisa held her for a few more moments before Pat spoke. "So, what now?"

"Corinne said you need to go to the crematorium."

Pat turned to look at Willow's head. It stared angrily, like it wasn't quite dead.

"That cuff will keep her from regenerating, but she won't be fully dead until I burn the body."

Lisa looked around the cemetery. "We have a lot of clean-up to do, don't we?"

"Think we can blame wild animals again?"

Lisa shook her head. "They're going to hunt down every wolf, cougar and bear in the tri-county area."

Pat sighed. "Alright. I'll get Fred's hearse and we can get started."

Pat hadn't been in the back of the funeral home since Fred had let her see Willow. The sterile white tiles and overwhelming smell of cleaners and embalming fluids tended to keep people away - even if you didn't get weirded out by people putting makeup on corpses.

She passed row upon row of *Most Efficient Funeral Home* certificates - awarded because almost no blood made it down the drain. Corinne had taken care of that. Pat skimmed her finger along the stainless-steel embalming table, delaying taking the neatly stacked pile of papers for as long as possible.

The first bore the bison head sigil of the RCMP - a copy of Lisa's medical discharge, dated for tomorrow. She no longer had a job. Pat wondered if Lisa knew that. A second letter was addressed to her parents, informing them that Lisa had been KiA. A yellow sticky note read *optional*.

Underneath those, she found the death certificates for Josh (CoD *smoke inhalation*), Bill (CoD *cardiac arrest*) and Jacob (CoD *envenomation - rattlesnake*), all signed and stamped with the coroner's seal. Pat smiled, imagining Corinne letting herself into the coroner's office to *borrow* his seal.

Beneath those, Pat found a copy of Fred's last will and testament, leaving everything to her, along with the deed to the land, the house, and the funeral home. And finally, Corinne's note.

The letter had no envelope. It was a simple folded piece of lined note paper. Understated and unassuming. Even in death, Corinne was unable to communicate the small gestures that might indicate she cared a little too much.

Pat unfolded the note.

Patrice,

If you didn't fuck it up, I will be gone and you will be left to clean up the mess. Of course, I've already done most of it for you. You're welcome. You could stand to be more grateful. But I know you won't be. You're a baby, still holding on to petty grievances. You'll come around in a few hundred years.

Lisa is too good for you. Yet for some unfathomable reason, she wants you. If only seeing ahead allowed me to see what she does in you. Alas, it does not. You have no idea what you've done. The first time may have been an accident, but if you piss away this second opportunity, I'll find some way to come back and make you regret it. You may have subverted the curse and every vampire after you will be happy, but don't forget that I was the one who helped you do it.

Don't celebrate too much, because now you're stuck here for the foreseeable future. You and Lisa will run this place like Fred and I did. You'll have to put up with these ignorant hayseeds for a while longer – no hiding in your weird little compound outside of town. Try not to kill everyone. Fred won't be there to bail you out if you hit someone with your truck again.

I know we weren't close. I know you had hoped I would show you the affection your own mother hadn't, even if you never said it. In that, I failed. I was angry that you got to enjoy what I never could.

Even my gift wasn't entirely selfless. There will never be another Fred. He was better than both of us. Don't waste his memory.

With regrets,
Corinne

Pat grabbed the keys to Fred's hearse and jammed them into her pockets, as if action could wipe the tears from her face.

epilogue

"You're sure you want to do this?" Lisa wiped away the ring of tea her mug had left on the oak table.

Pat could be heard in the kitchen, scrubbing incinerated bacon off of the cast iron pan.

Phaedra turned to her wife. "What do you think, Andi?"

"Honestly, I don't see a downside. Who doesn't want a hot vampire wife?"

"Sounds like something a lesbian would say," Pat yelled.

Phaedra pursed her lips, biting the inside of her cheek. The shaggy wolf cut Lisa remembered had turned greyer. Shorter, too – more of an overgrown pixie now. Pat may have her heart, but Phaedra was still hot. Lisa could picture twenty-something's throwing themselves at her. Andi probably had to threaten them away with sticks.

"Your heart is racing, dear." Pat yelled from the kitchen. "I can smell your blood from here."

Lisa blushed.

"Hands off my wife," Andi prodded. "Unless I'm there."

Phaedra swatted her. She always was quieter, preferring to let her expressions do the talking. That hadn't changed either.

Lisa took a deep breath. "Just so we're clear, you can't bite men."

Both Phaedra and Andi made faces.

Lisa laughed. "And turning more than one person will kill you."

"That had better be me, or I'll kill you." Andi shoved Phaedra. Phaedra shoved back.

Pat joined them at the table and sat beside Andi. "That would mean you would be the only one left who can."

"I think there's still one of the Himmel sisters who can. They came out for the last party." Andi laced her fingers through Phaedra's. Phaedra blushed. That had been one hell of a party.

Lisa caught it. "Whose toothbrushes are those?"

"Frida und Ida," Andi said in a fake German accent.

Phaedra smiled and shook her head. "You didn't seem to mind." It was Andi's turn to blush. She had been their donor for the evening.

Lisa frowned, feeling left out of the joke.

"Think of a jacked milkmaid with thick, blonde braids and her red-headed boyfriend with an obscene rack. Then add some teeth and kinks you've never heard of," Andi explained.

Lisa nodded slowly, trying to picture it. "I thought you called each other *mother* and *daughter*, unless they really *are* sisters?"

Pat shrugged. "Frida and Ida are different. They go back farther than any of us. You'd have to ask them."

"So, you…volunteer?" Lisa still wasn't sure how things worked.

"Venom is one hell of a drug." Pat poured herself a mug. "Plus, the pheromones that make you hallucinate. What Willow did to you? Most of what you think happened was in your head."

"So, she never…?"

"Oh, she did," Pat confirmed. "But she was just responding to what you wanted to happen. A repayment of sorts."

"It's not good for consent," Andi added. "Which is why we were fully informed before Pat let us join. Otherwise, it would be like trying to negotiate while someone is in subspace."

Pat set her mug down a little brusquely. "Put all the niceties you want on it, at the end of the day we're still monsters."

"Oh, shove it, Pat," Andi laughed. "No matter how many women show up at her door, she still can't believe that people are into that sort of thing."

"There's also that Romanian group that came the year before." Phaedra tried to change the subject.

"Yeah, you liked them. Three tiny short-haired goths with enough piercings to set off all the metal detectors in the airport at once," Andi teased.

Phaedra felt her cheeks heat. "They were just thanking me for my help with the play piercing suspensions." She took a sip to hide behind her mug.

Pat shook her head. "None of them can turn anyone else though. Alina was the last one of them and she tried to turn a man. I heard it from Maria a few months ago."

"What happened?"

Pat sighed. "Maria and Emilia pulled her away before she could finish turning him into ground beef. He went on a rampage with half an arm, took out four Politia and got shot enough times in the head that he went down long enough that they assumed he was dead. Maria got him into the crematorium early, so they couldn't autopsy, but the papers said contaminated drugs."

The table remained silent for a few moments.

"So, you're still sure you want to do this?" Lisa made sure to look Phaedra in the eyes.

Phaedra snorted a half-laugh. "A boy kissed me once. He smelled bad and I felt nothing, so you don't have to worry about me." She squeezed Andi's fingers. "What about you?"

Andi kicked her under the table. "I was married to a man *once*, but we got an annulment a month later."

"Yeah, but…" Phaedra started.

"I may be bi, but I chose *you*." Andi stared at Phaedra from under her brows. "And I always will."

Lisa slumped into her elbows on the table. "I can't believe it took me this long."

"It's really not that uncommon," Andi reached across the table to take Lisa's hand.

"But I wasted so much time," Lisa whinged.

Pat tried and failed to suppress a laugh. Phaedra hid behind her mug.

"I guess that doesn't really matter anymore, does it?" Lisa's eyes softened.

"The real question is whether you want to be stuck with me forever." Pat flashed a self-deprecating smile.

"You're asking me that after *this* long?" Lisa stared.

Pat raised her hands defensively. "How should I know? Maybe you were just in it for the thrill of the chase. Some people love slow burn romances."

Lisa leaned over and bit her.

"Ow," Pat whinged.

Lisa made a face. "Stop trying to be a victim."

Pat made a show of rolling her eyes to the rest of the table. "Yes, officer ma'am." Phaedra and Andi giggled. Lisa turned red.

"It's okay," Andi consoled her. "We know you'll make her pay for it later."

Lisa turned even redder.

"Change the subject," Phaedra warned. It was Andi's turn to blush. Pat bit her lips and exchanged glances with Lisa. They knew who was in charge.

"Does anyone else ever host parties?" Lisa came to Andi's rescue.

Phaedra and Andi looked at each other. "Pat makes the best furniture. And the best *furniture*. It can stand up to vampires a little better."

Pat swirled her tea. "I've sent a few things overseas. I'm sure they'll be hosting their own parties soon. With cooler music and continental nonchalance, I'm sure."

"I've never been outside of a couple of provinces," Lisa grumbled.

"That reminds me, we're going to Greece in October."

"What? You never told me this." Lisa jerked her head around.

"I'm sorry. I'm not used to making decisions for more than one person." Pat fiddled with the handle of her mug.

Lisa glowered.

"It's for Kyle's wedding. I *assumed* you would be my plus one, and yes," Pat placed her hands palms down on the table, "I know the thing about assuming."

"Someone's gonna catch a beating," Andi mumbled. Phaedra elbowed her in the ribs.

Lisa bit her lip. "I always did want to see Greece."

"Oh, thank god," Pat exhaled, tension relieving.

"Now." Lisa turned to look at Phaedra. "I believe you came here for a reason."

Despite never having worn a suit in her life, Pat managed to pull it off rather well. Lisa opted for a rich blue sundress that hugged her figure and flowed in the breeze like the azure waves just over the horizon. She caught Pat staring at her cleavage during the ceremony. Lisa shifted and hitched the bodice down just a little. Pat covered her mouth and had to look away.

Lisa leaned on her shoulder, baring the freckled column of her neck. "I can see your teeth pressing against your lip, dear." Pat took several calming breaths to no avail. "You should do something about that." Lisa trailed a finger up the tailored wool slacks.

"If I *do* something about it," Pat lisped, "Kyle will never forgive me."

She turned to look at the framed picture of Josh on the seat next to her. "I sort of owe him." Pat's fangs finally slid back into place. She stretched her jaw, relieving some of the tension. Pat was thankful that hadn't turned into a disaster.

Lisa prodded her ribs. "Why are you making faces? Everyone is looking at us?"

Pat glowered. "It's your fault," she mumbled.

Lucy trotted down the aisle with a ring pillow strapped to his back. He stopped to get a head scritch from Pat before she shooed him toward Kyle and Morris.

After the ceremony, Lisa handed the photo to Kyle. Pat hung back a few paces.

"Thanks for coming, Lisa." Kyle held the photo with both hands. "I know it didn't work out, but it means a lot to me."

Lisa struggled to maintain her expression. Kyle spared her the discomfort of trying to come up with something.

"It's okay. He knew. He just..." Kyle's voice faltered. "Josh was the best thing about that place. Everyone else was so mean and bitter if you weren't born and raised there. Or if you were different at all. Somehow, he kept believing that people could change. That the only reason they acted that way is because they were hurting. I could never see it, but he could."

Kyle looked past Lisa and caught Pat's eyes. Guilt shone through them. Kyle softened his stance.

"Get over here, Pat. Unless you're the one who set the house on fire, it wasn't your fault."

The corner of her lip turned up. She bowed her head and lumbered over to him, pulling him in for a hug.

"If it weren't for Pat and her damn Bronco, I never would have made it out of that place." Kyle pulled Lisa in with his other hand. "I'm glad you're together."

Pat and Lisa stepped back and glanced at each other.

"I also expect an invitation to the wedding."

"How do you feel about naked sunrise ceremonies?" Pat had found her voice. Kyle's eyes widened and Lisa covered her mouth.

"That's not too much for Northton, is it?"

"Uh..."

"Or is it *you* who has a problem with it?"

"Pat."

"I get it, you have a problem with tits."

"No, I..."

"It's your husband who has a problem with tits?" Pat tilted her head. "They're perfectly natural, Kyle."

Kyle looked over to Lisa for help. Lisa was trying to hide her face.

"Your mom has tits, doesn't she?"

"Oh my god, Pat."

"You've sucked on them too, haven't you."

"Please stop."

Lisa swatted her. Pat grinned.

"She *always* does this." Kyle glowered, but the slight upturn of his lip told her he missed it. "She loves making people uncomfortable."

"I'm truly a monster."

Lisa almost choked.

"I thought she threw herself off the Leucadian cliffs because she was in love with a ferryman?"

Pat looked at her like she had two heads.

Lisa shrunk. "What?"

"You fell for some top-tier straight washing, love."

"But she was married to a man, wasn't she?"

"You believe Sappho's husband was really named Biggus Dickus from Giant Dick Island."

"Uh," Lisa toyed with the hem of her sundress. "Maybe not."

"Also, those cliffs are nowhere near Lesbos. You'd have to cross the entire Aegean Sea *and* Greece to get there."

"So, why doesn't she have a tomb then? Or a memorial at least."

Pat opened her mouth, but Lisa stopped it with her tongue. Pat fell backward against the whitewashed stone wall.

"What was that for?"

"Are you complaining?" Lisa narrowed her eyes.

"I never complain."

"You were about to go on a rant."

"You don't like it when I rant?"

Lisa growled and bit her. Pat's vision blurred and warm glitter flooded her system.

"Oh, I see," Pat's eyes dilated. "My ranting turns you on." Her pulse sped. Lisa could practically taste her arousal perfuming the air between them.

Lisa gripped her shoulder and slammed Pat back against the wall. Pat hissed. "We'll lose our deposit if you damage the place."

"Shut the hell up." Lisa wrapped her hand around her throat. Pat choked. Lisa smirked. A last beam of brilliant tangerine flashed as the sun disappeared beneath the horizon. Lisa slipped into shadow.

Pat stumbled forward at her absence. She smiled, slipping away to give chase. Or at least she tried. The shadow wouldn't accept her. Pat lifted her arm to find a single silver cuff around her wrist.

Lisa's knee hit her spine, knocking her into the ground. Pat bared her teeth.

Lisa pressed her harder into the dust, triumphant over her prey. She leaned forward, pinning her to the ground. "Cute. What are you going to do with those?"

Pat bit her arm, but could produce no venom.

Lisa laughed. "I don't need it." She sunk her teeth deep into Pat's neck. Pat winced and then moaned as a new flood of venom flushed through her body.

Lisa pulled away, blood falling in fat droplets, splattering against the white tile. She cupped Pat's crotch forcefully. Pat could only whimper.

"You *are* packing," Lisa purred. "You always have to stand out, don't you." Lisa rolled her over and straddled her hips.

Pat's chest heaved. With the cuff, the venom and the blood loss, she could do little else but watch the blurry outline of the woman she'd been in love with for decades slowly kill her.

Lisa lifted the arm with the silver. "If I take this off, will you be good?"

Pat blinked.

The metal rang against the tile. Pat bolted upright and sank her teeth into Lisa's neck. Lisa wrapped her legs tightly around her waist and pushed her backward. Pat's teeth raked against her skin leaving an ugly gash.

"Good enough?"

"No." Lisa jammed her fingers between Pat's ribs. Her breath hitched, heart beating against her touch. "Bite me again."

Pat obliged. Lisa tore at her slacks, lowering herself onto the strap, pushing the air out of her lungs.

"Why does this feel so much better than before?"

Pat caught her lower lip between her teeth and grinned.

"How much venom did you use?" Lisa asked. Despite the tattered wool slacks, her thighs glistened in the starlight.

"Enough that this will feel good." Pat held the arm that Lisa had through her chest. "Do you want to try it?"

Lisa bit her lip and nodded.

The slight crack alarmed her, but it didn't hurt. It felt more like cracking your knuckles. An adjustment accompanied by a sense of relief. Like all of her needed to take all of Pat.

The first heartbeat brushed against the pads of her fingers. Lisa couldn't describe it, because words hadn't been invented for it. *Orgasm* is for bodies, the highest pleasurable feeling they can achieve. Whatever word could be coined for this would mean something else. Something only her and Pat shared.

The ricochet of Pat's heart against her fingers, echoed a moment later from hers. Lisa came apart. All of her. All that remained was her and Pat. All that would ever be was her and Pat.

It didn't matter that it had taken twenty years.

It wouldn't have mattered if it had taken another twenty.

Because forever is always longer.

About the Author

Marine lives in the wilds of Canada with her wife and cat. When not writing, she is riding her motorcycle, doing witchcraft in the woods or building a deck. Your mom probably told you to stay away from her at one point.

She was probably right.

This is an independently published book. You can help me and all other independent publishers by leaving a review.

Follow Marine on Bluesky
@marinestjean.bsky.social

Sign up for the newsletter at
marinestjean.ca

www.ingramcontent.com/pod-product-compliance
Lightning Source LLC
LaVergne TN
LVHW020656110826
845149LV00012B/2016

9781069318626